An ArtScroll Novel®

Conquer the

Published by

Mesorah Publications, ltd

Darkness

**A JOYOUS STORY
OF TEENAGE TRIUMPH
OVER ADVERSITY**

by Estie Florans

FIRST EDITION
First Impression . . . September 1991

Published and Distributed by
MESORAH PUBLICATIONS, Ltd.
Brooklyn, New York 11232

Distributed in Israel by
MESORAH MAFITZIM / J. GROSSMAN
Rechov Harav Uziel 117
Jerusalem, Israel

Distributed in Australia & New Zealand by
GOLD'S BOOK & GIFT CO.
36 William Street
Balaclava 3183, Vic., Australia

Distributed in Europe by
J. LEHMANN HEBREW BOOKSELLERS
20 Cambridge Terrace
Gateshead, Tyne and Wear
England NE8 1RP

Distributed in South Africa by
KOLLEL BOOKSHOP
22 Muller Street
Yeoville 2198
Johannesburg, South Africa

AN ARTSCROLL NOVEL®
CONQUER THE DARKNESS
© *Copyright 1991, by* MESORAH PUBLICATIONS, Ltd.
4401 Second Avenue / Brooklyn, N.Y. 11232 / (718) 921-9000

ISBN:
0-89906-134-6 (hard cover)
0-89906-135-4 (paperback)

Typography by CompuScribe at ArtScroll Studios, Ltd.
4401 Second Avenue / Brooklyn, N.Y. 11232 / (718) 921-9000

Printed in the United States of America by Noble Book Press Corp.
Bound by Sefercraft, Quality Bookbinders, Ltd. Brooklyn, N.Y.

This book is dedicated

לזכר נשמת

אבי מורי

ר׳ משה מרדכי בן חיים צבי סטבסקי ז״ל

Reb Moshe Mordechai Stavsky z"l

ולהבדל לחיים

In honor of:
my dear mother and her husband,
Rabbi and Mrs. Simcha and Chana Rubin,
and
my wonderful in-laws,
Rabbi & Mrs. Aaron and Frieda Florans

Acknowledgments

Many thanks to Mrs. Reyna Hisiger, Mrs. Miriam Weinreb and Mrs. Karen Kluger for reading and editing the original manuscript; to Rabbi Simcha Rubin and Rebbitzen Sara Ginsburg for their assistance in the research department, and to Mr. Ephraim Pollak and Rabbi Meir Gross for generously sharing their computer expertise with me.

I would like to express my appreciation to Rabbi Nosson Scherman, for his belief in this book and for making my "novel" experience into the literary field so gratifying, and to Mrs. Nina Ackerman Indig, for her professionalism in editing the manuscript.

My infinite gratitude to my darling *kinderlach* for their patience and devotion while Mommy was busy at the computer with THE BOOK and of course, to my very special husband, Shmuel Dovid, for ALL THE ABOVE and more. Without your encouragement and confidence in me, this work could not have been completed.

E.F.

. . . ki eisheiv bachoshech Hashem ohr li.
...when I sit in the darkness, Hashem is a light for me.
(*Michah* 7:8)

Prologue

It was at a quarter after ten in the morning when I received the phone call that would change my life forever.

I have no doubt as to the exact time. I had just placed a cake in the oven and closed the door with a satisfied smile. I glanced at the large grandfather clock that was sitting on the china closet, thinking happily and contentedly about how much I had accomplished in the last forty minutes or so, when quite suddenly the telephone rang. I wiped my hands on my apron, walked casually over to the telephone table and picked up the receiver.

As shocked as I was when I heard the caller's voice, I recognized it immediately. We spoke for approximately three minutes. In a mild daze, I calmly replaced the phone on its cradle, then slowly and thoughtfully returned to the kitchen. I began to wipe the counter carefully and deliberately, as if each protracted movement could stop the hands of the clock from moving on.

As I heard the rhythmic sound of the second hand gyrating around the clock, the calmness began to leave me. The old familiar feelings and fears started to return. What will we say to each other? What could we say, I wondered anxiously, not believing that this was happening after all these years. I could not restrain my thoughts from racing ahead, and could not control the tension that threatened to overwhelm me. It was a relief, however slight, that the children were out with my husband at the time and would not have to meet her. To have her visit when the children were home would have only made this awkward situation even more difficult than I already anticipated it would be.

I started to rush about nervously, picking up toys and various other items. Dovid's rubbers from the night before were in the hallway. I quickly pushed them aside. Tzviki's castle of blocks with the cute little "menchies" inside and around it would have to go. I remember sighing as I recalled how hard he had worked at building it that morning, and knew how disappointed he would be to find it gone. I'll explain the situation to him later on in the day, I reassured myself, and knew that even though he was only four years old he would understand. Ruchi, oh, my sweet little Ruchella, I thought, as I glanced down at the neat circle of dolls in the living room, waiting for their little "mommy" to come home and make a *Pesach seder* for them. I will help you set them up again, I silently promised my little daughter. Eli's truck, Dini's Big Wheel, the tall and elegant eucalyptus plant standing so proudly near the doorway . . . I quickly and efficiently moved everything and anything that might be in her way out of the room.

I kept thinking fondly of my darling children, and how disappointed they would be when they came home and found their neat little lives upset. I reassured myself that I would do all that I could to protect them and make things right again.

My eyes hurriedly scanned the living room for any other obstacles that might encumber her path, and stopped short at the sight of the children's play table right in the center of the room. How can I have forgotten that, I silently admonished myself. That will surely be in her way! I carefully pushed the table against the wall and sat down awkwardly on one of the children's chairs to catch my breath.

I looked across the living room towards the dining room table and I saw the *yahrzeit licht.* How coincidental that she should be coming on this very day, I thought. And then I reminded myself that nothing is coincidental. Who knows? Maybe it was destined for us to be together on this *yahrzeit* day. At the very least, I thought guiltily, it would certainly give us something to talk about. I rose slowly to get a closer view, but all I could think of was that SHE was coming.

I stared at the *yahrzeit* candle.

The flickering flame danced on the tip of the wick. Its yellow and blue hues were mirrored in the surrounding glass, giving the impression that it was not one flame but many, all wearing identical costumes, all dancing the same dance.

I stared at the *yahrzeit licht* and I remembered . . .

PART I

Chapter One

The world seemed pretty perfect, just then, as I sat on the fence with one foot intertwined in the gate to keep myself from falling, and the other foot dangling carelessly. The Catskill sun shone down brightly on us and I felt a soft warm wind lift my hair.

"Isn't it just great?" I said to my best friend, Nechama, who sat beside me sharing both the view of the sleepy lake and my ice cream cone. "I can't believe it, I'm really an aunt. I still can't believe it!"

"Oh, I believe it all right," she answered between licks. "You have not stopped talking about your new nephew for even a second in the last forty-five minutes, *Tante* Renie."

"That's right. I didn't even think of that. What will he call me? Maybe he should call me *Dodah* Renie, or how about

Tante Rena?" I said thoughtfully, "Or how about . . ."

"No, you're definitely too young to be a *tante*. Maybe 'aunt'?"

"Can't be 'aunt,' I answered. "There already is an Aunt Rena. What should I be called?" I asked worriedly.

"Maybe you should be called just plain Renie, or Auntie Renie . . ."

"That's it," I interrupted her, "I'll be *Tantie* Renie. This way my little nephew won't think of me as so old, but at the same time he'll still know that I am his aunt."

"Perfect!" Nechama said, jumping off the fence. "Now that your problem is solved . . ."

"And my mother said that the *pidyon haben* will be on the first day of *Chol Hamoed*. You'll come, Nechama, won't you?" I asked excitedly, as Nechama and I walked side by side along the edge of the lake.

"Of course I'll come," Nechama bent down to pick up a pebble and toss it into the water. "But how will you fit everyone into your *succah?*"

"Oh, I forgot to tell you. My father said that he'll be building the biggest *succah* we've ever had. It'll take up the whole driveway, and we'll pass the food in and out of the window. Oh, Nechama!" I squeezed her hand, "I don't know how in the world I'll be able to wait until then. I'm so excited!"

We walked slowly over the Old Mill Bridge, watching a mother duck lead her little ducklings in a perfectly straight procession. Nechama bent over the wooden fence and looked down at her reflection in the pond. I could see the expression on Nechama's face change as I peered at her image in the clear water.

"Nechama, what's wrong?" I asked hesitantly. "There's something bothering you, isn't there?"

"Oh, it's nothing," she said, still studying her reflection.

"Come on, Cham. You can't fool me. I know you long enough. What's bothering you?"

"Well, if you really want to know . . ." She swung around and blurted out, "You know that letter I just received from Etty? Guess what?"

"What?"

Etty Samuels had been with us for the first trip of camp and was also a classmate of ours.

"Renie, Etty heard from her father that Miss Einstein has to move back to Chicago for the year."

"What?!"

"That's right, you heard me correctly. Her sister is temporarily bedridden and someone is needed to care for the children. She's planning to return after *Pesach,* but in the meantime . . ."

"I can't believe it," I said with great emphasis. "Now, when we're entering eighth grade, the greatest year of our lives. Are you sure?"

"Sure I'm sure, and now what am I suppose to do?" Nechama started walking up the path leading to a shady cluster of trees as I hurriedly walked after her. "How will I run the G.O. without her?"

"And how will I manage with the yearbook?"

"Hey, what's bugging you two? You both look like the world just caved in and you're the only ones left!" We swung around to face Feigy and Suri, surprised expressions on our faces. We had not heard them come through the bushes. "Did the two of you have a fight?" Feigy could not help asking with a hint of sarcasm.

I felt my jaw tighten.

Ignoring her last remark, Nechama related the news. "And," she continued, "now with Miss Einstein leaving, who knows who will be our new eighth-grade adviser? What with graduation, G.O., the Mitzvahthon . . ."

"And the yearbook," I added.

"Well," Feigy said in that confident and irritating know-it-all tone of hers. "Nechama, I wouldn't worry about the G.O. if I were you, as I am sure that you will manage just fine, adviser or not. As for you," she continued coolly, turning to me, "that's another story." With that said, she tossed her long blonde hair over her shoulder, turned abruptly and continued on her way, with Suri at her heel toward the path leading to the rowboats.

"Creep," I mumbled under my breath.

"Just ignore her," Nechama suggested. "She doesn't really mean any harm. That's just the way she talks."

"Right," I said gloomily, "especially when she's talking to me."

"Come on, Renie, cheer up. She just wishes that she would have as special a friendship as we have."

"I guess you're right," I shrugged, my lips slowly spreading into a wide grin. "Not everyone is as lucky as we are."

We continued walking towards Treasure Island. This was really just a small peninsula, merely a few feet wide, jutting out towards the lake. As younger girls we would pretend that pirates had hidden treasures there, and many fun summer days were spent at this pleasant spot.

We sat down cross-legged on the warm green grass, content in each other's company, lost in our individual thoughts. I looked at Nechama. Her thick, wavy auburn hair was gathered into a ponytail with a thin blue ribbon tied into a neat bow, and her arms were wrapped around her long, folded legs, bringing them snugly against her chest. She turned her graceful neck towards the water, and her large brown eyes seemed to be concentrating deeply as she stared at one specific spot in the lake.

Indeed, I felt very lucky to have someone like Nechama Leverman as my best friend. Not only was Nechama the smartest girl in our class at Bais Yaakov of Barclay, but more importantly, she was one of the nicest girls around.

Nechama was the only person I knew who could be a "goody-goody" and still have everyone wanting to be her friend. The teachers loved her and so did all the girls. Nechama had this way of being able to stop people from speaking *lashon hara* without making them feel defensive and embarrassed. If someone would want to copy her answers during a test, she would not let them, of course, but she would not leave it at that. After the test she would go over to the girl and offer to study with her and help her so there would be no need for her to even contemplate dishonesty in the future. Whenever there was something to be done, Nechama was the first to volunteer.

And do it, she did — in the most efficient and organized manner imaginable.

Most of all, what impressed me about Nechama was that she was still so normal. We could have a great time together, fill our hours with loads of fun. There were no airs about her!

It was true, though, that until people got to know her they sometimes thought of Nechama as a cool, snobbish girl. They saw this very pretty girl, amazingly talented (if you could only hear her at the piano!), who seemed untouchable and distant, like an aristocratic princess. The girls would be so awed by this very special person that they were afraid to approach her.

And that is how we became friends in the first place. You see, I guess I was just not the type of person to be afraid of people and worried about what they would think of me. I would say what I meant, and mean what I said. Sometimes this trait would get me into trouble, but most of the time it enabled me to meet new people and make new friends easily. Especially if someone seemed rather lonely, and that is how I found Nechama when I first met her . . .

It was about three and a half years before that summer, right in the middle of fourth grade. I remember it was a beautiful winter morning. The snow was a clean white blanket stretched across our enormous schoolyard.

We were sitting in class learning *Chumash* with *Morah* Carlbowitz, stealing peeks through the windows, restlessly waiting for the recess bell to ring so that we could all run out into that glorious snow.

Suddenly, *Rebbetzin* Leibowitz, our principal, opened the door to our classroom and led an unfamiliar-looking girl to the center of the room. She excused herself for disrupting the class, introduced the new girl as Nechama Leverman, and requested that the girls show what a wonderful group they are and make the new girl feel welcomed and comfortable.

Of course, as soon as the bell rang we all ran off into the magnificent white snow, which sparkled like glitter glinting under the clear blue sunny sky. The air felt so crystal clear and refreshing, and we ran about merrily making "angels" in the snow, throwing snowballs and building snowmen.

It was not until I returned to class that I noticed the new girl again. She looked so neat, clean and refined compared to the rest of us lively, wet girls who were breathlessly scrambling into our seats. She also looked very lonely and shy. Her eyes met mine. I smiled at her encouragingly and she blushed and smiled back.

The teacher had seated her next to Feigy, and I could tell by the expression on Feigy's face that this poor girl was not going to have an easy time. After all, she had displaced Suri, Feigy's best friend, and as most of us knew, it was not wise to upset Feigy.

Morah Carlbowitz told us to take out our *Neviim*. We were then informed that we were having a *chazarah* in the form of a game. We were very excited because *Morah* Carlbowitz always had a way of making learning extra-special fun. So it was with much enthusiasm that *Morah* divided the class into teams and we took our places on the different sides of the classroom. Suddenly, I heard a groan from the other corner. It was Feigy, lifting her eyes heavenward then directing them back towards the new girl, thus expressing her discontent at having her on the same team. She was obviously worried that the new girl would not know the answers and would cause her team to lose. A flurry of whispers erupted, and it took a full thirty-five-second stare from *Morah* Carlbowitz to bring the class under control.

Morah proceeded to ask the questions and soon it was Nechama's turn to answer. I remember thinking that *Morah* would be very nice to this new girl and ask her an easy question. After all, she is the new girl. However, *Morah* is a fair person. What is good for one team is good for the second.

Morah asked the question. It was a real brain-teaser. Not only did you have to know part of the answer from before, but it also involved looking up the second part in *Rashi*. After a few breathless seconds, in a clear distinct voice, Nechama gave the precise answer. Everyone heaved a sigh of relief. It was at that moment that Nechama became "teacher's pet," and it was the next day, when Nechama helped Feigy with her math, that she won over Feigy's heart as well as the hearts of the rest of the class.

However, despite earning the respect of teachers and students alike, the girls seemed so awed by Nechama that no one really invited her over to their houses or played with her at recess. For her, it was like being this delicate butterfly, looked at and admired but not touched.

It was different with me. You see, I had always felt sorry for the new girls in school, and I guess I made it my sort of unofficial job to help each new girl break into the crowd. So it was without much thought and without any reservations that I quickly approached her when the bell rang and offered to show her to the lunch room, never thinking that this was the beginning of a very special friendship.

"A penny for your thoughts." Nechama playfully shook me. "Where are you, in China? I called you at least three times. I thought you wanted to go rowing before rest hour is over."

"Oh, Nechama," I shook myself out of my reverie. "I was just thinking about that first day you came to school."

"Don't remind me," she said with a look of mock horror on her face. "It was just awful until you came along and rescued me."

"Come on, Cham, you rescued yourself, by being so smart and so nice," I said nonchalantly. "I didn't do anything."

"My dear friend, Leba Rena, will you kindly stop being modest and acting like you're just this little nothing," she playfully admonished me. "If not for you, I would probably still be in this glass cage, for everyone to look at, but of course not to talk to or be friends with. Why, if not for you," she repeated, "I would still be Miss Lonely ... lonely like ..." her voice trailed off as she looked in the direction of the water.

I followed her gaze towards the lake and we both saw Miriam rowing in a boat by herself. Miriam had joined our class at the end of seventh grade and still seemed to be having trouble breaking in. I suppose that was the reason her parents decided to send her to camp, figuring it might aid her in her adjustment. Yet, even though we would try to help draw her into the crowd, she seemed to just melt away. She had a bad stutter, and was extremely shy, and to be quite honest, you had to have a lot of patience to hear her out.

My heart felt as if it would break when I saw her rowing by herself, looking so melancholy and lonely.

I called out to her and waved. "Hey, Miriam, hi! Do you mind if we join you?"

Her eyes lit up as she shook her head eagerly and brought the boat to the dock, where we carefully climbed on board and joined her.

"Hey, you guys, wait for me!" Chana Devorah came running down the path, heading towards us. "I'm comin' in." She clambered aboard none too cautiously, nearly throwing us all overboard. We laughingly screeched and managed to balance the boat to prevent it from tipping over. Chana Devorah Herman, or C.D., as she was affectionately called, was from St. Louis, Missouri, where her father was a *rebbi* in the *yeshivah*. We had been together for the last few summers and constantly wrote letters to each other throughout the school year.

We leaned out towards the wooden dock and together, with as much strength as we could muster, powerfully pushed the boat further away towards deeper waters.

I saw a bluejay dig its beak into the dark earth. It seemed to find its prey as it lifted its wings and flew off into the light-blue cloudless sky.

I sighed contentedly and began to remove my sneakers. I felt the softness of the warm water as we lazily dangled our feet over the sides of the boat, watching the shore slowly disappear from sight. I looked into the lake, its sparkling green water rippling as Miriam's oars expertly, rhythmically, dipped in and out.

"Oh, I almost forgot," Chana Devorah broke the silence. "I heard that you get a '*mazal tov*,' Renie. So, how does it feel to be an aunt?"

"Great, C.D. I can't wait to go home and meet the little fellow. The only thing sad about leaving," I continued, letting out a deep sigh, "is that means camp is over and you'll be flying back to St. Louis."

"True. But like I always say, c'mon over!"

"Very funny. How should I come, by foot or by bicycle?" I retorted.

"Renie, the truth is that it's very possible that we'll all see C.D. this year," Nechama joined in. "After all, this year is eighth grade and that means it is the year of the . . ." Nechama let the sentence hang in midair, dramatically.

"M-m-mitzv-v-vah-th-thon?" Miriam broke in hesitatingly.

"That's right, Miriam," C.D. answered kindly, "and it's supposed to take place in Barclay this year. I can't believe that I almost forgot about it. I'm sure I'll be going," she continued enthusiastically. "After all, our eighth-grade class is quite small. Oh, I'm absolutely thrilled!"

"Hey, what are you all so happy about?" we heard someone call out to us.

It was my cousin Lakey who was a year older than I and lived in Lakewood, New Jersey. In our excitement we had not noticed another boat full of girls coming closer. "*Mazal tov,* Renie. I just heard the news. How is Sima feeling?"

Miriam expertly maneuvered our boat alongside Lakey's.

"*Baruch Hashem,* she's feeling fine, and my mother said she can't wait to get home. And," I continued, "of course I'm just bursting to see her and the baby. Could you believe it, little old me, an aunt?"

"No, I can't believe it. I'm older than you, and I'll probably be a mother before I become an aunt. Unless Dovie decides to get married before me."

At that we all burst out laughing. Dovie was Lakey's little brother who had just turned three years old. Just the other day she was proudly showing off pictures taken at his "*upsheren.*" Dovie and Lakey were the only two kids of my mother's sister, *Tante* Rochel. My cousin and I had been close ever since I could remember, her family always having joined ours for holidays and celebrations. We were practically like sisters except for the fact that we lived quite a distance away from one another.

"Anyway, let us in on your secret. What were you people talking about so excitedly?"

"The Mitzvahthon!" Chana Devorah said ardently.

"Oh . . ." Lakey exclaimed, her eyes widening, "I could see why you are all so terribly thrilled. I remember last year's was fantastic," she said in a tone of voice that made it sound as if last year was an extremely long time ago. "Who do you think will be picked this year?"

Chanie, Lakey's good friend from Lakewood, who was one of the girls in the other boat, answered rhetorically. "C'mon, Lakey, who do you think?" Then she added, "Nechama, of course."

"Oh, I don't know," Nechama looked down, embarrassed. "There are a number of girls in our class who can very well represent us. Besides, we do have to vote, you know."

"Anyway, I don't know about you people, but rest hour is almost over and I am starved," I said, clutching my stomach in exaggerated, mock despair. "I feel as if it is a *taanis* today and I want to get back before the canteen closes. Let's race back to shore!"

"O.K." Chanie and Lakey eagerly said together. C.D. grabbed one oar, and Miriam continued rowing with the other.

"One, two, three — go!" we called out in unison, and with that we were off. After a few minutes of much splashing and maneuvering in different directions, we all laughingly climbed ashore and headed towards the canteen.

We cheerfully walked along to the Main House, talking and joking all the way. We were a lively, friendly group as we entered the canteen and took our places on line.

"I am going to have an ice cream soda," declared Chana Devorah. "How about you, Nechama?"

"Nothing for me, thanks. I just had an ice cream with Renie, and that's already more than I should have had in the first place."

"Oh, there goes my thinny-thin friend always worrying about her diet," I said good-naturedly. "Well, I think I'll have another ice cream cone, with a strawberry, chocolate and vanilla scoop."

"Renie, where in the world do you put it all?" Chanie asked, and we all started giggling. You see, everyone knew I ate like a horse, but supposedly I never seemed to gain an ounce.

"Renie, can't you think of anything besides food?" I turned around to see Feigy entering the room. "I never saw anyone visit this canteen as often as you do."

I felt my heart quickening with anger.

"Well, I never saw anyone who likes to make nasty comments as much as you do," I proudly retorted.

There were a few embarrassed snickers and everyone looked around uncomfortably.

Before Nechama joined our class, Feigy and I got along, well, not great, but O.K. However, when Nechama and I became best friends, that was the beginning of the end. Feigy and Nechama lived near each other in Rorey, which was about a fifteen-minute drive from Barclay, where I lived. It was much newer and more modern there, and quite frankly had the reputation of being the wealthier side of town.

Feigy could not understand what a girl like Nechama could see in me. You see, we were very different and sometimes I could not understand it myself. Feigy and Nechama were excellent dressers, and I guess I was just a bit more easy going about my looks. I was not the neatest, most organized person either. And even though I did all right in school, I was not at the top of the class as they were. It was true that I drew and wrote well, and that was why I was chosen to be the editor of the yearbook. But I was not into dance, music and drama like the two of them. Sometimes I worried and wondered whether a friendship like ours could last.

"Can you believe it?" Nechama attempted to change the subject. "In less than a week, camp is over!"

We all groaned.

"And at this time next week we'll all be doing homework!"

More groans.

"Not me," I said, my cheerful mood returning. "Next week at this time I will be preparing for my new nephew's *bris.*"

"And I'll be helping you," added Lakey.

"So will I," said Nechama.

"At least you guys get to see each other at the mini-reunion on *Chol Hamoed Succos,* when you go on the hayride and everything," Chana Devorah sighed. "Poor me has to wait until next summer, or if I'm in luck, *Purim*-time at the earliest — that is, *if* I get to go to the Mitzvahthon."

"That's what you get for being our 'out-of-towner,'" Lakey said affectionately, and we all laughed.

"REST HOUR IS NOW OVER, REST HOUR IS NOW OVER," we heard the head counselor, Ruchi, and her assistant, Sara Leah, announce over the loudspeaker. "EVERYONE PLEASE GO IN FRONT OF THE APPLE TREE FOR LINE-UP. WE HAVE A VERY SPECIAL SURPRISE FOR YOU!"

We heard excited cries of delight and eagerly joined the throng of girls pouring in from various directions, all heading enthusiastically towards the tall apple tree.

I felt exhilarated and carefree as I ran happily along, unaware that this happy-go-lucky existence was soon to come to an abrupt end.

Chapter Two

I t was soon afterwards, on a sunny Sunday afternoon, that Nechama and I were companionably rowing down the usually calm river near our homes, taking advantage of our free time. Feeling relaxed, we were enjoying the beautiful scenery and discussing the exciting changes that were taking place in school now that we were in the eighth grade. We let the boat drift as we chattered away, oblivious to the fact that we were fast approaching the dangerous water-falls.

Suddenly, without warning, we felt the small boat lurch forward sharply in response to the strong pull of the current. Horrified, we realized that in a matter of seconds we would be thrown over the rocks along with the cascading waters. We grabbed the oars and wildly tried to paddle against the current. With my strength ebbing away, I madly grabbed hold of a rock protruding from the water.

As soon as I secured my hold on the rock and turned around, I tried to discern where Nechama was. I could hardly see anything. Water was spraying into my eyes, and the noise was deafening.

All at once I saw her. She was about to go over, her eyes wide with shock and fear. I screamed and tried to stretch my hand towards her, but my fingers slid off the slick rock and I felt myself slipping and slipping and . . .

. . . Thump, bang. "OUCH!"

"Hey, Renie, are you all right?" I heard my brother Shimon's voice through the door.

I looked around through sleep-filled eyes. I was on the floor in my room next to my bed, clutching my damp pillow tightly.

I can't believe it — I'm alive and in my room, I thought shakily. It was just a dream and I actually fell off my bed! Incredible!

"Yes, *Baruch Hashem,* I'm O.K.," I called out to him, still trying to shake myself awake and away from that awful nightmare. "I guess I sort of took a tumble."

"Anyway, Sleepyhead, Mommy said it's time for you to get up already. Do you have any idea what time it is?"

"No," I called through the door. "My watch stopped. What time do you have, Shimon?"

"It is five minutes and thirty-two and a half seconds to eleven o'clock, my dear Miss Slumbering Princess," my brother said teasingly. "By the way, you had a phone call . . ." I heard his voice trail away as he went down the steps.

"Yikes, I'm suppose to be at Nechama's house by 11:30!" I reminded myself suddenly. I quickly stood up and put my pillow back on my bed. I washed *neigel vasser,* finished saying *Modeh ani,* threw the covers over the bed, and grabbed my denim skirt. I slipped my pink sweatshirt over my head and was about to run out the door, when I caught sight of my reflection in the mirror.

Of course, I had never been the vain type, but for some

reason, lately I had become a bit more conscious of my looks. I guess that it is not so unusual, when you're turning thirteen years old, to suddenly find yourself more aware of your brown, thin, straight, shoulder-length hair that would neither curl neatly nor stay up in a ponytail, and little red pimples that seemed to just pop out overnight. And so, that morning, I spent an inordinate amount of time peering at myself in the mirror, searching for pimples and deciding that I did not really mind my green eyes and dimples, even if they made me look cute and young, instead of pretty and sophisticated.

I opened the door of my attic room, and delightedly inhaled the wonderful aroma that floated upstairs. When did my mother do it all, I marveled, as I ran down the steps. We had been up late the night before, baking all sorts of pastries and desserts for the *pidyon haben* and *Succos* and now she was at it again. I breathlessly came into the kitchen and saw the counter top filled with pies, cakes and cookies.

"Mommy, everything looks and smells wonderful," I said, giving her a kiss on the cheek. "I can't wait to make it disappear," I added, rolling my eyes and playfully patting my stomach.

"Well, before you disappear from here this morning, *zeeskeit*," my mother reminded me, "make sure to take a *siddur* and *daven Shacharis,* before it will be too late."

I took my *siddur* from the shelf in the *sefarim shrank* in the living room, and carefully completed *Shacharis*. When I finished and returned to the kitchen, I saw that my mother had prepared some cereal and juice for me. There was a basket of fresh rolls in the center of the table.

I happily greeted my brothers Shimon and Yerucham, who were quickly finishing their breakfasts. They were eager to go outside and join Naftoli, who was in the midst of building the *succah*. It was a treat to have their company during breakfast, as I usually did not get to see them on Sunday mornings. Normally they were in *yeshivah* at that time. However, it was *bein hazmanim,* and I was excitedly looking forward to tomorrow night, when Lazer and Yehuda would be returning from their *yeshivah* in *Eretz Yisrael.*

Squeezing some chocolate syrup onto my cornflakes, I cheerily remarked to my brothers, "I'm so excited about *Yom Tov*. Naftoli is back home now from Lakewood Yeshivah, Lazer and Yehuda will be back, *im yirtzeh Hashem,* tomorrow night, and, of course, I'll even get to see you guys, too. And, wow, Sima and Yisroel and the baby will be here, also! The whole family will be together — isn't it just wonderful?" I bubbled.

"Yes, it's wonderful. Maybe, we will even get to see a little bit of you, too. That is, if you could stay put for more than a minute or so, Miss Leba Rena Greenberg," Yerucham teased affectionately, calling me by my full name.

Leba Rena, I mused. I proudly recalled the reason my parents had given me that name. "When you were born," my mother had once explained to me, "*libeinu,* our hearts, were full of *rena,* such joy." You see, my six older siblings were all born within a period of seven years, and then, after Shimon was born, I did not come along until eight years later. And, as my father had explained to me, I am their little miracle, their *bas zekunim.*

"Leba Renala, finish your breakfast quickly. Nechama called while you were *davening* and wanted to know why you're not there yet. And," my mother said, as she placed a generous slice of warm *kokash* cake in front of me, "she said something about a *Chumash* sheet that's due tomorrow. I explained to her that you were helping me with all the preparations for *Yom Tov* until late last night, and that you overslept."

"O-o-o, Mom, this is delicious," I burbled, washing down the *kokash* cake with a tall glass of milk. "I've gotta run now." I said a *brachah acharonah,* grabbed my shoulder bag and jacket, and was off.

❀ ❀ ❀

By car, the ride to Rorey usually took only about fifteen minutes. Since I was going by bus, however, it took me fifteen minutes just to get to the bus stop on Main Street as I had not seen the Barclay bus and was forced to walk to town. I had missed the last express bus to Rorey, and, with all the extra stops, it took a full forty-five minutes of travel time to reach my destination. I whiled away the minutes by looking out the window, watching as the stores in town disappeared and made room for a mile or two of woodland. As we neared Rorey, signs of affluence became apparent — the homes were more modern than those in Barclay, spread further apart, and set on wide, lush lawns.

It was a pleasant five-minute walk to Nechama's house from where I had alighted from the bus. As I neared her split-level, modern home, I heard the musical notes of a classical overture vibrating through the air.

I could have stood at that doorway forever, stiff and still with my finger frozen over the bell button, listening to Nechama's music. But Nechama's mother, Mrs. Leverman, opened the door just then, an amused smile on her face. She had on a beautifully coiffured wig, the same color as Nechama's hair, and her eyes — a deep, electric blue — matched the royal-blue suit she was wearing.

"Renie, how nice to see you. Please come in," she said graciously. "Nechama is expecting you."

"Sure, Mrs. Leverman, thank you," I said, as I entered the elegant hallway, carefully wiping my feet on the welcome mat. "Don't you just love the way Nechama plays piano? You probably never want her to stop," I said fervently.

"Yes, Renie, she does play beautifully," her mother answered proudly, still smiling at me. "Come, take off your coat. I'll tell Nechama that you are . . . "

The beautiful musical passage that had been building to a crescendo came to a sudden halt in mid-note. Nechama walked into the hallway gaily. She was wearing a beige cowl-necked sweater with a matching brown-and-beige tweed skirt. Her hair was pushed off her face with a headband, leaving a few wispy bangs gently fringing her forehead.

"Hi, Renie, I thought I heard voices," she greeted me warmly. "We have loads of work to do. Go to my room," she gestured with her hand in the direction of the bedrooms, "and I'll get some *nosh*. Then we can get started."

Feeling at home, I walked towards Nechama's room. I knew Nechama wasn't getting any food for herself; after all, she was always so diet conscious. Not that she had to be, of course, but that was Nechama. Yet, knowing what a *nosher* I was, she enjoyed indulging me.

As usual, I could not help marveling at the beauty and femininity of Nechama's bedroom. Her canopied bed was in the center of the room, covered with a grey-and-mauve print bedspread. A solid plum-colored ruffle surrounded the lower part of the bed, hiding a high-riser bottom for sleep-over guests. Matching throw pillows and lace cushions were artfully arranged near the fluffy pillow sham as well as on the lovely window seat. Standing in one corner was a large wooden dollhouse that Nechama used to play with when she was a child. There was a wide, grey-lacquered Formica desk with a hutch in the other corner, and a matching dresser against the wall between them. Pretty mauve tulips and grey stripes covered the walls. A large, luxurious plum-and-grey shag rug sat in the middle of the shiny parquet floor.

I walked over to the cozy window seat and, pushing aside some of the cushions, sat down and assumed my favorite position, leaning back and hugging my knees. I gazed out of the bay window which overlooked the green manicured lawn and thought about the last few weeks.

It was hard to believe that so short a time had elapsed since we had been in camp. What with preparations for the *bris, Yom Tov,* the *pidyon haben,* loads of schoolwork, the yearbook — it sure felt like a different world! I was eagerly anticipating the mini-reunion that would be taking place on *Chol Hamoed.* Fortunately, it was to be a day after the *pidyon haben,* and I would not have to miss any of the exciting events.

"What is my philosopher friend thinking about now?" Nechama asked teasingly. She entered the room carrying a tray laden with two cans of soda, one diet and one regular, a bowl of potato chips, a box of peanut chews, some fruit and two straws. She carefully laid the tray down on the desk, and in that getting-down-to-business tone of hers, declared, "O.K., Renie, let's begin our homework."

"Sure," I replied breezily, opening up my pocketbook. "That is, if I can find it."

I started to rummage through the many papers and objects in my pocketbook. "I'm absolutely positive it's here. I know I put it in as soon as *Morah* gave it to us because I didn't want to lose it. It's got to be here!" I exclaimed.

"O.K.," Nechama sighed patiently. "Let's empty everything out and then we are sure to find it. That is, if you say you're sure you put it in."

"Sure I'm sure," I grinned. This reply had always been a staple of our playful banter and, despite the delay I was causing, Nechama laughed aloud affably, comfortable in its familiarity.

I proceeded to dump the precious contents of my shoulder bag on the floor. A comb, three neatly folded articles for the yearbook, two pieces of chewed bubble gum in their original wrappers, a card that I was saving to give Nechama on her birthday, a "To Do" list that I had made the day after camp was over and was planning to use to get myself organized — but had totally forgotten about until now, a few sheets of crumpled paper that had not yet made it to the wastebasket, a letter on my new stationery to Chana Devorah, and a few other papers and odds and ends.

"Renie," Nechama exclaimed, "how does so much fit into something so small?"

"Um-well," I started to search for an explanation.

"Never mind," Nechama broke in. "Let's just try to get all this stuff sorted out."

She began to sift through the various items, arranging that which deserved to make its home in the wastebasket in one pile, neatly straightening out papers of importance in another, sorting personal items in yet a third pile, and basically just getting me organized. Suddenly she exclaimed, "Here it is. Here's your *Chumash* sheet. Now let's sit down and complete this assignment before the whole afternoon is gone."

I sauntered over to the desk and sat down next to her as we proceeded to work on our sheets together, answering one question at a time, looking up the explanations in the different *mefarshim,* and gradually overcoming the difficult challenges of this work sheet.

The clock ticked on, and as the hours passed I began to resent being cooped up doing homework on this beautiful Sunday afternoon.

Munching on my third peanut chew, I complained, "Boy, this is really hard stuff and so time consuming. We didn't even learn the answers to all these questions."

"Come on, Renie, we're almost finished."

"But why does she have to give a bunch of thirteen-year-olds so much work? We're busy enough as it is!"

"Renie, *Morah* wants us to learn how to find answers on our own, not just be fed everything like babies," Nechama explained patiently.

"Nechama," I said, attempting to change the subject, "what do you think of our new English teacher?"

"Huh?" Nechama was still diligently working on her *Chumash* work sheet. "Oh, you mean Mrs. Ross? Fine. I think she's very nice. Why?" She put down her pencil and turned to face me.

"Well, I think there's something very strange about her," I said. "You know, she seems so out of it when you try to have a simple conversation with her, and yet . . . when she teaches, she's brilliant! And her *sheitel,*" I paused for a moment, "it's blonde."

"So what? What is so strange about a blonde *sheitel?*"

"Cham, don't you see? She has dark eyebrows, dark eyes and a dark complexion. It's kind of queer that she wears a blonde *sheitel,* don't you think?"

"Actually, Renie, I really couldn't care less what color *sheitel* she wears, and besides, it's not exactly right that we should be discussing our teachers."

"I still think there's something peculiar about her, even if she is a terrific English teacher." I was reluctant to get back to our homework, so I abruptly changed the topic and continued talking. "I can't believe it's almost *Succos* already."

"Me neither. Time flies when you're having fun."

"Not that schoolwork is so much fun," I made a face, "but

at least we have the camp mini-reunion on *Chol Hamoed.* I'm so excited about the hayride!"

"So am I!"

"And you know what's going to be on the first day of *Chol Hamoed !*"

"What? I just can't imagine," Nechama said jokingly. "Could it be, could it actually be the *pidyon haben* of," Nechama began to imitate me, "the one and only most lovable, most adorable nephew in the world?"

"Hey, don't make fun of me," I said, giggling. Opening the wrapper of another peanut chew, I continued, "And I am absolutely thrilled! All my brothers will be home from *yeshivah;* Sima, her husband and the baby will, of course, be staying with us, and Lakey and her whole family will be coming for the first days and staying for *Chol Hamoed* as well. And," I went on breathlessly, "a bunch of my father's students from his *shiurim* will also be coming and going, and Abe . . ."

"And I am absolutely so jealous of you, Leba Rena Greenberg."

"What, you jealous of me?"

"Well, not exactly jealous, but, yes, I really envy you."

"*You* envy *me?*" I asked with disbelief.

"Yep," she nodded, her lips pursed together knowingly.

"But why?" I was incredulous. "You've got everything a girl could dream of." I gestured with my hand towards her night table. "Your own telephone, a gorgeous room, talent, you're the most pop . . . "

"Oh, come on, Renie. These things aren't so important. What counts the most is what *you* have," she said fervently.

"What's that?"

"Besides the fact that you are the warmest, friendliest person I know," I felt myself blushing and she continued, "you're never lonely."

"That's true," I said, still unsure of what she was getting at. "That's why you envy me?" I asked skeptically.

"Your home is always full, either with your own family or with loads of guests. There's always so much laughter and fun. Renie," Nechama said in such a serious tone that I was beginning to feel uncomfortable, "you don't realize what you have."

"Well," I admitted, "I never really thought of it like that. Thanks, Nechama, thanks loads," I said appreciatively. "I guess I . . ."

I never did get to finish my sentence, because just then the telephone on Nechama's night table rang. Listening to Nechama's side of the conversation, I could tell that it was Feigy on the phone, and as they continued to talk I felt my bubble of euphoria slowly burst.

". . . Yes, of course I had a great time at your house on *Shabbos.*" Pause. "Sure, I would love to, but . . ." she stole a quick glance in my direction. "Sorry, today isn't good. Renie and I are in middle of doing our *Chumash* sheets."

"Cham, if you want to go someplace, it's all right with me," I broke in.

She covered the receiver. "It's Feigy. She wants me to go shopping with her for a dress for *Yom Tov.* You're sure you don't mind?"

"Na, no problem," I said with a wave of my hand. "I can spend the day with Miriam, or Etty or . . ."

"Great," she said, turning back to the phone. "I can go with you, Feigy. I'll meet you, now, let's see . . ." she said, looking at her watch, "in about half an hour at the corner of Riverside and Maple?" Pause. "Sure, no problem, glad to come. I need a few things, too." Pause. "O.K., great, I'll see you. Bye."

She turned to me. "Renie, we'll have to finish up real quickly. Otherwise, I'm afraid that the stores will close before we get there." She looked at me directly, seeing for the first time the resentful expression on my face. "You're sure you don't mind? Maybe you'd like to join us?"

I laughed bitterly, shaking my head in the negative. "Come on, Nechama, you should know better than that. Putting Feigy and me together is like combining fire and water. Besides, Feigy knew I was here, and if she wanted me to come along she would have said so. No, thanks," I could not help adding with a twinge of sarcasm, "I have other things to do besides shopping all day for clothing."

"O.K., if you say so," Nechama looked at me seriously, "but I really wish the two of you would at . . ."

Mrs. Leverman knocked at the door just then and entered. "Renie, you have a telephone call on the kitchen phone."

"Thanks," I said to Mrs. Leverman, following her out of the room. And then, poking my head back through the door, I could not help adding to Nechama, "Saved by the bell."

I entered the state-of-the-art, all-white, tastefully decorated kitchen and casually glanced at the glimmering counter tops and shiny white-tiled floor. I picked up the receiver.

"Hi," I said, and instantly recognized Sima's voice at the other end of the line. Sima is my sister, my only sister, and, in my opinion, definitely the best big sister anyone could possibly ask for. "What's doing?" I asked eagerly.

"I'm sorry to bother you, Renie, but Mommy told me I could catch you at Nechama's house. Yisroel is in *yeshivah* right now and I don't want to disturb him while he is learning, but I am so worried . . ."

"What's wrong, Sima?" I broke in, my heart pounding.

"It's the baby. Now, don't panic," she stopped me from interrupting her. "Maybe I'm just being overly cautious — first-time mother, you know — but Mommy said that just so I shouldn't be too anxious, I should ask you to stop off at the drugstore on the way home and detour around to my house."

"Sure, what would you like me to get? Some medicine or something?"

"No, hopefully he's all right, and I'm being worried over nothing. I called the doctor and when I told him that the baby was crying all day and felt a bit warm, he asked me whether I took his temperature, and, Renie, I felt so foolish when I told him that I don't even have a thermometer," Sima ran on nervously.

"O.K., no problem, I'll pick up a thermometer for you. Anything else?"

"Well, let me think . . . Yes, as long as you're going anyway, I could use a large box of Pampers, and let's see . . . another box of Wet Ones, and, h-mm . . . that's about all. Are you sure you don't mind, Renie?"

"Of course I don't mind. Besides I can't wait to see the baby."

Nechama and I quickly finished our *Chumash* sheets, said our good-byes, and I ran off to catch the bus back to Barclay. This time I was lucky, and caught it just as it was about to leave.

❧ ❧ ❧

The ride back was uneventful, and I sat with my elbow on the windowsill, my chin resting in the palm of my hand, staring at my melancholy expression reflected in the glass.

I was in a sour mood, thinking about Feigy and Nechama shopping together. Lately, Nechama was spending *Shabbos* afternoons with Feigy, and in school Feigy was constantly writing notes to Nechama. The two of them went to swimming and dance classes together, and Nechama was even teaching Feigy how to play the piano. Well, I thought bitterly, if Nechama would rather have Feigy as a best friend, that's fine with me.

Lost in brooding thoughts, I missed my stop. I had to ask the bus driver to let me out in the middle of the block, in order that I would not have to continue on to the next town.

After purchasing the baby items and a chocolate bar for myself, my mood changed as I thought about my new nephew. My enthusiasm returned as I looked forward to going to Sima's apartment and seeing her and the baby.

I was standing at the corner of Main Street and Elm, waiting for the light to change. Putting my packages down, I reached for the chocolate bar and was about to take another bite when, suddenly, there was a tap on my shoulder. Startled, I quickly turned around to face a little old lady whom I had never seen before.

"Oh, I vedy sorry to frighten you, young lady," she said in accented and grammatically incorrect English. "You look like a fine *Yiddishe maidel.* Maybe, you could help me to cross de street?"

"Sure," I smiled and took her arm as we proceeded to cross.

"Dank you, dank you vedy much. Vat's your name, nice girl?"

"Renie. Renie Greenberg. What's yours?"

"Pleased to meet you, Miss Renie Greenberg. My name is Mrs. Finkelman. I tell you a secret, Miss Renie, come . . ."

I bent down conspiratorially. She cupped her hand around her mouth and, leaning towards my ear, said in a not-so-very-low whisper, "I'm starting to get a little bit old now, so . . ." she lowered her voice a bit more, "I don't see so good no more. I vasn't alvays dis vay," she said apologetically. "Just now ven I starting to get a little bit old."

"Oh, that's O.K.," I looked at her, my face full of understanding. "Do you live far from here?"

"No. I live just around dat corner."

"You know what?" I asked. "It would be my pleasure to walk you home. Is that all right with you?"

"Oh," she smiled up at me. "It vould be my pleasure, too."

Arm-in-arm, the two of us walked along chatting like old acquaintances. Turning the corner to Wilson Street, we saw a slightly dilapidated apartment house. I was about to say good-bye to Mrs. Finkelman as we approached her house, but the lonely look on her face stopped me.

"Mrs. Finkelman," I asked, "would you mind if I walked you to your door?"

"Oh, I vouldn't mind at all. It vould be my pleasure," she said proudly, emphasizing the word "pleasure" and smiling broadly. She continued, "Lately I have so much trouble vid mine key."

She led me up the stairs to her apartment. "Here ve are, number E. Dis is my apartment. It vould give me great pleasure," again she emphasized the word "pleasure," "for you to be mine guest."

Fishing in her bag for her keys, she suddenly called out in delight, "Ah, here it is."

She proceeded to stick the key in the keyhole and try to turn it. The key would not budge. I tried it. The key came out. I tried again, but it would not turn. I tried again. It still would not turn.

"Mrs. Finkelman, is there something wrong with your door?"

"No, nuding is wrong vid mine door," her forehead creased

in a worried expression. "Maybe, dis silly key. Someding wrong vid dis silly old key."

I tried again. I pushed my body against the door hoping to nudge it open. It would not budge. In frustration I banged on the door. I then pushed the key in again and turned it back and forth, pushing the door at the same time. Suddenly the door flew open, and I went tumbling into the apartment. I just missed crashing into a tall, lanky, stern-faced elderly man who fortunately managed to dodge me.

"WHAT IN THE WORLD?" he yelled and then stopped short when he saw Mrs. Finkelman. "You again?" he asked angrily, eyes blazing. "Don't you know where you live? Can't you leave me in peace?"

"Oh, come come, Mr. Petrovsky, don't be so upset," Mrs. Finkelman said soothingly. Still on the floor, I looked with disbelief from one to the other. "You going to frighten my friend here," she looked at me affectionately. "Come, Renie, let me in-tro-duce you to my downstairs neighbor, the very gentle-man-ly Mr. Petrovsky."

I started to rise, dusting myself off and apologizing. "I am very sorr . . ."

"DON'T GO APOLOGIZING TO ME, YOUNG LADY, GET OUT, BOTH OF YOU, GET OUT!"

I hurried out the door, while Mrs. Finkelman lingered on, calmly taking her time. "Anyvay, Mr. Petrovsky, maybe tomorrow you come vid me for a valk?"

"GET OUT!"

"Have a nice evening," Mrs. Finkelman smiled sweetly, "and be vell, Mr. Petrovsky." She closed the door softly and smiled up at me, her face flushed, her eyes shining.

We started walking up the stairs to what I hoped was truly Mrs. Finkelman's apartment. We heard Mr. Petrovsky open his door and yell up to us.

". . . AND REMEMBER, YOU LIVE IN 2E, NOT 1E. I LIVE IN 1E, NOT YOU. SO STAY IN 2E. AND DON'T BOTHER ME ANYMORE!"

I looked at her, shocked. "What a rude . . ."

"No, no, no, Renie. You too nice not to like somevone. He

just a vedy, vedy lonely old man."

I helped her get settled in her apartment, and declined her offer to stay for dinner.

"No, thank you," I told her. "My sister is expecting me to bring her — oh, no! I forgot the packages on Main Street."

With a quick good-bye, I was off and running. I raced down the two flights of stairs, sprinted through the hallway, and was just emerging from the lobby when I unexpectedly collided with someone. She had been looking down as she hastily made her way into the building. She was carrying a large suitcase and had not seen me coming. I mumbled a quick apology and was ready to break into a run, when my eyes widened in surprise as I recognized her.

"Oh, hi," I said breathlessly to my English teacher, Mrs. Ross. "Sorry, but I was in a tremendous rush. How are you? Do you live here?"

"N-no, oh, I mean y-yes. I do live here," she said nervously, her dark eyes widening and darting from side to side. "I am sorry. I wasn't really looking where I was going. I do apologize, but I must go now."

She looked shaken and upset, and without any further conversation hurried away. Watching her dash up the steps, I shook my head slowly, wondering what was wrong. Convinced that there was something bizarre about this woman, I was gripped by a sudden sense of foreboding.

Chapter Three

The next few days flew by quickly and *Succos* finally arrived.

This had always been my favorite *Yom Tov,* besides *Purim,* of course, and as the solemn period of *Yom Kippur* departed, we happily ushered in the joyful days of *Succos.*

In truth, according to the Torah, it is always a *mitzvah* to be happy, but *Succos* is a *Yom Tov* that specifically is known as *zman simchasainu* — the season of our rejoicing — and this year the preparations for *Succos* had an especially festive air. We had an extra *simchah* to look forward to, the *pidyon haben* of my nephew, Shuey.

Under my father's watchful eye, Shimon, Yerucham and Lazer were building the biggest *succah* I had ever seen. Our *succah* had always been large to accommodate our family and guests, but this year we had to expand it even further to make room for the people who would be attending the *pidyon haben* celebration.

Yehuda and Naftoli were constantly going in and out of the house, carrying packages, picking up orders, stacking crates of soda and making sure that my mother had all the food supplies she needed.

Besides taking care of the new baby, and recuperating from just having given birth, Sima was trying her best to make herself useful in the kitchen. Finally, after much convincing, by my mother, she agreed to sit down and just peel potatoes.

My brother-in-law, Yisroel, was sitting by the table with a few open *sefarim,* taking notes, preparing the *devar Torah* he would deliver as the *baal simchah.* At the same time he was making lists and telephone calls, and, in general, making sure that everyone who had to be informed about the *pidyon haben* was notified.

And I was sprawled out on the kitchen floor, busy making posters to decorate the longer walls of our expanded *succah.*

The vacuum cleaner was humming in the background, and I could hear the gentle bubbling sounds of a pot roast simmering on the stove, as well the pleasant voices of my father and brothers through the open window. As I applied the finishing touches to the border of my latest "masterpiece" with a red magic-marker, I heard the sounds of a car motor and tires crunching against gravel, and Shimon's excited voice exclaiming, "They're here."

I heard car doors slamming, voices greeting each other, and my father's warm and hearty *"Shalom aleichem."* I was out the door within seconds.

I ran over to *Tante* Rochel and kissed her, and then turned excitedly to Lakey. Shimon was holding Dovie high up in the air, Uncle Tzvi was shaking hands with my brothers and Yisroel, wishing them all *mazal tov,* and now my mother was hugging *Tante* Rochel.

I grabbed Lakey's arm, pulling her forward, and with my other hand I lifted her suitcase.

"Come on, Lakey, I'll show you the baby, before Sima has to feed him again," I exclaimed.

"O.K., O.K.," she said, laughing. "Let me just get the rest of my stuff."

"Me too, me too!" Dovie cried. "I wanna see the new baby, too!"

"So do I," *Tante* Rochel said, "but first we must go into the house and take off our coats. And then we will ask Sima if the baby would like visitors."

"Of course he likes visitors. He's the friendliest baby you ever met," I said proudly.

"And of course, you are the proudest aunt I ever met," Shimon teased me affectionately.

"Of course," I grinned, and we all laughed and trooped into the house.

❀ ❀ ❀

Later that evening after our mothers had lit the *Yom Tov* candles, Lakey and I set the table and then went into the living room to find *siddurim* to *daven Maariv* for the *Shalosh Regalim*. My mother was sitting on the chair in the living room, the baby in her arms. His eyes were opened wide and he seemed to be staring straight into my mother's eyes. She sighed contentedly.

Tante Rochel smiled and looked proudly at my mother, at her older sister's radiant face. "Dina, you are the most beautiful *Bubby* I have ever seen."

"I agree," I said, as I walked over and kissed my mother on her cheek. I felt very proud of my never-complaining, hardworking mother who somehow always maintained a positive attitude. "I am so happy to have you for a mother."

"And I am so happy to have you for an aunt," Lakey added.

"Enough, enough," my mother said, feigning annoyance. "Let's go, girls. Finish *davening* and prepare the salad. *Abba* and Uncle Tzvi and all the boys will be home from *shul* soon, and I don't want us to keep them waiting."

It took an unusually long time for everyone to assemble, but at last we were all standing around the table waiting for my father to begin *Kiddush* for the *Shalosh Regalim*. Actually, the *succah* contained three tables in a row, all covered with white tablecloths, and giving the impression that they were really one long table. Shiny silverware, crystal glasses, fresh flowers in vases and my grandmother's china were neatly set out on the tables. In the center, my mother's silver candelabra stood proudly.

I looked around appreciatively at the well-adorned *succah*, the colorful pictures and flowers on the walls, the ceiling with the *schach* trimmed with fruits. I saw the enthusiastic smiles on the faces of my siblings and our guests, and felt the air of contentment that emanated from my parents.

The air was crisp and chilly, and so it was with great satisfaction that we warmed ourselves with the steaming stuffed-cabbage rolls that my mother always made for *Succos,* as well as the *divrei Torah* and *zemiros* that poured forth.

My father reminded us that the *succah* is reminiscent of the *ananei hakavod,* the clouds of glory. Just as the Jewish people were surrounded by them and protected throughout their years of wandering in the desert, we enter the *succah* and surround ourselves with the *mitzvah* of the *succah* as a reminder that we too can enjoy the Divine protection as long as we remain loyal Jews, faithful to *Hashem* and our Torah.

There was always a lively crowd at each meal. Besides my family — my parents, five brothers, Sima, Yisroel, and the baby — and Lakey's family, there were other guests, too. My brother Naftoli, who learned in Lakewood, brought home a friend from *yeshivah.* Chaim lived in South Africa and could not make it home for the *Yamim Tovim.* And of course, some of my father's *talmidim* joined us, too.

Although my father had retired from his job as a school teacher two years before, he had accepted a position in a local *yeshivah* that was geared towards adult male *baalei teshuvah.* These were men who were highly intellectual and intelligent, successful in their careers or businesses, but unfortunately had not received a religious upbringing. To their credit, they felt that something was missing from their lives, and decided to temporarily put their careers on hold in order to study Torah full time and commit themselves to a Torah way of life. Abba would give a *shiur,* in English, three times a week, and he claimed that he learned more from his students than they did from him.

We always had at least three *bachurim* from the *yeshivah* as guests at our *Shabbos* and *Yom Tov* meals. Their presence enhanced the *kedushah* that we all felt at those times.

One of the boys who was particularly close to us had become engaged during the summertime, and was planning to get married right before *Chanukah.* Abe was a *ger,* and Linda a *baalas teshuvah,* and therefore neither of them had family to help them prepare for the *simchah.* My parents were planning to take care of everything.

It was a wonderful *Yom Tov* evening and despite the crisp air, I felt enveloped by the warmth of close friends and family. I could not suppress a deep sigh of happiness.

Oh, how I wish it were possible to take time by the forelock and save it; to go back to the way things were. How could I have known then that I would soon make the dreadful discovery that what can commence as a dream, a figment of the imagination, can terminate as a catastrophic nightmare of reality? But just as the sand gravitates to the bottom of the hourglass without stopping, I now know that what I . . . what we . . . had to face was destined to be.

❦ ❦ ❦

During the afternoon on the second day of *Yom Tov,* Etty came to visit me, and one of Lakey's friends from camp came over to see her. At my suggestion, we all decided to go over and visit my new friend, Mrs. Finkelman. She had not accepted my invitation to come to us for *Succos,* claiming that she did not want to leave Mr. Petrovsky to eat in the apartment building's *succah* alone. Such a sweet elderly lady, I thought to myself. I had not realized that Mr. Petrovsky was even Jewish.

We cut through a few back yards to shorten the walk to town, and half an hour later we were standing in front of the three-story-high building on Wilson Street.

"Is this where she lives?" Etty asked incredulously, noting the slightly dilapidated look of the building.

"It's really not as bad inside as it seems from the outside.

Come on in, I'll show you where she lives."

We climbed the steps, passing the first floor, making sure not to mistakenly knock at Apartment 1E. I did not want to face the mean-tempered Mr. Petrovsky again.

"Who dere?" Mrs. Finkelman asked in response to our knock.

"It's me, Renie Greenberg, and some friends. We've come to visit."

The door swung open, and Mrs. Finkelman, with a most flustered look, greeted us. "Oh, children, I am so so happy to have you. You came just ven I needed you. I have a very big problem. I can not find mine glasses anyvere in dis house. And vidout mine glasses, I can't see nuding. And I can't look for mine glasses, because I don't have dem."

Etty and I exchanged anxious looks.

"Don't worry," Lakey said comfortingly. "I am sure we'll find them."

"Ah, such vonderful girls," Mrs. Finkelman smiled delighted. "I vill give us some tea and biscuits — ven I can find dem, dat is."

We all laughed, and started a thorough search through her apartment. It was really quite small, and we figured that in no time at all we would be sure to find Mrs. Finkelman's glasses. Etty and I covered the bedroom, Lakey searched the living room — or, as Mrs. Finkelman called it, the parlor — and Lakey's friend, Baila, went with Mrs. Finkelman to the kitchen.

Suddenly there was a loud bang from the kitchen, and we all rushed in to see what had happened. With relief we saw that Mrs. Finkelman, in her attempts to take out a tray from the cupboard, had accidentally knocked down an old, unused kettle. Although a bit shaken, she was quite fine. She was smiling mischievously, and pretending to talk to the kettle, saying, "I'd been vondering vere you ver hiding . . ."

Her words were interrupted by the unexpected opening of the door, and Mr. Petrovsky's fast and heavy footsteps brought him straight into the tiny kitchen.

"Mrs. Finkelman, are you all right?" I could not have mistaken the worried tone I heard in his voice. "I heard footsteps and a loud noise and . . ."

I gasped as he suddenly noticed us and looked straight at me. "YOU AGAIN. WHO ARE YOU ALL, AND WHAT ARE YOU DOING HERE?"

"Oh, Mr. Petrovsky, no need to yell. Ve can all hear you very good. Maybe, I cannot see so vell vidout mine glasses, but I sure can hear. These nice girls have come to visit me and now they help me to look for mine glasses."

His shoulders fell backwards and I saw him sigh with relief. He said in a somewhat more subdued voice, "Oh, well, maybe next time you look for something you do it more quietly, and don't disturb an old man from his nap. Don't you learn anything about being respectful in those schools of yours?" He started to leave and then turned to face Mrs. Finkelman, his mouth twitching as he tried to repress a smile. "By the way, those glasses of yours. They are on your head."

All eyes turned to Mrs. Finkelman and we all burst out laughing when we realized that, sure enough, the shiny pair of spectacles was sitting proudly on her head, almost invisible against the flowery print of her kerchief.

We were so overcome with gales of laughter that we did not even hear Mr. Petrovsky leave the apartment, and it took quite a while for us to calm down. Mrs. Finkelman was a good sport and giggled along with us as we joked and told stories throughout the afternoon. I knew Mrs. Finkelman adhered strictly to *Kashrus* laws and therefore, we were able to enjoy some of her delicious biscuits. She treated us to a choice of several different types of herbal tea. It was a wonderful day and we made sure to remind Mrs. Finkelman to come to the *pidyon haben* the next day.

❁ ❁ ❁

Early the next morning, relatives and friends began arriving with cakes and pastries and wishes of "*Mazal Tov.*" The air of festivity grew stronger as more tables were brought into the *succah*. A large *challah* was placed at the head of the table, and *bilkalech, challah* rolls, were placed at each setting. Lakey and I filled the cups with fruit salad, while Lazer placed bottles of soda, wine and *schnapps* on all the tables. *Tante* Rochel was busily arranging cake platters, while my father and brother-in-law prepared for the actual ceremony.

It was very exciting as we greeted all the guests, and I was happy to have Nechama there with me. Dovie and a few other little cousins were mischievously running around and under the tables, helping themselves to candies and cookies, thinking that none of us older people saw them.

Sima was glowing, smiling and enjoying the company, and Yisroel, the proud father, was shaking hands with the men and accepting their congratulatory pats on the back. I was the radiant, exhilarated and doting aunt. My parents were in the background *"shepping naches,"* accepting *"Mazal Tovs"* and making everyone feel warm and welcome.

My father had explained to me that the *pidyon haben* takes place thirty days after the birth of a first-born baby boy — that is — providing that neither the father nor the maternal grandfather is a *Kohen* or a *Levi,* and that the mother gave birth in a natural way.

"Originally," I explained to Nechama, "all first-born males were to have been consecrated — that means, set apart in a holy kind of way — as *Kohanim* in the service of *Hashem.* But because they participated in *chait ha'egel, Hashem* gave this special job over to the *Levi'im* and . . ."

"And yet the *bechor* is still special to *Hashem?"*

"That's right," I continued, feeling very knowledgeable. "And their special sanctity can only be removed by their redemption. That's why it is called *pidyon haben. Pidyon* means redemption and, of course, *ben* is son," I said proudly.

"But how do they get redeemed?" Nechama asked, a puzzled look on her face.

"The father may give the *Kohen* goods, like jewelry or whatever is equal in value to five *shekalim,* but he may not give bills or checks. By giving this redemption money to the *Kohen,* this sanctity that I told you about now gets transferred over to the *Kohen.* But by performing this ceremony the father is still considered to have dedicated his son entirely to *Hashem."*

"I guess it is not such a bad job to be a *Kohen,* getting all this jewelry and stuff," Nechama giggled.

"That's just what I said to my father when he explained it to me, Cham," I laughed. "But do you know what he said? He said that nowadays, the *Kohen* usually gives the money or whatever was used back to the father as a present."

Our conversation came to a halt when we suddenly heard someone exclaim, "They're bringing the baby!"

We saw that the men had crowded into the *succah* as the baby, dressed in a brand-new *Shabbos* outfit, was carried in on a silver tray filled with jewelry and precious coins.

I squeezed Nechama's hand as we watched Yisroel walk up to the *Kohen*, place the goods before him and say in *Lashon Hakodesh*, "My wife, who is like myself, a '*Yisrael,*' has borne me this first-born son and I hereby give him to you."

"What happens if the *Kohen* won't accept the goods and wants to take Shuey instead?" I jokingly whispered to Nechama.

Nechama smiled and gave my hand an extra squeeze as we continued to watch the ceremony and listen to the *Kohen's* words.

"What do you prefer, your first-born son or the five *shekalim* which you are obliged to give?"

As Yisroel handed the money over to the *Kohen,* he recited two *brachos.* When he finished, we saw the *Kohen* take the money and, over wine, recite the appropriate *brachah.* He then took the money, and, holding it over the baby's head, said:

"This is instead of that, this is in exchange of that, this is in remission of that. May this child live, may he learn Torah, and may the fear of Heaven be upon him. May it be G-d's will that even as he has been admitted to redemption, so may he enter the gates of Torah, the marriage canopy, and a life of good deeds. *Amen.* "

Everyone joined in by answering "*Amen.*" The *Kohen* then placed his hands on Shuey's head, and *benched* him.

After the ceremony, people returned to their seats to partake of the *seudah,* since the washing for *challah* had taken place before the ceremony began. As my mother and aunt dished the hot meats and *kugels* onto platters, Lakey, Nechama and I carried out of the kitchen trays of sliced *gefilte* fish that had neatly been arranged around cups of *chrain* earlier in the day.

Busily running back and forth to the kitchen, handing platters to my brothers in the *succah* through the open window, rushing about breathlessly making sure that everyone had a seat, I felt exhilarated and was thoroughly enjoying myself. I wished fervently that this time would never end.

When the food had been served and all the guests made comfortable, Nechama and I finally managed to grab the last two seats available at the end of the table where some of Sima's friends were sitting. After helping myself to a slice of meat, coleslaw, and some other delicacies, and heaping salad onto Nechama's plate, I complacently proceeded to consume the edibles that I had so meticulously helped to prepare. I looked around at the faces of Sima's friends. Some girls were still single, a few were married, and two already had babies. Was it really just a few short years ago that these same girls were sitting around our basement preparing for color-war, practicing for choirs, playing the guitar? Does time really fly by so quickly and do people truly grow up so fast?

I asked Freidy, Sima's best friend, to pass some ice cubes my way. Taking notice of me, the "little sister", Freidy and the others wished me *"Mazal Tov"* and asked the usual questions: How does it feel to be an aunt? Does the baby keep Sima up nights . . .? They then went on to discuss the new baby.

"He's so cute, that Shuey. Did you see his dimples?"

"And his green eyes. He looks just like a Greenberg, yes, most definitely he's a Greenberg."

"No, he has the Greenberg eyes, but certainly the Bradsky lips."

"Yisroel's chin."

"Sima's nose."

Nechama and I looked at each other and exchanged grins.

"Promise me, Cham, that when we get old, we won't be like them," I whispered to Nechama conspiratorially.

"Don't worry, Renie. I can't imagine ever getting old like that anyway."

🦋 🦋 🦋

That night Nechama stayed over, as it was quite late and we

would be leaving early the next morning for the Camp Bas Tzion's mini-reunion trip. After we helped clear away the dishes and sweep the floor, my mother hurried us upstairs.

"O.K., you two, you've done more than your share. The boys will help me with the rest," she said wearily, turning to us with tired but smiling eyes. "Go, get ready for bed, you'll have to be up early in the morning for your trip."

We knew she was right, and, sorry to see such a wonderful evening come to an end, we slowly climbed the stairs to the attic.

"Thanks for everything," I heard my brother-in-law, Yisroel, call from downstairs, "and, *im yirtzeh Hashem,* by you two."

"Our pleasure," I called back down to him. Turning to Nechama and trying to stifle a yawn, I added, "I feel like it'll be a million years until we'll be old enough to get married and be mothers."

"And I hope I'll have loads of kids and a family just like yours. And," she added, "I hope I'll be just like your mother."

I thought of Nechama's mother, always meticulously and fashionably dressed, coordinated and organized, serene and young looking; a woman who through the years worked full time, yet managed to always be available when needed, and who somehow seemed able to combine career and family perfectly.

"Why?" I asked, once again surprised that Nechama could want something that I have, something that I had always taken for granted.

I led the way to my room and comfortably sprawled out on my bed. With my chin resting in the palms of my hands, and my elbows leaning on a cuddly, peach-colored pillow, I gazed at Nechama inquisitively.

"Because that is the way it should be," she said adamantly, sitting down on the open high-riser next to me. "That's what brings true happiness and contentment."

"I don't know what you are talking about." I laughed uncomfortably, trying to lighten Nechama's mood. "I would be plenty happy having a gorgeous room like yours and plenty content having my own phone, too."

"Come on, Renie, be serious," she inched closer to me. "You always think that nice clothing, piano lessons, and things like that are what makes a person happy. Whenever I come to your house it's always so full of life, so much action, such cheerfulness . . ."

"Wow, gosh, I must admit, I use to feel kind of embarrassed!"

"You, embarrassed? About what?" She casually tucked a strand of auburn hair behind her ear.

I sat up, hugging my knees, and easily replied, "When I would come to your house I would see everything so neat and orderly and shiny. And then you would come here, and . . ."

"Oh, Renie," Nechama tossed a pillow at me, "you've got to be kidding. Lots of things are here today and gone tomorrow, but cheerfulness and happiness," she paused, looking around my room, "that's something that no one can ever take away from you."

I allowed my eyes to roam around my room. The walls were old, and the furniture was not new, but, somehow, with Sima's help, we had turned it into a warm and cheerful place. One Sunday we had gone to the department store and purchased a few large sheets that were on sale. They had peach daisies printed on a mint-green background, and Sima made a quilt cover, throw pillows and café curtains to match. Two coordinating sheets, with peach and mint-green dots, were carefully stapled to the walls and sewn as a dust ruffle. We took some lace ribbon that we found in the basement and managed to trim everything with it. Using my pastels, I made a large picture of a daisy that one of my brothers graciously framed for me. In the center of the room was a shaggy mint-green area rug that I had found at the local flea market. The slanted attic ceiling was painted a bright peach-parfait color that contributed to the room's warm feeling.

"H-m-m-m. Maybe you're right," I admitted as I walked over to my dresser to find my pajamas, "but boy, you sure are in a serious mood tonight."

"I don't know. It's just that sometimes I think and wonder about what it would be like to be older and grown up. Like today, seeing your sister's friends . . ."

"Yes, I think I know what you mean."

"And I become a little afraid. I wonder about what things will be like for me . . . what kind of home I will have. I wonder how much of the future *Hashem* just makes happen, and how much I can shape it and control it to be the way I want it to be."

"Wow, Cham, you have such grown-up thoughts!" I was definitely impressed. "I never think about such things," I added, rather ashamed.

"Oh, that's because you are so easy going and carefree. You're probably never afraid of anything."

"That's not really true," I said slowly, sitting back down on the bed, holding my pajamas tightly. "There is something that frightens me terribly . . . and that I try not to think about. Something I never told anyone before."

Nechama's big brown eyes widened. "What?" she asked in a whisper.

My eyes darted from side to side, even though I knew that there was no one around to hear me. "Promise not to tell anyone?"

She nodded.

"I sometimes worry — well — I don't know if I should say."

"Tell me," she pleaded, her face intently earnest.

"I am afraid," I swallowed hard, "that my parents, th-that one day, one of th-them, you know, might d-die." There. I said it.

"Oh, Renie," Nechama seemed relieved. "Everyone always worries about that. We all want our parents to live forever, but eventually . . ."

"I know what you are going to say," I broke in. "I remember once when I was little, having a terrible nightmare about my father dying. And then when I cried out at night, and my father came to comfort me, he explained that he might not be around forever, but that he and my mother will be around for as long as I need them."

"So what's the problem?"

"I'll need them forever."

Chapter Four

I know now that even the minutest details of what happened that day will remain clearly in my mind forever.

Very early the next morning we met Lakey, who had stayed overnight at the home of a friend from camp, and the three of us proceeded to school, where the rest of the girls were assembling. If it had not been for the excitement we felt about the reunion trip, I do not know how we would have been able to drag ourselves out of bed so early in the morning. Nechama and I had continued talking and talking until very late the night before. Finally, we decided to say *"Hamapil"* and get a bit of sleep before we had to rise in the pre-dawn hours.

The bus made two stops before reaching us. It started out

from the Bais Yaakov in Brooklyn, picked up a group of girls at the camp office in Manhattan, and then continued on to Barclay where we happily joined the other girls from camp.

Every year, Camp Bas Tzion had a mini-reunion during *Chol Hamoed Succos* for the girls living in the tri-state area: girls from Brooklyn, the Bronx, Washington Heights, Barclay, Monsey, New Jersey, and whatever other location was within an hour or two traveling time.

This was the first time my age group was able to participate, as the trip only included campers in the eighth grade and up. This year an exciting one-day excursion upstate was planned with, as its highlight, a trip to the Wrangler Ranch, which specialized in different types of hayrides.

It was great to see my friends who lived in other neighborhoods, and I had a wonderful time on the bus. Nechama and I sat next to each other, singing and clapping and talking all through the ride. We watched dawn turn into morning and stopped in Square Town to *daven Shacharis* and *bench lulav* and *esrog.* We had lunch in the *succah* in Summerville and took a tour of the glass factory in nearby Corning.

We continued on as far as the picturesque town of Pleasantville and drove along its winding roads until we finally arrived at the Wrangler Ranch. It was usually closed during this time of the year, and we were fortunate that our camp made special arrangement for our trip there.

We settled down in a clearing alongside a crystal-clear lake. To this day I can still recall the feeling of peacefulness, of serenity, which surrounded and encompassed us there. Later I was to tell myself that what we experienced that morning was the calm before the storm. However, at that time I was still carefree and happy-go-lucky, unaware of what lay ahead.

I saw that there were some terrific trees for climbing and I raced Etty to the top of the tallest one. I dared Nechama to join us, but she smilingly declined. After a while, Ruchi asked Nechama to play the guitar, and we all gathered around and sang. There were "*grammin,*" stories, jokes and much laughter.

It was soon announced that it was time for the hayride. Three separate wagons had arrived, and we were divided up according to age groups. As soon as we were assigned our wagon we climbed aboard, flip-flopping all over the hay, scrambling for spots. When I sat down and turned to see whom I was sitting next to, I saw my disappointed expression reflected on Feigy's face.

Suri was sitting on the other side of Feigy and seemed relieved to be next to her. Those two remind me of a panther and her shadow, I thought sourly. Wherever Feigy went, Suri was sure to follow. And Feigy seemed to enjoy it. Suri was not the only one. There were many girls from camp and from school who wanted to be part of her clique, and although she was not the sweetest person I knew, even I had to admit that Feigy was as loyal to and protective of her friends as a mother bear is to her cubs. And the fact that Feigy was the best dancer in the whole eighth-grade class did not hurt, either. If I was to be honest with myself, I would have to concede that I would not have minded if she liked me, too. From the corner of my eye I saw her turn to Suri. Nodding her head in my direction, she icily said, "And I came on this trip to enjoy myself . . ."

That did it! I had heard enough. I stood up and placed my hands firmly on my hips. Without looking at her, I spoke in an unnaturally loud voice. "Anyone in the back want to switch seats with me? It's more bumpy over there, and I like the bumps!"

"I'll gladly switch, Renie," Nechama called, and began to pick her way towards the front. "I get so nauseous in the back," she whispered as she drew near.

"Thanks, Cham." I lowered my voice, but intentionally kept it just loud enough for Feigy to hear me. "Maybe the queen bee won't sting you."

Glancing in Feigy's direction with as icy a stare as I could muster, I triumphantly took my place in the back of the wagon, next to Etty. I hoped that the smile I gave Etty concealed the quivering sensation I was experiencing in the pit of my stomach. I was feeling slightly guilty over having made that snide remark, but then again, tactfulness had never been my strong point. Anyway, I reminded myself, Feigy really deserved that comment. So why was I still feeling so miserable? I suppose that what was really disturbing me was the knowledge that Feigy and Nechama were sitting together during the hayride.

Not one to let myself be down for long, I successfully pushed that troubling feeling out of my mind as soon as the ride commenced.

We sat comfortably on bales of hay that had been piled high in an open wagon which was now being firmly pulled forward by a farm tractor. As we bumped along the winding country roads, I could not help but marvel at the brilliant colors of autumn which surrounded us, and I watched the many-colored leaves fall gently in the wind.

Prior to that *Chol Hamoed* trip, I do not remember ever having wished so hard that I was already an accomplished artist, able to capture the beauty of the surrounding countryside on my canvas. Words, I felt, would be inadequate to describe the breathtaking scenery that we were all privileged to enjoy that day. I pictured myself at work in my "studio," filling the empty canvas with the brilliant and dazzling colors that I was presently observing.

There was a tiny little room — really, a walk-in closet with a window — in the attic in my large home. Once, when I was a little girl of about seven years old, my parents presented me with a wooden easel. My happiness knew no bounds when my father carried it up to that little room and told me that if I cleaned up and emptied out the paraphernalia that was up there, that space could be my special studio.

Buoyed with determination, I threw myself into the task of scrubbing, dragging, dusting and rubbing, until at last I had a shiny, but empty, little haven. I proudly placed my easel in the center of the room. I moved it closer to the window, then opposite, concerned about sunlight and view, and then finally decided on the perfect spot where a stream of sunlight shone on my easel. I then lugged up some empty crates from the basement, and piled them up one on top of the other, thereby creating shelves for my paints and brushes. My mother gave me some old ceramic cups — that she no longer needed — for mixing colors and soaking brushes, and I happily arranged them nearby on an overturned crate.

I dreamily thought back to that evening when all was finally in place. My brother Yerucham was down on one knee, connecting some wiring. He finally finished, stood up, dusted his pants, wiped his hands together and flipped on the switch. The room was suddenly illuminated. As the strong light glowed down on my little studio, my heart glowed with such pride and happiness that I must have been grinning from ear to ear.

Yerucham walked over to me and, pulling a beret all the way down on my head, over my eyes, chuckled and said, "O.K., my little sister, the artist. I expect no less of you than a Rembrandt."

"Oh, Yerucham, thank you, thank you, thank you!" I cried over and over again. "Call Mommy and *Abba* up to see it, please. Oh, I can't wait to get started."

I carefully placed a large board on my easel and dipped my brush into the paint and, feeling very much the professional, I confidently began. I was working with such determined concentration that I did not hear my parents come up the stairs and enter the room until my father intentionally coughed and cleared his throat.

I swung around and ran to my parents. "Oh, Mommy, *Abba*. Thanks so much! I love it and I'm so happy. Thanks, thanks, thanks!" I hugged them gratefully. "You're the best mother and father in the world!" I exclaimed.

"Well, we are very proud of you," my mother said, smiling as she appreciatively surveyed the room. "You worked hard and did a wonderful job."

"And you'll see how spotless I'll keep this room."

"We're sure you will."

"And I'll never paint anywhere else. I'll just keep everything together neatly over here," I said, pointing to the crates.

She walked over to the organized shelves and turned to me approvingly. "Renie, we're truly impressed with how responsible you have shown us you could be."

"And," my father continued, his eyes twinkling, "indeed, if you show us how serious and diligent you actually are about this art, we will see about art lessons."

My parents understood what a hopeless case I was when it came to being organized and neat, and this was one way they tried to encourage improvement on my part. I felt so fortunate to have parents who, instead of nagging me and trying to force me to become something I really was not, could think of creative ways to motivate me to want to be more responsible on my own. And so, knowing how much I loved drawing and mixing colors, they gave me that room — which, of course, was much more than a room — to help develop my talents as well as my personal growth.

I laughed aloud, reliving it all with pleasure.

"What's so funny?" Etty, sitting beside me, asked.

"Oh, nothing," I said, suppressing a smile. "I was just thinking about my 'studio' and how much I love this scenery. Isn't it gorgeous?"

"Sure is," she said, grabbing her camera. "Smile, Renie, this is a great picture for the yearbook."

I turned around fully to face Etty and spread my lips into a wide grin, making sure that my dimples would show.

"Hey, just because she's the editor . . ."

That came from Feigy. Here I was, enjoying the scenery, dreaming of painting this panoramic view. I had all but forgotten Feigy's initial nastiness to me. It was not until that moment, with her sarcastic comment about the yearbook pictures and her blatant jealousy that Etty was photographing me and not her, that I was bluntly brought back to reality.

I need not have worried about formulating a retort, since Etty liked her just about as much as I did.

"If you want to start dancing now, Feigy, I'll be glad to take a picture of you, too," Etty said sarcastically. Feigy was Dance Club head and eventually would have her picture taken formally for the yearbook.

As editor, I had appointed Etty to be the official yearbook photographer, as she was always taking candid shots of us girls throughout all our years in elementary school. Etty and I lived around the corner from each other and were great friends ever since I could remember. When Nechama and I became best friends, Etty and I still remained close. Etty liked Nechama, and of course Nechama accepted Etty, and so we sort of became a threesome with me in the middle.

I threw Etty a grateful look. There were a few snickers and Feigy blushed.

"C'mon, girls, this is a camp trip. No school politics, please," Aliza Katzman, one of the girls from Brooklyn, remarked.

Another girl began a lively song and soon we were all joining in. It really was true that the back was my favorite spot, and we all shrieked in delight each time the wagon lurched over a bump. I sang and clapped along, happy to be there with my friends.

Etty and I smiled at each other as we sang. Miriam was sitting next to me on the other side and was also clapping and singing. She had made more friends in class since camp, and was spending a lot of time at my house. I had noticed that the more comfortable she became with the *chevrah*, and the less pressured she felt, the less she stuttered. Peshy, the new girl from Israel, was right next to Etty, and Chavy, Zehava, Rochel Leah, Rivky, and the whole gang from camp and school were there, too. I looked around at my friends contentedly and was only saddened by the fact that Chana Devorah had not been able to join us.

"Which part of today did you like best?" someone from the front of the wagon called out to no one in particular.

"The *kumzitz*," I heard someone say.

"I loved the tour of the glass factory," another girl declared.

Nechama said, "I always enjoy the bus rides with everyone having a good time together."

"The tree climbing," I laughed. "That's my favorite part."

"Figures," Feigy said sourly. "You would like that sort of thing, Renie."

Etty, chewing her gum noisily, cut in, "Well just because you don't know how to have a good time and you're always afraid of getting yourself dirty . . ." She let the sentence dangle, and snapped her gum.

"Boy, I am so excited about the Mitzvahthon," Nechama attempted to change the subject.

She was answered with many cries of "Me, too!"

"What is the Mitzvahthon?" Peshy asked, her English flavored by her Israeli accent.

"You mean you've never heard of the Mitzvahthon?"

"How could she have heard of the Mitzvahthon?" Etty asked. "After all, it only involves the Bais Yaakov schools across the United States and Canada, not Israel."

"It's like this . . ." I turned to Peshy. "It's sort of similar to what the seniors have in high school, the Bais Yaakov Convention. But this is for all the Jewish Girls' Day Schools across North America."

"Every year, around *Purim* time, it takes place at a different Bais Yaakov. Girls from every eighth-grade class are picked to represent their class."

"Represent them — how?"

"You're supposed to use a talent. It could be anything. Singing, dancing, acting, painting, music, sewing . . . anything . . ."

"And," Etty continued, "you take a *passuk* from *Tanach* or *Pirkei Avos* and somehow, with creativity and imagination . . ."

"You tie it together," I completed the sentence.

"You see, the purpose of this," Nechama explained, "is to take a talent, a gift that *Hashem* gives you, and use it to glorify Him, because everything a person does is supposed to be done *leshaim Shamayim.*"

"There is a panel of judges," Zehava continued, "who decide, based on educational and spiritual content, who the winner is."

"The winning school is awarded a grant that is used to fund special programs to benefit the students," I exclaimed. "It's so exciting. The host school — that's us this year — plans the program, and to top it off, we get to miss a lot of school." I giggled.

"Speaking about school," Etty said. "What do you think about . . ."

The topic of conversation turned into a discussion of subjects so dear to typical eighth-graders — tests, extracurricular activities, yearbook, favorite and least desirable classes, and of course, teachers.

"I think Mrs. Ross is an excellent English teacher — but she seems so strange, and she dresses funny." A few snickers.

"Well, I think that she is kind of peculiar," I said mysteriously. "Dark eyes, dark skin, and yet, she wears a blonde *sheitel*."

"Do you think she is a spy?" Peshy asked, her voice suspicious.

"I think that she is just plain weird," Feigy said flatly.

"I think we should talk about something else," Nechama's tone was gentle. "Oh, look, we are starting to climb Buttercup Mountain," she exclaimed happily.

There was a chorus of exciting "ooh's" and "ah's" as we began our ascent, slowly and carefully worming our way up to the top of the mountain. We could see the small sleepy town spread beneath us like toy dollhouses in a sandbox. The lake twinkled as it caught the reflection of the setting sun.

As if at a prearranged signal, we began to sing slow, soft songs, rocking back and forth, arms around the waist of the nearest person, softly harmonizing with each other. Surrounded by beautiful scenery, singing familiar songs with close friends, I remember thinking that it could not be possible for anyone to be happier than I was at that very moment.

And then it happened.

Thinking back, I am amazed at how much can pass through the mind at such a moment. I pictured my mother and father, my brothers and sister and little Shuey. And I wondered if I would ever see them again. In that terrible, horrific moment I honestly believed that this was the end.

It was so fast, just a matter of seconds . . . probably less than a minute or so . . . and yet, when I envision it, I remember every detail — in slow motion, as if it took much longer to occur.

We had been traveling slowly and peacefully, when suddenly a small green car came whizzing towards us from up the mountain. Our driver, trying to avoid the car, swerved into a tree. I felt myself being thrust forward with tremendous force, and then thrown back again. I saw Nechama fly out of the wagon, tossed like a rag doll onto the grass a short distance away from the truck. Another girl was hanging dangerously by her leg from the wagon. I remember the pain-filled and shocked expressions on all the girls' faces. But most of all, I remember the silence. The awful, incredible silence.

As the seconds ticked by, I heard soft moaning as one girl began to cry. And then another. And another.

Slowly, girls began to shakily climb out of the wagon. Some girls were limping, leaning against their friends for support. I stood up weakly and looked around. Pocketbooks, brushes, pocket *siddurim,* bags of *nosh* and cans of soda were strewn all over.

I stepped down and moved forward. And there, on the ground before me, I saw Nechama's *siddur*. Small and leather bound, it had Nechama's name printed on the cover. I bent down to retrieve it, but as I was about to put it to my lips to kiss, I suddenly froze. I gasped, horrified. The sight that met my eyes was one that I will remember forever.

Nechama was lying still on the ground, her big brown eyes staring straight ahead.

I began to tremble violently. In a daze, I felt a protective arm slip around my shoulders, and I allowed myself to be led away and guided to a spot where some girls were sitting with the assistant head counselor, saying *Tehillim.*

I glanced towards the side of the road and saw that the wagons carrying the rest of the group had pulled over. The older girls emerged from the wagons silenced by the shocking scene that met them. They stood around numbly, over-whelmed by the gravity of the situation.

The shrill sound of wailing sirens reached us from far away, becoming louder and louder with each passing second. A few unfamiliar people — locals who had already, somehow, heard about the accident — were moving quietly among us, dispensing blankets, warm drinks, and reassurance. I could see our driver sitting on the ground nearby, his head in his hands, sobbing.

It was already dark. By this time the ambulances had arrived, their blinking lights flashing eerily on the people's faces. I saw one of the medics examine Nechama, and then hold his walkie-talkie to his mouth and mumble something. Within minutes there was a tremendous rush of air as a helicopter noisily landed nearby.

I saw two frightened girls, crying in pain, being helped into the helicopter.

And then I saw Nechama. She was lying, silent and unmoving on a stretcher. I watched as the emergency team carried her carefully into the waiting helicopter, the sounds of its motor deafening, its rotors still moving.

I wanted to run after them, to call out to Nechama, but I could not move and I could not utter a sound. I watched helplessly as the helicopter lifted off the ground, and saw it slowly disappear into the dark, black sky.

I wondered if I would ever see my friend again.

PART II

Chapter Five

"Please, Renie, you must eat something," my mother said, placing a cinnamon bun and a glass of orange juice before me.

It was late *Shabbos* afternoon and I was sitting at the table in my mother's warm kitchen.

I shook my head. "I'm not hungry."

"Leba Rena, you can't go on like this," my mother pleaded, a worried look in her eyes. "You did not touch anything at the *Shabbos seudah* this morning . . . Please, darling, just a little something."

"I'm not hungry," I answered with a shrug, "and I really don't feel like eating."

Sima walked into the kitchen just then, holding Shuey. She

was wearing a blue velour robe, and a blue and white polka-dotted kerchief covered her hair. She headed towards the electric percolator to get hot water for a glass of tea.

Taking the baby from her, my mother asked, "How did you sleep, Sima?"

"*Baruch Hashem,* great!" she smiled, "I guess when a baby keeps his mother up all night, he can do her a big favor, and let her nap for an hour on *Shabbos* afternoon." She laughed. "Anyway, how's his favorite aunt doing?" Sima asked, turning to me.

I did not reply, but continued staring glumly at nothing in particular.

My mother threw Sima a concerned look. Taking the cue, Sima took Shuey from my mother's arms and brought him towards me. "How would you like to play a game with *Tantie* Renie?" Sima asked brightly, trying to hand him over to me.

"I would rather not," I answered flatly.

My mother and Sima exchanged worried glances. Sima cleared her throat. "Renie, you know you really cannot go on being depressed forever," she said guardedly.

"Leave me alone," I mumbled .

"Things go on . . . Mommy could use your help. Behaving like this won't help Necha . . ."

"Would you just leave me?" I cried out, pushing my chair back and heading towards the door.

"No, Renie, wait . . ."

She tried to come after me as I ran from the room, but I heard my mother's concerned voice telling her to let me be.

I let the side door slam behind me, not caring if the loud noise awakened someone. I rushed on unhappily. I knew I had to be alone, but I also feared being by myself with my troubling thoughts.

I walked quickly, knowing exactly in which direction I was heading.

For as long as I could remember, the brook had always been my special place. I turned onto the path at the side of my house and hurriedly headed towards the small brook that ran through our back yard. My father had called it my "thinking spot, and somehow, I felt, all problems could be resolved there. Only now, I thought, nothing will ever be the same again, and I was overcome by a feeling of resignation.

I felt a deep kind of agony inside me, as if there was a lump in my throat that could not come out. It was as if my heart was a large ice cube that would not melt. I wished I could cry.

I looked around and saw the bare trees; the ground was covered with a blanket of leaves.

I sat down on the ground, not caring if my *Shabbos* dress would get stained, and heard the crunch of the leaves as I found a comfortable position. I looked at the brook and watched the bubbling waters weave their way around the rocks. I suddenly found myself wishing that I was that water and not me. At least the water knew where it was going, I thought, and what it had to do. I felt so useless and helpless and I wondered if I could ever feel like a normal human being again.

As much as I tried not to think about the accident, I felt as though I were watching a film of it, over and over again. I squeezed my eyes shut, but could not erase that image of Nechama lying so still on the ground. The picture of those big, brown eyes staring unblinkingly ahead into the dark night will forever be imprinted in my mind.

I remembered the crush in the emergency room, the nurses and aides in their starched white uniforms gently examining us, filling out forms and quietly reassuring us. Thank G-d, there were no major injuries, that is . . . besides Nechama. I had a sprained ankle, Feigy's leg was broken, there were many bruises, sprains, and black-and-blue marks, but the injuries were relatively minor. It was mainly for shock that most of us needed treatment.

We returned to the loving arms of our grateful parents who tried to make the remainder of *Succos* as festive as possible. However, dancing in *shul* and the liveliness at home did not lighten my mood of despondency. It was the first *Simchas Torah* that I was not filled with *simchah*.

School was not a help and did nothing to alleviate my depression. My teachers and friends regarded me with great compassion, but I could only stare back at them helplessly.

During one discussion at recess, I overheard a girl ask who will be G.O. president now. With my usual lack of tact, I bluntly told her to be quiet, and sharply reminded her that Nechama was still president and that I never wanted to hear her or anyone else speak like that again. Even as I spoke I knew that I was embarrassing her, but felt too argumentative to apologize, too angry to feel guilty.

I started to walk around the brook. I sighed heavily, remembering the incident that had occurred in *shul* earlier that morning. I had been sitting in my seat following the *laining* of the Torah, when I heard two ladies who were sitting behind me discussing the accident. They had no idea that I had been on the hayride, and therefore were not very careful when they talked.

I sat rigidly, listening in stunned silence as I heard Nechama's name mentioned, and heard one woman's comments about the "poor Leverman parents, who were beside themselves and just falling apart. After all," she went on, "this girl is their only child."

"And who knows," I heard the other lady say, "if the poor child will ever awake from the coma."

I felt myself stiffen.

"And even if she does," the first woman continued, "they say there is a great chance that she will be brain damaged."

I closed my *Chumash* with a loud bang and, without thinking, I quickly turned around. Blazing with anger, I let the words tumble out, "You have some nerve speaking like that about someone . . . especially in *shul*. Don't you know that *tefillah* can always change things? Instead of gossiping, you should be praying!" I shouted at them and, with tears streaming down my cheeks, I grabbed my coat and ran out of *shul*.

Remembering this incident, I stared into the waters of the brook, feeling desolate. I recalled their dumbfounded expressions, how they had stared at me open mouthed, and now I felt totally embarrassed by my outburst. I wished fervently that I could erase what had happened. If only I could learn to think before I spoke, I thought, and not always get myself into trouble with my temper. If only I could be more like Nechama.

Nechama. Oh, Nechama, will I ever see you again? I wondered. My best, best friend, Nechama. Please, if you could stay alive, I would do anything for you . . . But now there is nothing I could do. I cannot even visit with you, since they will not let anyone but family see you.

I felt a breeze and shivered. I looked up. The sun was setting and I knew that it was almost time for *Havdalah*. I had forgotten how short the days were, now that the clock had been changed back to Eastern Standard Time. I slowly rose and walked back towards the house.

As I neared the kitchen I could hear my mother and Sima talking. I froze in place when I heard my name mentioned and stood very still in order to hear what was being said.

" . . . She really must pull herself together. It's just wrong, walking around that way . . ."

" Sima, you must be more understanding about what Renie is going through."

I edged closer.

"I know, Mommy, but you work so hard . . . and now, with Linda and Abe's wedding and *sheva brachos* coming up . . . "

"*Abba* said that what Renie needs right now is our patience, Sima. We must give her time," I heard my mother say.

"But, Mommy, it's two weeks already. I never saw Renie act like this before. She keeps getting into fights with everyone. In fact, just this morning in *shul*, " I heard Sima say, "she yelled at two ladies, just because they were talking about Nechama."

I heard my mother sigh and say anxiously, "I must discuss it with *Abba* after *Havdalah*. Perhaps he will know what to do."

"She can't just sit around brooding," Sima continued. "She should do something about it."

Enraged, I could no longer hold myself back. I burst into the kitchen.

"Renie, I didn't hear . . ."

"Well, what do you want me to do?" I spit out angrily, "I say *Tehillim* all day . . . what do you expect of me? You can't understand how I feel . . ."

"Renie," my mother cooed, putting her arms around me, "it's all right. Hush, my child, everything will be all right."

The dam finally burst and I could restrain my tears no longer. Secure in the warmth of my mother's embrace, I laid my head on her shoulder, and felt the sobs rack my body. As I wept, my mother continued to speak soothingly to me, all the while stroking my hair. It felt so good to get that lump out of my throat, to let that ice cube in my heart melt. When I pulled myself away from her, she wiped the tears from my cheeks.

I looked up and saw Sima's face twisted into a pained expression. She came closer to me.

"Renie, I-I didn't mean to sound so callous." She hesitated briefly, then continued, "but seeing you so depressed, so hopeless," her voice suddenly broke, "makes me so afraid. It-it's like y-you're somebody else," she stammered.

I edged closer to her. Within seconds we were tearfully hugging each other.

I sniffed and she held my hand. "Sima, I do feel so helpless," I said hoarsely, "and I know how inconsolable I've been, and what a pain it must be to be around me."

"Renie, don't say that . . . it's O.K." She squeezed my hand tightly. "You have a right. I shouldn't have . . ."

"No, you're really right," I looked her directly in the eye. "I so much wish there was something I could do to help Nechama."

" I-I was thinking," she hesitated.

"Yes?"

"Remember when I was in Seminary? My teacher's son was very ill."

"Yes, I remember," I replied, wondering what Sima was leading up to. I let go of her hand and walked over to the counter where a box of tissues was sitting.

"Well, we started this *shmiras halashon* club," she went on, a bit more certain. "To be part of it, each person had to commit herself to abstain from talking, writing, or listening to *lashon hara* for a certain amount of time each day."

"So . . . how does that help?" I asked doubtfully.

"Well, you see, you are doing it on behalf of the ill person," she continued. "It is the hope that, in the merit of *shmiras halashon,* of guarding one's tongue, the sick person will recover and have a *refuah sheleimah.*"

"And you think that we could do this for Nechama?" I asked guardedly. "You think it would work?"

"Sure," she answered a note of triumph in her voice. "After all, you know the *passuk*, '*Mi ha'ish hechafetz cha'im . . . netzor leshoncha mei'ra . . .*'" She sang the words to the familiar tune.

"That's true . . ." I was still doubtful. "A *shmiras halashon* club? Hm-m-m . . ."

"And, of course, you know the *passuk*, '*Maves vecha'im beyad halashon,*'" she added reassuringly.

"But a club? I wouldn't even know how to start."

"I would be glad to help," she offered.

"You would?"

"Sure," she replied breezily. "It would be my pleasure."

It was as if, suddenly, a heavy load was lifted off my back. I looked at Sima and felt overwhelmingly grateful to have this woman as my big sister.

"Oh, thank you, Sima, thanks so much," I said appreciatively. We went towards each other and once again we were hugging, only this time comfortingly and full of hope.

My mother had not said anything to us during this whole exchange. Shuey began to cry and she went to lift him out of his infant seat. I could see the pride in her eyes when she turned to us, but at the same time, I detected a note of worry in her voice.

Softly, she said, "Renie, I want you to be hopeful, to pray and to do whatever you can to help Nechama. A person must do whatever is possible, and then *Hashem* helps. But," she hesitated, "I also want you to realize that at the end *Hashem* knows what is best . . . and," she paused, her forehead creased in concern, "you must be ready to accept whatever *Hashem* has in store for Nechama."

"Oh, Mom," my voice was full of renewed enthusiasm. "Don't worry about a thing," I reassured her. "This *shmiras halashon* club is definitely going to help." I went to my mother and gave her a quick hug. It felt so good to be full of hope again, to be rid of that helpless feeling.

I took Shuey from my mother and swung him gently in the air. "Nechama is going to get better quickly," I sang, feeling wildly optimistic. "You'll see she will. You'll see."

Chapter Six

I was still talking on the telephone when the doorbell rang. Seeing that it was Etty, I motioned for her to join me in the kitchen and have a seat while I finished my conversation. Absently, I pointed to the plate of chocolate chip cookies that my mother had baked early that morning and gestured to Etty to help herself.

Tapping the "flash" button on the telephone pad, I waited until I heard a dial tone. "O.K. Just two more calls left," I told Etty, "and then we're off to Sima's."

"Oh, that's all right with me," Etty answered, munching a cookie contentedly. "Take your time. I'm enjoying myself immensely!"

I smiled at her and proceeded to make my calls. When they

were done, I scrawled a few circles around some names on my list and checked off the last two.

"O.K. That about does it," I said happily. "Ten for-sures, five question-marks, three can't-make-its, and two. . ." I shrugged.

"Two?"

"Feigy and Suri."

"You called them, too?" Etty asked incredulously.

"Sure did." I replied. "Sima insisted that I call everybody."

"That's interesting," Etty said, still puzzled.

"I wonder. . ."

Just then my mother walked into the room. After greeting Etty warmly, she reminded me to take the remaining cookies to Sima and proceeded to pile them into a Tupperware container.

Swinging my pocketbook over my shoulder, I zipped up my parka and took the package from her.

"Don't forget to drop *Abba's* letters in the mailbox," my mother reminded me as we neared the back door. "They're either on his desk in the study or on the shelf in the entrance hallway."

"Oh, thanks for the reminder, Mom!" I said, as I ran quickly up the steps, taking two at a time. I headed straight towards my room in the attic.

"I'll be back in a minute," I called down to Etty, breathlessly pushing the door open at the same time. I hurried to my desk, and hastily looked up Chana Devorah's St. Louis address in my telephone/address book, and wrote it clearly on an envelope. Carefully, I folded the letter I had written to C.D. late the night before and placed it inside.

I stopped by my father's study on the way back to the kitchen and made sure that there were stamps on all the envelopes. Then Etty and I said our good-byes and we were off.

We decided to walk to Sima's, cutting through backyards, instead of going by bus. It was a sunny autumn day. The streets were full of colorful leaves, and the cool, brisk air made us feel energetic and refreshed.

Sauntering along, I smiled to myself as I recalled the events of the previous night. Only twenty-four hours ago I would not have believed that my mood could improve so drastically in such a short time.

It had seemed like ages until the men finally came home from *shul* and *Abba* made *Havdalah*. Buoyed with renewed enthusiasm, I was eager to start working on our *shmiras halashon* campaign as soon as possible. My mother and Sima excused me from helping with the dishes, and I sat down at the kitchen table, pen in hand, a fresh sheet of lined paper in front of me. I began to take notes as Sima dictated instructions from where she was standing by the kitchen sink. Carefully and meticulously, I wrote down everything, feeling very proud of my newfound organizational skills.

" . . . And you will have to call everyone in your class. You all may come to my apartment tomorrow afternoon for a planning meeting to discuss ideas and strategy," Sima said authoritatively.

"O.K. I'll start a chain call tonight, and I'm sure that I'll be able to reach most of the girls."

"You have to make sure that everyone is contacted, Renie."

"Fine," I said, beginning to doodle in the margin of the paper. "I'll make sure to get in touch with most of the girls in the class. But," I said determinedly, "I am not calling someone," and I emphasized the word "someone."

"Renie." She put down the towel. "You have to call everyone." She emphasized the word "everyone."

"Well, why should I call Feigy?" I asked stubbornly, continuing to doodle. "Anyway, she probably won't want to come."

"That doesn't matter." Sima retrieved her towel and began to vigorously rub a plate. "That will be her decision, and besides, you never know."

"I do know," I put down my pen purposefully. "She hates me and I ha . . . don't like her. She'll never want to do anything with me and besides, she'll probably think the idea is — corny."

Sima walked over to where I sat, the towel and plate still in her hand. She had a hurt look on her face. "Do you think it's corny?" she questioned, looking me directly in the eye. "Because if you do we could st . . ."

"Well, n-no, n-not really," I stammered. "If your class was able to do it, and you were Sem girls . . . " I felt the tears welling up in my eyes. "O-of course, it's the right thing to do. It has to work, I-I guess. It is just that Feigy and I . . ."

"It does NOT matter," Sima said vehemently, "what you and Feigy think, or rather thought, of each other. If you want this to work, Renie, you have to be prepared to forgive. Part of *shmiras halashon* is also being '*dan lechaf zechus.*' You have to be ready," she continued, "to judge a person favorably."

"Well, how do I judge Feigy favorably?" I asked, not really expecting an answer. "Whatever I say, whatever I do, she puts me down. I don't know what she has against me, anyhow."

"Who says that she has anything against you? It could be that she is just a very sad person. Maybe she is just very envious of you, Renie," she said, looking at me steadily.

"Feigy? Envious of me?" I laughed. "Feigy, rich Feigy, who has everything, who gets great marks, who is the most graceful dancer in the whole sch . . ."

"Renie," Sima lifted up her eyes despairingly, "come on! Just because a girl is talented and smart, it does NOT mean she has everything. Maybe she's really very insecure and feels that she has to put you down for that reason."

"Insecure? What could she be insecure about?"

"Well, I remember that when we had our *shmiras halashon* club, we learned that many times the people who feel compelled to put other people down are those people who feel they are most lacking."

"Come on."

"Suppose," Sima continued determinedly, "that despite everything she has, she is really quite lonely. Perhaps she wishes that she was best friends with Nechama, or who knows? Maybe she wishes that she could be as close to you two as you are to each other."

"It's funny — Nechama once said something like that to me," I said softly.

"It's possible that if, instead of always answering her in a nasty tone, you would respond kindly, perhaps you would see a gradual change in her attitude towards you."

"I don't know," I said doubtfully. "I can't be so sweet and charming to someone when that someone is always so mean to me. I just don't know."

"Well, Renie, if you want this to be successful, you cannot just work on it with half a heart. If you are going to be preaching to others and trying to get them to work on their *midah* of *shmiras halashon,* you are going to have to work on yours plenty hard, too."

Of course, I ended up calling Feigy. At first we were awkward with each other. I spoke in a very matter-of-fact, business-like voice, and she responded a bit coolly. But I reminded myself sternly to be nice, and when I told Feigy the reason for my call, she surprised me by taking down Sima's address and offering to call Suri. By the time we hung up, she still had not committed herself to joining us at the meeting, but I detected a slight softening in her attitude towards me.

"I wonder how many girls will show up," I said aloud, a note of concern in my voice.

"Well, out of a class of twenty-one, I'm sure that we'll have, at the very least, half," Etty replied, pushing her fingers through her jet-black short hair. "And stop worrying, Renie. I never saw you like this."

"I can't help it. I never had my best friend in a coma before," I muttered sourly.

The expression on Etty's face brought forth an immediate apology from me. "I'm really sorry, Etty, you didn't deserve that. It's just that," I admitted uncomfortably, "I suddenly feel so responsible for Nechama . . . It's like I know for sure that if this *shmiras halashon* club is successful, then Nechama will get well, and then I worry that if it is not . . . "

"Don't think like that," Etty said comfortingly. She bent down to pick up a russet-colored leaf, and held it out admiringly. "It *is* going to be successful. It has to be."

We rounded the corner and waved as we saw Miriam and Peshy coming from the bus stop. They joined us and we all walked together towards the building in which Sima lived.

The meeting turned out to be more successful than I had

expected. Incredibly, seventeen girls came. Over my mother's chocolate chip cookies and cups of hot cocoa, Sima explained how we were all there, not just for Nechama, but for ourselves, too. She told us many stories of how people's lives had improved when they judged others favorably and were careful with the way they used their gift of speech.

I watched Sima admiringly. This is my sister, I felt like shouting to everyone, feeling possessively proud. This is MY wonderful sister! I looked at her appreciatively. We both have the same green eyes and brown hair. But where I had always thought of Sima as being much prettier than I, I now thought of her as beautiful. She was wearing a wig that was a light shade of brown with reddish highlights. It brought out her high cheekbones, and its fringed bangs emphasized her long eyelashes. Her green eyes were luminous against her clear, milky-white complexion as she excitedly spoke to us.

Engrossed in animated discussion, many of us enthusiastically told our own stories and contributed ideas, all the while passing around popcorn and potato chips. We decided that besides accepting the responsibility of keeping a specific time of each day "*lashon hara* free,' each of us would have a *chavrusa*, a study partner, with whom to review the laws of *lashon hara*. We would also be able to work on a *shmiras halashon* project together with our partner. This way, besides growing spiritually, we would have fun, too.

Sima suggested that we all put our names in a pile and randomly pick a partner. I saw her tear a paper out of her spiral notebook. First she bent it in half, and then proceeded to fold the half into tenths. After carefully cutting the paper into twenty even pieces, she handed them out to all the girls assembled there. When we finished passing around the pens and printing our names, the folded papers were placed in an upturned hat.

Etty went first. Theatrically, she swished her hand through the air and then let it fall into the hat. She took out a folded paper. Slowly, dramatically, she read the name of her new study partner. It was Yocheved. We all giggled and then it was the next girl's turn. Zehava ended up fishing her own name out of the hat, and had to pick again. And so it went until it was Feigy's turn.

There were only four of us left by then: Feigy, Suri, Ahuvah and I. I saw Feigy and Suri exchange hopeful glances as Feigy placed her hand in the hat. I sat rigid, waiting.

I watched the expression on her face change as she looked at the name on her paper. At first her eyes widened in disbelief, and then I saw her nose crinkle in disappointment as she glanced once again at the note, as if to make sure that she was seeing correctly. I sat tensely and stared, open mouthed, as she raised her blue eyes and, looking directly at me, prepared to read the name from her unfolded piece of paper.

"It says here . . ." she pointed to the paper and continued warily, all the while looking at me. "It looks like Renie Greenberg and I are going to be partners."

Chapter Seven

"Come on, Renie, you can't let it get you down."

"That's easy for you to say, Etty," I said dryly. "You'll be working with Yocheved."

Etty and I had left Sima's apartment and were walking down the steps of the large apartment building. Some girls had lingered behind to discuss ideas for projects with Sima, and some to consult with their partners. I was in no mood to hang around with the others.

"Listen, Renie, that's just the way things turned out," she commented, matter-of-factly. "You've got to try to make the best of it."

"Yeah, right," I brooded. "Anyway, if Feigy would rather work with Suri, I don't see why Sima won't let her. After all," I continued adamantly, "I sure wouldn't mind working with Ahuvah."

I angrily pulled open the heavy outer door and let it bang. We walked out into the crisp autumn air and, momentarily, I allowed myself to enjoy the feeling of the warm sunshine on my face. Then, remembering my morose mood and bitter feelings, I hastily pulled up the zipper of my parka, sighing noisily.

"Well," Etty continued steadily, "before we even began drawing lots, Sima explained the rules . . . whoever's name you picked, that's the girl you get to work with. Oh, look," Etty whispered softly, "there are Feigy and Suri."

Turning my head slightly, I could see Feigy and Suri standing under a large maple tree on the corner, engrossed in deep conversation.

Sima, why must you be so mean? I thought sulkily to myself. Why can't you make an exception for your own sister? I had been so excited about the project, and now, with my luck, out of seventeen girls, I get Feigy. Sima knows that we don't get along, so why force the two of us to work together? It's just not fair, I thought resentfully.

We walked on in silence. I guess in my heart I knew she was right and, I reminded myself sternly, the reason for this *shmiras halashon* club was as important as ever.

"There's Yocheved now."

We had reached the bus stop. I turned and saw Yocheved hurrying towards us.

"I was hoping we could get together this afternoon, Etty," she began breathlessly, "to start working on ideas for the *shmiras halashon* campaign."

"I know. I would love to," Etty replied eagerly, "but I have my cousin's shower today. If you don't mind, tomorrow after school would be fine with me."

"Great. I was thinking of an idea." She turned conspiratorially towards Etty. "Do you suppose . . ."

I walked away gloomily, figuring that they probably would not even notice my absence. I found myself brooding.

Everyone was enthusiastically involved with their own *chavrusas,* and here I was, alone, and in a despondent mood. Well, at least I helped get things started, I reminded myself bitterly, so I guess now I won't be needed anymore. As I walked on, I concluded that since no one would miss me anyway, I would visit Mrs. Finkelman instead of returning directly home. At least there, I comforted myself, I would be appreciated.

I suppose I'll work on my own, I decided sullenly. It won't be as much fun, but . . .

I was interrupted by the sound of a cough directly behind me. Surprised, I whirled around and was astonished to see Feigy standing there, a look of discomfort shadowing her face.

"Um, Renie," she began awkwardly, "I know you aren't happy about it, and I can't say that I am too thrilled either, but . . ."

"But we're supposed to be *chavrusas,* " I finished her sentence with some asperity.

"And even though I could think of at least fifteen other girls I would rather work with . . ."

"You're stuck with me." My tone was icy.

"Well, after we finished picking the names out of the hat," she told me, "you went into your nephew's room, and I," she paused, then continued a bit more gently, "had a talk with your sister."

"You spoke with Sima?" I demanded.

"Yes," she hesitated, then added more softly, "and she's very nice. You're really very lucky to have someone like her for an older sister."

"Thanks, I know," I admitted. "But what did you discuss?" I asked guardedly, unable to hide my uneasiness. How could my sister be so disloyal to me as to have a talk with my archenemy behind my back?

"I went to her to find out why we can't switch partners. I would work with Suri, and Ahuvah would be your *chavrusa.* I figured that with that change, at least two of us would be a lot happier."

"I can guess what her answer was," I muttered, my voice hardly audible.

"Of course, she said that it wouldn't be possible." Feigy paused, and then continued more mildly. "But you know something? Believe it or not, I think she's right."

"You do?" I asked incredulously.

"Yes," she replied slowly. "After all, if the *shmiras halashon* club is to be successful," she hesitated again, and swallowed uncomfortably before going on, "then we'll have to put aside our feelings for each other and try, for Nechama's sake, to get along. And as your sister explained, to be *'dan lechaf zechus.'*"

"I guess you're right," I admitted uneasily. "We could try working together, that is, *for Nechama's sake.*"

"Yes. *For Nechama's sake.*"

We stood together silently, smiling uncomfortably, for a few awkward moments. In spite of the warm feeling that was beginning to spread through me, I said, more coldly than I had meant to, "I've got to run now, Feigy. A friend of mine is expecting me. Perhaps I'll be free one day after school this week." And then I added for extra punch, "I'll have to check my calendar." "Er-um, Renie," Feigy faltered, "I thought the meeting was going to take much longer, and I told my parents that I wouldn't be home until much later."

"Yes?"

"They went away for the day and," she admitted, "I forgot my key."

"Do you need a place to stay today?" I asked, more kindly.

"If you don't mind, just for a short while." She blushed furiously, unaccustomed to admitting that she needed a favor. "I can go to Suri in about two hours, but right now she's going away with her mother. Or one of my neighbors might be home by then."

"Oh, it's no problem at all." My voice sounded positively benign. "You can come with me to visit Mrs. Finkelman. She's an elderly woman with whom I am very friendly, and she loves to have company."

"Are you sure it's O.K.?"

"Of course! She always likes to meet new people," I said eagerly. As an afterthought I added, "How about we first go for pizza?"

"That sounds great," she grinned shyly.

We crossed the street together and I could not prevent a small sigh of relief from crossing my lips. Feigy looked at me and smiled. We headed towards Main Street and, upon reaching the small but cozy and warm pizza shop, ordered a couple of slices of pizza and two medium Cokes.

We did not say much to each other at the time, although we sat there amiably, comfortable in each other's company. I guess we were still feeling a bit awkward about the sudden transformation in our attitudes towards each other. To be quite honest, I must admit that I was feeling a bit self-conscious, too. I wanted Feigy to like me, but at the same time I knew that we were very different. And yet, I thought, Nechama and I are very different, too, and somehow that did not matter.

Washing down my last bite of pizza with the remainder of my soda, I suddenly had an idea. "Feigy, how about coming to my house to work on the *shmiras halashon* campaign after we visit Mrs. Finkelman? You could stay for supper."

"That sounds nice." Feigy's smile lit up her face. "But are you sure your mother won't mind? I mean, don't you have to ask her first?"

"I guess it would be proper if I did," I answered with a laugh, "but then she would probably think that I wasn't feeling too well. You see, I never have to ask my mother permission to bring someone home for supper, for lunch or whatever. There's always plenty of food in our house, and we always have guests coming and going."

"Really?" Feigy asked incredulously.

"Sure. Mind you, it isn't always so formal and it's not exactly fancy . . . "

"Nechama used to always tell me how much she loved going to your house . . ." She smiled, and her smile was warm. "I would like to come," she hesitated for a moment, "if you're sure it's O.K."

"Sure, I'm sure it's O.K.," I replied breezily.

"Renie," she reminded me, "I think that if we want to get all this accomplished today, we'd better get going."

We said our *brachos achronos* and were out the door. When

we reached Wilson Street we turned the corner, and I led Feigy down the block to Mrs. Finkelman's home. She stopped short when we reached the front of the apartment building, and I saw her blue eyes widen in surprise as she surveyed the slightly dilapidated building that we were about to enter.

"Don't worry," I assured her, feeling a bit embarrassed. "It's really clean and neat inside. I-I guess that this is all she can afford," I stammered.

I was annoyed with myself for feeling so defensive, and yet, I could not help feeling ashamed in front of Feigy.

Slowly we began to climb the stairs. I was about to warn Feigy about Mr. Petrovsky, but two things stopped me. First, I remembered that it would be considered *lashon hara* to discuss someone else and then — as if to strengthen my resolve — we suddenly heard a loud, ferocious groan from the hallway below.

I gasped, horrified. I saw Feigy's white face and trembling lips and knew that she depended on me to find out what had happened.

Carefully, on tiptoe, I inched my way into the shelter of the shadows in the hallway. I saw that Feigy was following quietly behind me, her eyes shadowed by fear. Slowly, we edged closer.

To this day, I still do not know what made me do it or how it happened, but all of a sudden I tripped. There was a loud bang. Someone must have heard me and was heading towards us. Feigy grabbed hold of my arm and I froze in fear as we heard the hurried footsteps getting louder and louder. Suddenly, a tall shadowy figure loomed before us. It was Mr. Petrovsky and he was heading straight in our direction.

He had his shirt sleeves rolled up to his elbows and his hair and shirt were soaking wet. The skin on his face was dripping with perspiration.

"Oh, er, um, Mr. P-p-etrovsky," I stammered.

"YOU AGAIN?" he bellowed.

"I am s-s-sorry if we dist-t-urbed you," I went on nervously, "but we heard a sh-shout, and we thought someone might n-need help."

"Oh, so you heard someone SHOUT?" he growled.

We nodded.

". . . and YOU thought YOU could be of some help?"

We continued to nod our heads vigorously, as if our lives depended on it.

"Would YOU like to see what kind of HELP is needed?" his voice throbbed.

"Y-yes." My voice was hardly audible.

"Then come with me," he commanded.

We followed obediently. He led us into his apartment. It had the exact same layout as Mrs. Finkelman's, but it lacked the warmth and friendliness that permeated her home. He opened the door to his kitchen . . . and then, we saw it.

There were torrents of water pouring down from all sides, from the corner of the wall to the cracks in the ceiling. I could not believe what I was seeing.

"Oh, you poor man," I said compassionately, forgetting my fear of him. "No wonder you're so upset."

Feigy didn't say a word. She was dumb with shock.

"I am standing by the sink, innocently washing my lunch dishes, minding my own business, when suddenly, this . . ." he lifted his hands upward.

"Oh my goodness!" a thought suddenly struck me. "We must make sure that Mrs. Finkelman is all right. Doesn't she live right above you?" I asked worriedly.

"She sure does live on top of me, and she never lets me forget it! Don't think that this is the first time she let her sink overflow," he continued angrily. "It's the third time this month!"

"Yes, but I hope she's O.K." I was still anxious.

"Well, maybe we should give a look . . . just in case," he murmured under his breath. "But, boy, does she deserve it this time!"

We hurried up the stairs. I glanced at Feigy following behind, as if in a daze. Well, I thought, there goes the end of what might have been the beginning of a beautiful friendship. I don't think she'll ever want to do anything with me again.

When we reached the door of 2E, we saw water rushing from

under it. Now I was really concerned, and by the expression on Mr. Petrovsky's face, I could see that he was, too.

Without bothering to knock and waste precious minutes, Mr. Petrovsky threw his large frame against the door and pushed it open. Breathlessly we rushed inside, unsure of what we would find.

The living room was empty. Water was gushing out through the kitchen doorway and we could hear the loud sound of the faucet turned on full force.

We hurried into the kitchen. A waterfall was cascading from the basin of the sink onto the floor, covering it and moving it towards the doorway, reminding me of a river flowing downstream.

And sitting cozily on a chair, her feet on a stool, deeply engrossed in a book and oblivious to us all, sat the subject of our worry — our dear Mrs. Finkelman.

Mr. Petrovsky waded into the room and turned off the faucet. The sudden quiet jolted Mrs. Finkelman back to reality. She blinked rapidly and, upon seeing us, the corners of her mouth curved upward into a wonderful smile.

"Oh, how nice," she exclaimed, her eyes sparkling. "I have company. Oh, dis is just vonderful! Mr. Petrovsky, Renie, and how sveet, you brought a friend," she concluded happily, greeting Feigy with a broad smile.

I looked around at my companions. Mr. Petrovsky's face was turning red, Feigy was staring, wide eyed and open mouthed, and I was trying to think of something to say, when Mrs. Finkelman stood up.

"Oh dear me," she said looking down, a worried expression on her face, "I must have left dat plug in de drain again." She waded through the water to the sink and triumphantly pulled out the stopper. "Did it leak into your house, Mr. Petrovsky?"

He just ground his teeth together furiously, but remained silent.

"I guess it must have," she commented, with a note of concern in her voice. She walked over to a corner cupboard and took out four towels. Handing one towel to each of us, she said calmly, "And now ve shall clean up here and den ve vill go downstairs and make Mr. Petrovsky's house beautiful!"

I took a cup and began to scoop up water and pour it into a pail. I saw Feigy put her towel on the floor, wait for it to soak up some water and, a few moments later, lift it carefully and squeeze it into the sink. Mr. Petrovsky found a mop and pushed the water from the hallway back into the kitchen. Mrs. Finkelman went to her old phonograph and put on a record with *chazanishe* music. Every few minutes, while the cantor was on a high note, the needle would reach a scratch on the record, and we would hear it over and over again. It must have taken us a full hour to complete the job.

Mrs. Finkelman offered us some lemonade to refresh ourselves before we went down to Mr. Petrovsky's place. She gave us some delicious blueberry pie, too. I have to admit that I was having a pretty good time. Mr. Petrovsky, it was proven to me, could be a pretty pleasant fellow when he was around Mrs. Finkelman. He was telling us funny stories about the "old country" and we couldn't help giggling when Mrs. Finkelman added her comments in her accented English. However, I could not help but feel sorry for poor Feigy. She must be having a terrible time, I figured. After all, her mother has live-in help, and she probably never has to do anything to help out at home. I was sure that a girl like Feigy probably found an afternoon, spent with elderly people, boring.

On the way down to Mr. Petrovsky's apartment, I managed to get a few private moments with Feigy. I threw her an apologetic look, and began to excuse myself.

"Sorry, Feigy," I said defensively. "If I'd known what would happen here today, I never would have dragged you with me ."

"You didn't drag me here," she whispered back to me. "You did me a favor by taking me along with you and besides, I wouldn't have missed this time for anything in the world!"

"You mean you're enjoying yourself?" I asked incredulously.

"Sure am," she grinned.

I could have danced down the rest of the steps and through Mr. Petrovsky's apartment, I felt so light hearted. It took much less time to finish off Mr. Petrovsky's kitchen, since only that room was affected and his floors were not flooded.

We returned to Mrs. Finkelman's apartment to tidy ourselves up and to taste some of her homemade ice cream. Feigy was in the living room, combing her hair by the mirror. I was in the kitchen, chatting with Mrs. Finkelman while she scooped the ice cream into sundae cups. I watched her lift a small saucepan from the stove and pour some hot fudge onto the ice cream. As she busily squeezed some whip cream on top, I told her about Nechama and the *shmiras halashon* club. Feigy returned to the kitchen and let out a whistle when she saw what Mrs. Finkelman had prepared. We eagerly sat down at the table, and Mrs. Finkelman placed the ice cream sundaes before us.

"No, no, no, not yet," Mrs. Finkelman stopped me as I was about to dig my spoon into it. "Vone more ding," she said, wagging her forefinger and hurrying off to the refrigerator. "Now let me see," she wondered aloud while looking inside. "Ah, here it is," she exclaimed triumphantly, as she removed a jar of juicy, red maraschino cherries from the shelf. With a small flourish, she placed a cherry on top of each sundae. "*Now* you can eat!"

We enjoyed the heavenly treat, and after saying *"Borei nefashos"* we regretfully said our good-byes. We chatted with great animation as we walked downstairs and were surprised to see that it was already dark when we reached the outside. It was still difficult for me to get used to the time change. I looked upwards towards the sky, and saw dark clouds hovering above.

"Time flies when you're having fun," I said gaily.

"Oh, my goodness," Feigy said looking at her watch, "I don't believe it. It's already six o'clock. My parents must be home already and are probably frantic with worry."

"Do you want to call them and ask if you can come to my house?"

"Thanks, I would love to, but I didn't do my homework yet, and it's already late in the day. It looks like it's about to rain," she spoke quickly. "How about tomorrow after school?" Her question came easily.

I was about to answer her that of course, it wouldn't be a

problem, when suddenly we saw our English teacher, Mrs. Ross.

She was walking towards the building, with the same worried expression that I had become accustomed to seeing on her face. Walking with her was a tall, broad-shouldered man. He was wearing a black coat with its collar pulled up over his chin. Sunglasses hid his eyes, and a hat was pulled down low over his forehead. He walked quickly, alongside our teacher, hunched over, his hands in his pockets. They must have been so engrossed in their own affairs, that when I called out her name as they passed us, they just continued walking on as if they did not hear me.

As they walked away I watched them mysteriously disappear into the shadows of the building.

Suddenly the dark clouds opened, and like a waterfall, the rain came pouring down.

Chapter Eight

"Renie, are you all right?" *Morah* Fischer asked me kindly.

"Yes, I-I'm sorry, *Morah*," I murmured, looking back into my *Chumash.*

If earlier that Monday morning I had remembered that this was the day of elections, I probably would have not gone to school. As it was, I had been so preoccupied with the *shmiras halashon* club that I had completely forgotten about the Mitzvahthon. That is, until *Rebbetzin* Leibowitz came into our class and instructed us to remain in our room, after the bell rang, to vote. She explained to us that we were to pick a girl who was not only able to perform well, but was someone we could feel proud of as the representative of our school.

I had always been fascinated by the democratic process of voting, of majority rule; but that day I wished with all my heart that there was a different way.

It was hard for me to concentrate on the *Chumash* lesson. I kept replaying the accident over and over again in my mind. I knew that had the hayride never taken place, Nechama would be the unanimous choice to represent our school. I also knew without a doubt that Nechama would have made our school the national winner.

I imagined that night of triumph. I pictured our principal, Nechama's parents . . . I pictured myself, and the girls in the class. And I pictured Nechama smiling shyly, embarrassed by all the attention, but proud that all her hard work, the years of lessons, the training and practicing at the piano resulted in this great public achievement and *Kiddush Hashem.*

My heart sank lower and lower as that picture quickly faded away and was replaced with that image of Nechama which, to this day, I still cannot erase from my mind: Nechama lying on the grass, her auburn hair spread out around her face, her large brown eyes staring straight ahead. And now she'll never have that glory, none of us will, I thought guiltily, and it is all my fault.   "Renie Greenberg, what do you think the answer is?"

I looked up at my teacher, a blank expression on my face.

"Are you sure that you're O.K., Renie?" *Morah* asked again, compassionately.

"Yes! Yes!" I repeated turning away, struggling to hold back my tears.

I did not know how I would get through that day; but while *Morah* taught *Chumash,* I reached a decision. I intended to do all that was in my power to make Nechama the winner. With my whole heart, I knew she was the right choice. Accident or no accident, Nechama would be on that stage, in the spotlight, playing piano as the representative of our school for the Mitzvahthon. I was determined to make that dream a reality. When the bell finally did ring and the class remained in their seats as instructed, I was prepared.

Morah Fischer, as our homeroom teacher, organized the vote. My heart pounded as she requested nominations.

My hand shot up. Glad to see my enthusiasm, *Morah* called on me first. She turned towards the blackboard, smiling. With a piece of chalk already in her hand, she was prepared to write down my suggestion.

In a clear voice I declared, "I nominate Nechama Leverman to play the piano at the Mitzvahthon."

A hush fell over the classroom. *Morah* swung around, her eyes and mouth opened wide in surprise. The stillness was so intense that we were able to hear the soft sound of the chalk dropping onto the stone floor.

I broke the silence. "Well, why not?" I demanded. "We all know that Nechama is the best!"

"Because we also know, Renie," *Morah* replied, regaining her composure, "that Nechama is ill." She walked over to my desk and added softly, "Very ill."

"I know that she is in a coma," I said with some asperity. "But I also know that she is going to get well soon. Very soon," I added with emphasis.

"Of course we hope and believe that Nechama will have a *refuah sheleimah bekarov,* but . . ." *Morah* looked around the room at her students who were quietly sitting on the edge of their seats, waiting expectantly for her reply. "But we have to also be realistic. Even if Nechama was to come out of the coma today," she paused uncomfortably, "we do not know what kind of condition she would be in."

"She'll be fine," I said indignantly, "and she'll be the grand winner of the Mitzvahthon." I knew that *Morah* could see the steely determination in my eyes and was beginning to feel frustrated by the position in which she found herself.

"Renie," *Morah* sighed, "I, too, want the best for Nechama . . . but I also want what's best for the class . . . for the school." She paused to collect her thoughts, and looked searchingly from one face to the other, obviously uncertain whether our youthful minds could grasp what she was about to say. She spoke slowly, weighing each word carefully as she paced up and down the aisles. "Girls, I hope with all my heart that Nechama will be able to join us soon. But, you see," she said hesitatingly, "she received a severe head injury . . . there was some internal bleeding and the doctors don't know at this time whether any part of the brain was permanently damaged. Even if she was to come out of the coma . . . " She paused. The girls were absolutely silent. The only sounds we could hear was the ticking of the clock that hung over the blackboard and the clicking of our teacher's heels against the stone floor. She continued, her face drawn, "We don't know what kind of condition she would be in. The doctors just can't say for sure . . . what will be. She might require months, or even years, of therapy . . . " Her voice suddenly broke and she was unable to continue.

Without raising my hand to be called on, I said hoarsely, in a very low voice, "But, *Morah,* the *shmiras halashon* campaign . . . Nechama *will* get well soon. She *has* to."

Morah looked at me, her eyebrows raised inquisitively.

"*Morah,*" I heard a voice from the other side of the room. We all turned in its direction and I was surprised to see that it was Feigy who had spoken. She cleared her throat and continued, "It's like this. Yesterday, most of us gathered at Renie's sister's house and . . . " Feigy glanced in my direction and I threw her a grateful look. "And we began a *shmiras halashon* club."

It took fifteen minutes for the girls, with Feigy at the helm, to eagerly explain to *Morah* Fischer what our *shmiras halashon* club was all about. *Morah* seemed a bit surprised but definitely very pleased, and happily told us that she would be very proud to inform *Rebbetzin* Leibowitz about our project. She was sure that the principal would want to expand this campaign throughout the school.

She concurred that since we all unanimously wanted Nechama to represent our school, she would consent to it; however, we would have to be realistic and agree to choose a runner-up. Feigy, reluctantly and with great embarrassment, accepted our vote.

The rest of the day passed by routinely. The only change was in me. Contrary to my usual, somewhat haphazard system of note-taking, I sat in class, a sheet of carbon paper carefully placed between two looseleaf pages, studiously, meticulously, taking notes. I was careful not to miss anything. After all, a heavy responsibility weighed on my shoulders. I felt that it was now my job to be here, in class, for Nechama. I intended to be fully prepared with everything she missed while ill, in order to help her upon her recuperation and return to school.

❦ ❦ ❦

When the four-thirty bell rang, indicating that school was over, I eagerly met Feigy at the school entrance. I saw that we were not the only partners getting together that afternoon to work out our *shmiras halashon* ideas. I saw Suri wave to Feigy as she and Ahuvah headed towards the bus that went to Rorey. Etty, Yocheved, Miriam, Feigy and I began the short walk in the direction of our homes, talking excitedly about the *shmiras halashon* club and exchanging ideas on how to turn this into a successful school-wide campaign.

When we reached my corner, Feigy and I waved good-bye to the other three as we turned to walk towards my house. Alone with Feigy, I suddenly felt unusually shy. What if we have nothing to say to each other, I wondered. And worse: what if Feigy thinks my house is too noisy or too messy?

I waved nonchalantly to my neighbor, Mrs. Eidelstein, as we passed her house. We heard the gleeful cries of another neighbor, little Yanky Beer, as he and his friend raced around us, dodging a third child who was chasing them. I laughed aloud, remembering my own days of playing "tag."

From the corner of my eye I stole a quick glance at Feigy, and I could not stop my own feelings of inadequacy from creeping up on me. With her long, blonde hair swept up into a neat ponytail, its golden highlights shimmering in the sun, she looked so sleek and pretty. We were wearing identical outfits, as it was a school day and uniforms were required. Her brand-new navy jumper fitted her smoothly and neatly, but as for me, although I had tried taping it up with masking tape the other day, the hem was constantly coming down and my jumper was pilled from wear, slightly creased, and not exactly stain-free.

I sighed noisily. What's going on with me? Why do I suddenly have these feelings of inferiority, I wondered sulkily.

suddenly have these feelings of inferiority, I wondered sulkily. I never worried about things like this before. Other types of girls were always concerned about what they looked like and what others thought of them, not down-to-earth girls like me. So what in the world was happening to me now? Will I ever be my carefree self again?

As we opened the door and entered my home, we were greeted by the wonderful aroma of *challah* baking in the oven. My mother gave us a plateful of her famous chocolate chip cookies that she had just removed from the cooling rack. We sat down at the table and munched our cookies, washing them down with tall glasses of fresh milk. Contentedly, we watched my mother continue baking, and chatted comfortably with her.

Feigy was incredulous as she observed my mother removing pan after pan filled with *challos.* As my mother wrapped them in aluminum foil and then placed them in plastic bags, she explained to Feigy that these *challos* were to be put away and frozen until *Shabbos Chanukah.* She was preparing in advance for Abe's and Linda's *sheva brachos.* And then I had to explain to her who Abe and Linda were. She could not get over the fact that my mother was like a mother to them and that they were so much a part of our family. I laughed and told her that they were not the only ones, and that there were many people like them, people who were not related to us, and yet considered this their home.

Just as we were about to go upstairs to my room, my mother invited the awed Feigy to come to our house one Friday morning when we were off from school for *challah*-baking lessons. She eagerly accepted.

Before long we were comfortably sitting cross-legged on the floor in my room, surrounded by fresh sheets of oak tag, markers, pens and papers. A container of orange juice, two paper cups and a bag of corn chips were nearby.

"We need publicity," Feigy said thoughtfully. "We have to think of an idea that will make the whole school want to participate. Something . . ."

". . . that will really turn everyone on," I said fervently.

"Yes, something attractive, and . . ." Feigy said, her blue eyes opening wide with excitement, "yes, something with a theme."

"A theme?" I asked speculatively, chewing on the top of my pencil.

"Yes ... We need something common, recognizable — something that normally is presented in a certain way. Then what we do," Feigy smiled slyly, "is convert it to our theme of *shmiras halashon.*"

"H-mmm . . ." I allowed my eyes to roam around my room. They stopped short at the sight of a poster that Nechama had brought back from her trip to Israel the year before. It read: *TIZAHER GVUL LEFANECHA* — Hebrew for CAUTION: BORDER AHEAD. "Do you mean," I asked, my voice rising with excitement, "something like that?" I pointed to the poster. "We could use this idea but change the words to CAUTION: *LASHON HARA* IS DANGEROUS TO YOUR HEALTH — or something like that."

"Or," Feigy continued animatedly, "we could use a stop sign. But we would write: STOP! speaking *lashon hara.*"

"Or," I continued, catching Feigy's enthusiasm, "we can use a traffic light. Red light — Do not go ahead with *lashon hara*! Green light — GO! no *lashon hara* spoken here! Yellow light — Slow down, conversation is changing!"

"And we could use a No-Smoking sign. You know, the ones with the circles around a cigarette and a slash right down the middle. Only," Feigy laughed, "instead of using a picture of a cigarette, we can make a picture of a tongue."

"Oh, Feigy, it's great!" I was thrilled. "We can think of a million ideas." I visualized the school's hallways covered with *shmiras halashon* signs . . . I imagined two girls in conversation . . . one girl about to say something about another, when suddenly her eyes catch sight of one of our signs and she stops . . . "All we have to do is think of a typical sign and then convert it to our theme. Using this concept," I said breathlessly, "it's simply unlimited!"

"That's true," Feigy said, smiling at me, "you thought of it and," she added fervently, "you must be a genius!"

"Come on," I said, blushing modestly, my heart soaring, "you were the one who gave me the idea."

The hour that followed was full of the excitement of sudden brainstorms, laughter and activity. Our only interruption was for a delicious supper of fried chicken cutlets and mashed potatoes. We continued working diligently until a quarter to nine, when Feigy's father came by car to pick her up and take her home. Grudgingly we parted, eager to continue working together again, soon.

❈ ❈ ❈

After I finished washing the dishes I returned to my room to do my homework. Looking over the carbon copies of the notes I had taken for Nechama, I realized that she probably would not be able to read them since, admittedly, I have never had the greatest handwriting, especially, when rushed. Taking a few pieces of fresh looseleaf paper, I concluded that I must rewrite the notes neatly for her.

Two pages were completed when my back started aching. I decided to continue working in bed. Carrying my notes and a few more sheets of looseleaf paper and a heavy notebook to lean on, I climbed under my covers and placed a pillow comfortably against my headboard and continued to work.

I went on writing, determined to keep Nechama's notes neat and legible to enable her to keep up with the class when she returned. I kept writing. My eyes kept closing. I continued to write until finally my eyelids felt so heavy that I just let them stay closed.

I must have been half asleep when, a short time later, my mother tiptoed softly into my room. She removed my notebook and papers and placed them on the night table beside me. Tucking the fluffy quilt under my chin, she reached over carefully, switched off my lamp and left the room quietly, leaving me contentedly lying in my warm bed with a kiss lingering on my forehead.

Chapter Nine

A strange incident occurred in school the following day.

It was late afternoon, the last period of the day. Since we were presently part of the elite and oldest group in our school — more commonly known as eighth grade — we were now worthy of one free period a week. This time was to be used to work on the yearbook, clubs, or anything else that was considered to be academically or spiritually constructive.

As I have previously mentioned, I had been chosen as editor-in-chief of our yearbook. And it was for this reason that I found myself sitting up front, at the large teacher's desk, with our new English teacher — who also served as our yearbook and G.O. adviser — Mrs. Ross. Despite the fact that out of school she came across as a suspicious character, she proved herself to be quite brilliant and witty as a teacher. Speaking to her informally during these weekly free periods, while working on the yearbook, I discovered that she was also gifted with a splendid sense of humor. I found myself liking her more and more.

That Tuesday the two of us sat there discussing the placement of an essay that had just been given to me. On the desk were piles of articles and assorted photographs that were waiting to be selected and arranged. I was in the midst of explaining why I thought that this particular article belonged in a specific spot, when Mrs. Ross interrupted me with a strange request.

In a low voice, just a pitch above a whisper, she turned to me and asked, "Renie, I have a favor that I need to ask of you."

"Sure," I replied, my eyebrows raised curiously.

"I-I was wondering, Renie, do you ever baby-sit?"

"Sure," I answered again, but this time a bit more speculatively.

"I have a three-and-a-half-month-old little boy," she whispered. "I-I need to go somewhere Thursday evening." She looked around the room to make sure that no one could hear her. "Would you be free to watch him for me?"

"Of course, no problem," I said reassuringly, although I was still puzzled.

"But, Renie, there are two things I must ask of you," she looked me directly in the eye, a troubled expression on her face. When I nodded, encouraging her to go on, she continued, "Firstly, to please not tell anyone anything about this, and secondly," she paused, weighing her words carefully, "I know that this might seem odd, but," she hesitated, "I need you to watch him in your own home, not mine."

She was right. It did seem odd. Very odd. As I walked home from school late that afternoon, I pondered the possible reasons for this strange request. I knew that someone had to watch her child during the hours that she taught in school. But who? And why could she not turn to that person now? Mostly, though, I was puzzled as to why I had to watch the child in my own home. She knew that I knew where she lived, so what was she trying to hide?

Ironically, as strange and suspicious as her actions appeared to be, I found myself worrying and feeling protective towards her. Somehow I knew that whatever trouble Mrs. Ross was in, as peculiar as she might seem, this lady needed my help . . . and because she had asked me for it, I was going to be there for her.

I was walking home from school with Etty. I was about to tell her about the strange conversation I had with our English teacher that afternoon when I remembered my promise to Mrs. Ross. I also reminded myself sternly that it would be considered *lashon hara*, and I remembered what had happened much earlier in the day.

Morah Fischer, true to her word, had spoken with our principal about our new project, and so, first thing that Tuesday morning, *Rebbetzin* Leibowitz, beaming with pride, spoke to our class. After praising us, she suggested that each morning another girl from our class should say a *din* from *sefer Chofetz Chaim* over the loudspeaker to enable the whole school to participate. The girl would be responsible to prepare it ahead of time as she would have to translate the *din* from the *sefer* and give examples, too. This, our principal told us, would be a wonderful way of beginning the school day.

Since none of us were prepared that morning to speak, *Rebbetzin* Leibowitz surprised us by volunteering to address us herself. She explained to her enraptured audience that disclosing private information about someone is considered *lashon hara,* even when the person himself did not tell the one to whom he was speaking to keep it a secret. By doing so, one might cause embarrassment to the person who had confided in him.

"Hey, what are you so pensive about?"

I looked warmly at pixie-like Etty, with her short black hair and dark, penetrating eyes and smiled. "It's so weird." I tried to explain. "So much is happening in such a short time. I feel like it's been ages since seventh grade . . ."

"I know what you mean," she said, shifting her heavy briefcase to her other hand. "Last year all we could think of was eighth grade, and now that we're here . . ."

". . . It's different than what we expected."

"That's probably because of what happened . . .", she hesitated.

". . . to Nechama?" I asked challengingly.

"Yes. Well, Renie," she said guardedly, "you've changed so much. You used to be so carefree, so much fun to be with, and now . . ."

"I'm so serious?" I asked, with a hint of sarcasm. "Well, that's just too bad," I said stingingly. "If I'm not so much fun anymore, then I think you should just go ahead and find somebody else to be friends with."

"Come on, Renie," Etty's voice was defensive. "That's not what I meant."

"Well, quite frankly, Etty," I looked at her coldly, "I don't care what you had in mind." By this time we had reached my corner, and without turning to her to say good-bye, I rushed off to my house.

In school the next day I basically ignored Etty. She tried to approach me several times but gave up after being rejected each time. During lunchtime I sat with Feigy and Suri. I felt a slight stab of pain when I saw Etty's hurt look, but I told myself that I did not care.

When I came home from school I was greeted with the news that a letter from C.D. was waiting for me. I quickly tore open the envelope and eagerly devoured the contents of the letter.

> . . . And when I heard about what happened to Nechama, I immediately thought of you, Renie. I know how close the two of you have been for years and I'm worried about what this must be doing to you. Our whole school says *Tehillim* for Nechama daily and we pray for her speedy and complete recovery. It probably seems easy for me to say, sitting comfortably here in St. Louis, and not having to face the situation on a daily basis like you must . . .

but Renie, please try to remember that *Hashem* gives and takes and that everything is in His hands. Don't let this break you. Continue to be the great kid that you are.

On a more cheerful note, GREAT NEWS! I'm coming to Barclay. My principal said that our school received enough slots to enable our whole eighth-grade class [all nine of us, that is!] to go to the Mitzvahthon! Don't tell anyone because really I'm not supposed to tell — and it's supposed to be a surprise at the Mitzvahthon itself — but remember I told you about the talented twins in my class, Tzirel and Mirel Grossman? They have the most hysterical performance planned. They'll be the ones to represent our school for drama. Oh, Renie, I can't wait until the Mitzvahthon! We're chipping in to rent a van, and Rabbi and Mrs. Hershkowitz will be driving us to N.Y. I am so-o-o-o excited, I'm already counting the days . . . Take care.

Love,
C.D.

P.S. By the way, I hope I get to stay at your house. My best friend, Leah, wants to be placed with me . . . so request us!

P.P.S. Make sure to send regards to Lakey, Miriam, Zehava, Feigy, Suri, Etty, and everyone else. Can't wait to see you all!

I neatly folded her letter and placed it back in the envelope. I had just written C.D. on *Motzaei Shabbos,* a long letter all about the *shmiras halashon* campaign and knew that it was impossible for her to have received it yet. And so, I decided, I would let this letter go unanswered for now.

Walking slowly up the steps, there was one sentence that she had written that I could not erase from my mind. "Continue to be the great kid that you are." I did not know what she meant by "great kid," but I did know that she was telling me not to let this incident change me. That's sort of the same thing that Etty was trying to tell me. Oh, well . . . I felt my jaws tighten. It's easy for them to say don't change, when one of the biggest changes in my life was taking place. They just can't understand what I am going through.

❧ ❧ ❧

Early the next evening, Mrs. Ross brought over her baby son. He had curly black hair, large dark eyes and the most adorable smile. When I had first mentioned to my mother that I thought it odd that my teacher had asked me to baby-sit her child in my own home, she did not seem to think it strange at all. In fact, she warmly welcomed Mrs. Ross as if they were old friends. She left us a large, red, quilted, baby bag filled with some things that she thought he might need. Laughingly, I reassured her that whatever she might not have included we were bound to have in our own pantry as, in recent days, we kept ourselves well stocked with baby items.

When she left, I carefully emptied the contents of the baby bag and lined them up neatly on the kitchen table. There was a bottle filled with formula, two jars of baby food, a bib, a stretchy, a few diapers, baby powder, and two toys. There was also a sheet of paper covered with neatly written instructions regarding the baby's schedule.

I carefully strapped him into Shuey's infant seat, slipped on his bib, and fed him his cereal and dessert. I then took him to the living room and, putting him on his stomach, placed him on a clean blanket with his two little toys in front of him. I took out my notebooks and continued my project of copying over notes for Nechama, all the while listening to his joyful gurgling sounds as he talked to his little toys. Uninterrupted, I worked diligently for almost an hour until the baby began to cry. I picked him up, changed his diaper and put a clean stretchy on him. After warming his bottle, and testing it to make sure it was the right temperature, I sat down on the rocking chair and, cradling him in my arms, fed him his baby formula.

I looked down into his large dark eyes and he stared straight back into mine. Taking care of this little baby made me feel so grown up and responsible. I was also overcome with a sensation of peace and contentment as I smoothed back his curly hair. His rhythmic sucking relaxed me and I felt myself drifting off to sleep as I watched his eyes begin to close.

Just then my mother came into the room.

"Renie," she said softly, "you are so tired, why don't you go to bed now? I'll put the baby into his carriage, and don't worry," she added, "your teacher should be back soon."

"O.K., Mommy. If you're sure you don't mind," I yawned and stretched out both my arms heavenward. "I really am awfully tired."

I gave the baby a kiss on his cheek and proceeded to drag my tired body up the two flights of stairs. I slipped on my yellow pin-striped flannel nightgown and matching yellow fluffy slippers, and went to the sink to brush my teeth. Peering at my face in the mirror, I noticed a new red blotch on my chin and made sure to dot on some acne cream. Where did these things come from, I wondered, and why have I never noticed them before? Then I bared my teeth and, leaning closer to the mirror, I checked to see if the yellow was gone from my teeth and if they were getting any whiter. I smiled at my reflection and then, not liking what I saw, I tried a different pose, smiling a different smile. Finally, I decided that despite my imperfect teeth and that new pimple that had popped out of who-knows-where, maybe I was not so bad looking after all.

I washed my hands and sat down on my bed to say *Krias Shema al hamitah.* I was looking into my *siddur,* saying the words carefully when suddenly I heard the doorbell ring and voices coming from below. It must be Mrs. Ross, I mused, and my mother is probably entreating her to have some tea and *ruggalech.* After completing the prayer, I tiptoed over to the top of the staircase and tried to catch the gist of the conversation, but I could barely hear their hushed voices. I was very curious to know what they were talking about. After all, Mrs. Ross was my teacher!

I crept down to the second-floor landing, trying to remain quiet and unnoticed. But, unfortunately for me, our house is old and creaky and, despite my caution, they must have heard me, because a second later I heard my father's voice.

"Renie, is that you?"

I quickly ran back up the steps to the attic, embarrassed to be caught in the act of eavesdropping. I sat down for a few minutes on my bed and then restlessly went to the window.

Looking down at the street below, I was surprised to see my mother, her coat on and pocketbook in hand. She was walking alongside Mrs. Ross, who was carrying her baby, towards our family's car. I saw them both get in. My mother started the car and I watched as she drove off, the large blue station wagon disappearing into the dark night.

❁ ❁ ❁

The next week flew by rather quickly. During the day I sat in class, studiously taking notes. At break time and after school Feigy and I were busy with our *shmiras halashon* project, and any free time in-between was filled with homework, yearbook, *Tehillim* for Nechama, and rewriting her notes. To say that I was busy would be an understatement! And so, when the following Sunday came around, I could not believe that it was already two weeks since the day we had all been at Sima's.

It was an unusually warm and sunny day for late autumn and after a surprisingly uneventful visit with Mrs. Finkelman, I happily ran up the steps to my front porch and swung open the door to my house.

It was then that we received the phone call.

PART III

Chapter Ten

My mother had the receiver to her ear, a somber expression on her face. She was nodding and apparently trying to grasp something the caller was telling her.

After a short while she politely thanked the caller for contacting her. Slowly, my mother put the telephone receiver back on the hook and turned to me, her eyes shadowed with worry. I realized then that as much as I wanted to hear what that telephone call was about, I was filled with dread. From her serious reaction I understood the news could not be good.

I waited uneasily, afraid to break the silence. The only sound we could hear was the quiet simmering of the vegetable soup on the stove.

Finally, my mother said quietly, "That was Nechama's aunt."

My gaze met hers. I felt myself stiffen. "Don't tell me," I cried out in alarm, my eyes wide with fear. "Is-is Nechama d-dea . . .?" My voice trailed off. I could not bear to say the word.

"No," my mother continued, her eyes filling with unshed tears, "*Baruch Hashem*, Nechama is out of the coma."

"So what's wrong?" I almost laughed with relief.

My mother just shook her head sadly. She could not tell me.

"Oh, no!" the thought suddenly shook me. "Is-is she brain damaged?" I was afraid to ask the question . . . but I had to know the truth. "Or . . ." I decided on something a little more positive, something temporary. "Does she have amnesia or something like that?"

"No, no . . . it's nothing of that sort." My mother turned away, her eyes unable to meet mine. "She knows what's going on. Her intelligence is fine," was the mechanical and only answer she could give me.

My heart was beating quickly. I had never seen my mother this way. Slowly she shook her head and walked over to the table, pulled over a chair and sat down. With her elbows leaning on the table for support, she held her head in her hands and closed her eyes. Helplessly, she sat there, as if holding a heavy burden in her head, unable to tell me something she knew she had to say.

I hurried over to the table and, leaning down towards her, pleaded, "Mommy, what's wrong? What aren't you telling me?"

She looked at me, shaking her head back and forth sadly, but could not say a word.

"Mommy," I begged, the tears rolling slowly down my cheeks, "if Nechama is out of the coma, and she's not brain damaged, what could be the problem?" I paused for a moment. "Oh, I know," I said, heaving a sigh of relief. "She can't walk . . . now she won't be able to dance."

Again, my mother shook her head.

"She has a problem with her hands? Oh, no . . . she'll never be able to play the piano again!"

"No, Leba Renala," my mother walked over to the window. "It is something else, something terrible . . ."

I walked over to her and took her cold hands in both of mine. "Mommy?" I questioned searchingly, my eyes pleading. I could no longer continue this macabre guessing game. I just wanted to learn what was wrong, for I knew that whatever it was, I had to know.

Her troubled gaze met mine. "My darling, dear Renala," my mother looked at me compassionately, and put her arm around me. I took a deep, apprehensive breath. I knew that she was about to tell me the news that I so dreaded hearing, but was determined to learn.

When she spoke her voice was quiet, but I could feel the tension in the arm that encircled me. "Your friend, Nechama," her voice suddenly broke, "Renie . . . Nechama is . . . blind."

I gasped, horrified. Blind. I was desperate to escape what I had just heard and, irrationally, I ran out the back door, heading towards my brook. Blind, blind, blind, blind. I felt the words repeating themselves quickly, synchronized with the rapid beating of my heart.

The tears were streaming down my cheeks. I looked up at the beautiful sun shining in the blue sky . . . the sun and the sky that Nechama would no longer see. I watched a group of birds flying in perfect formation, probably, I guessed, heading for a better climate down south. I wished then with all my heart that I, too, could fly away and escape the bitter winter months that lay ahead for me. And perhaps, when I would return in the springtime, it would be to learn that all these dreadful events had not really occurred. I turned away and looked down. The ground was covered with colorful crisp autumn leaves . . . colors that Nechama could no longer enjoy.

Blind. That horrible — and, yes, scary — affliction.

I remembered the time, when I was about five years old, when I was taken on my first visit to Manhattan. I was bubbling with excitement as we emerged from a tall building where my mother had some business to take care of. We walked along Fifth Avenue, and I was mesmerized as I observed the colorful arcade of characters roaming the streets. There were those busy, sophisticated businessmen and elegantly dressed career women rushing off to work, the eager and curious tourists examining their maps and taking pictures, messengers on bicycles and then, of course, there were the entertainers. I recalled how I had laughed in glee as I watched the black juggler expertly toss the balls in the air and rhythmically, without fail, catch each one of them, all the while carefully balancing a glass bottle on his head. Further down the block I heard music. I tugged at my mother's hand, eager to move on.

And then, suddenly, I saw him. His hands were moving back and forth. He was playing an accordion and had a copper cup on the floor nearby. As I approached him to hear his music more clearly, I looked up at his face. He was staring straight ahead, his pupils out of focus. I looked more closely and thought how lifeless his eyes were. And when he said, "Little child, do you like my music?" I looked into his sightless eyes and screamed. I kept on screaming until my mother grabbed my arm and dragged me away from there. And even though my mother sat me down and explained what was wrong with him, I could never get over my fear of blind people. I never forgot how he bent his head down to me, and although he could not see me, knew that I was there.

As the years passed, my feeling towards blind people did not change. If I saw a blind person walking down the street, I would nervously cross to the other side. And if ever I was in situation from which I could not run away, I made sure never to look at the blind person's face. It was a horrific fear, tainted perhaps with an irrational prejudice. Nevertheless, it was a real phobia from which, I knew, I could never escape

And now, my best friend was blind.

I shivered despite the warm sun. Suddenly, I felt the weight of my parka on my shoulders. I turned around. My mother stood behind me, a sympathetic expression on her face. She had wrapped a winter coat around herself, too. Carefully, she lowered herself to the ground and sat next to me.

We sat silently for a few minutes. Finally, I turned to her. "Mommy," I cried, "tell me it isn't real . . . tell me that this whole thing is just a terrible nightmare and I will soon wake up."

"I wish I could, Renie. I wish I could comfort you as I did when you were a little girl, and I would hear you cry out at night, and

I would come to you, sit on your bed and tell you . . . Don't worry
. . . All this . . . it didn't really happen."

I felt my tears flow freely as sobs shook my body. My mother
sat silently beside me, allowing me to cry undisturbed. Finally,
when I felt that there were no more tears left, I accepted the
handkerchief that she offered me.

"I don't understand." I looked at her helplessly, still sniffling.
"How does a person go on? How can *Hashem* do this, especially
to a person as good and special as Nechama?"

My mother did not respond immediately, but when she did
she spoke gently but firmly. "As hard as it is to understand,
Renie," she hesitated a moment, "we must remember what
we've been learning and believing all these years. Whatever
Hashem does is for the best."

"I know that is what I have always been told, and until now I
really did believe it . . ."

"Yes, Renie," she continued softly, as she soothingly
smoothed my wet hair behind my ears. "It's easy to believe in
Hashem's ways when everything is going well for us. The hard
part, the real test, my darling," she looked me directly in the
eye, "is having faith when things are not so good for us."

"But Mommy, this is terrible," I cried out despondently. "She
had her whole life before her . . . and now, nothing. Maybe it's
even worse than dying."

"Don't ever say that, Renie," she shook her head vehemently,
"*Hashem* has His plan. And Nechama has a future. *Hashem*
never sends anything to anyone who cannot deal with it. What
is most crucial is for you and your friends to be there for
Nechama. If you thought you were friends before, now is your
real chance to prove yourself. Now, when it *is* the toughest."

"Oh, Mommy . . . I don't know how I will do it! I won't even be
able to look at her."

"I know it will be difficult at first . . . but eventually things will
work themselves out. The important thing is to make the best
of the situation, to treat Nechama as a regular friend."

I sat there silently, thinking, trying to grasp all that my
mother was telling me . . . trying to come to terms with
everything that was going on around me. Suddenly as if stung,

I cried, "Oh, Mommy, I don't know what I would do if something bad ever happened to you! I don't think I could go on!"

"Don't worry, Renie," she smiled at me, understanding, "I'll be here for as long as you need me, *Zeeskeit.* Come," she said rising, "let's go inside, now. It's beginning to get chilly."

"Mommy." I, too, rose, walked over to my mother, and appreciatively slid my hand into hers. "I love you so much," I whispered hoarsely, a sob caught in my throat. "Thanks for being the greatest mother in the world."

❧ ❧ ❧

When I went upstairs to get ready for bed that night, I turned off all the lights in my room, then made sure that my door was closed, allowing not even a glimmer of light to shine into the room. Groping in the darkness, I found the dresser in which I kept my pajamas. Pulling open the second drawer, I reached for my nightgown and slipped it on and then, with shaky fumbling fingers, I awkwardly buttoned it up. Next, I tried to find my brush. There was a loud bang as I knocked down a flowerpot, but I was still determined to continue my quest in the dark. After another few minutes of bumping into furniture and knocking down some more objects, I finally gave up. I opened the door to allow the light from the hallway to guide me to my lamp. After turning it on, I lay down on my bed staring up at the ceiling, not bothering to clean up the mess I had just made.

How will Nechama manage, I wondered despairingly. How will she get dressed, find things she needs, brush her hair, *daven* from her *siddur,* ride her bike . . . How will she do anything?

Will her sightless eyes have that lifeless look in them, wandering in no particular direction? Will they look horrible and frightening? Will she now have that eerie sixth sense that blind people have, and know where others are and what they are thinking without being told anything?

There was a knock on my door and I turned onto my side as my mother entered, carrying a steaming mug of warm milk on a plate. "I figured that you might need something to help you sleep," she said softly as she placed it on my night table. She sat down on the edge of my bed and said gently, "Renie, there is something else that I have to tell you."

"Yes?" I questioned, sitting up abruptly.

"Tomorrow, I would like to keep you home from school. I think you need the break."

"Thanks for your understanding, Mommy," I said with relief. "I guess I'm not really ready to face the rest of the girls right now."

"There's something else, too."

"What?" I asked anxiously.

She took a deep breath. "We are also going to the hospital tomorrow to visit Nechama."

I felt my lips go dry. "No, I can't. I'm not ready."

"Renie, I cannot stress enough how important it is for you to go . . . both for your sake and Nechama's."

"No, not yet," I said adamantly. "I still need more time."

"Renie, you'll push it off one day and then you'll procrastinate the next. That's what happens when we postpone doing something that we don't want to do — but should."

I knew she was right . . . but I tried to think of excuses anyway. "Maybe she's still too tired for visitors. Perhaps . . . "

"You're just trying to justify delaying something you will have to eventually face, Renie. I know you are worried and uncomfortable about your initial meeting with Nechama." She reached over and softly touched my cheek. "But despite these feelings, as a true friend, visiting her now is something you must do."

She lifted herself off the bed and walked over to my dresser, where she noticed the fallen flowerpot. "Maybe it will turn out better than you expect." She bent down to clean away the debris. Swiftly I was by her side, wiping up the dirt so that she would not have to. She straightened herself, and wiping her hands on her apron turned to me and said steadily, "I'm planning to go to the hospital at eleven o'clock in the morning, with or without you, Renie. I won't force you to come with me, but I sure hope that you will. I know how proud it would make *Abba* and myself to see how brave, caring, and selfless you are . . . thinking of your friend and not just yourself."

I did not say anything. I was too ashamed of myself to talk. Leaving me with a kiss on the forehead, she walked out of the room and closed the door softly behind her.

I returned to my bed and, crossing my arms behind my head, resumed staring at the ceiling. I knew that this was going to be a sleepless night. The only sound in the room was the ticking of my alarm clock.

I recalled the conversation that Nechama and I had had in this room the night before the hayride, the night we had stayed up so very late talking. It seemed so long ago, yet only a month had passed since that time. Nechama had been thinking about the future and I remembered commenting that she had such grown-up thoughts. Oh, Nechama — I felt the tears rolling down my cheeks — what kind of a future will you have now?

I watched night turn to dawn and dawn become morning before I finally dozed off. When my clock's alarm rang at seven thirty-five, I groggily reached over to press the button and turn it off before falling back asleep. At ten o'clock my mother woke me and reminded me that she would be leaving within the hour. Immediately, I sat up and said *Modeh ani,* washed *neigel vasser* and quickly got dressed. After *davening* and hastily gulping down a glass of juice, I walked with my mother to the car.

I sat next to her in the front seat, strapped myself in and rolled down the window. I needed the air. As the car started up I felt my stomach begin to churn. I was so nervous that my throat felt numb. What will I say to her? Will I be able to look in her direction? Will she blame me?

The car continued its journey down the turnpike. It was only one exit to the hospital and I sat there apprehensively, trying to swallow the lump in my throat, my heart beating quickly.

In too short a time my mother turned into the hospital's visitors' parking lot. There was no turning back now. Tensely, I looked ahead.

Looming before us was the hospital building, forbidding and grey.

Chapter Eleven

O ur footsteps echoed loudly on the shiny tiled floor of the hospital corridor, each step bringing us closer to Nechama.

The hospital walls were a freshly painted white and the air smelled from some antiseptic cleanser. We passed the nurses' station and I saw two nurses laughing over coffee and doughnuts. How can they be so happy and go on with life as usual when the people around them are sick and dying, I wondered bitterly.

I wanted to turn around, run back to the car and wait there until my mother would return. I thought of rushing off to the rest rooms and hiding. I wished for something to happen that would prevent me from having to enter that room where Nechama lay.

My wish was not granted. We turned left at the end of the hallway and I saw Nechama's mother and father talking to a nurse outside her room. I stood still and felt my mother's soft touch on my elbow nudge me on. We came closer.

Nechama's mother, although slightly pale, was immaculately put together, as usual. Her auburn wig was well coiffured and she was wearing a slimming navy-blue tweed dress with a thin leather belt of the same color around her waist. She did not look like a woman who was falling apart. Her father, on the other hand, appeared drawn and tired and had the dark growth of a five-o'clock shadow on his chin.

We went forward and I saw Mrs. Leverman's eyes flicker uncomfortably as she recognized us. Without saying a word, my mother touched her empathically on the shoulder and I heard her stifle a sob. Immediately, however, she composed herself and turned to me.

"Renie, I am so happy you could come. Nechama is expecting you."

Looking at the floor, I numbly nodded.

As my mother opened the door she touched me lightly on my back, prodding me on. We walked inside. Nechama was propped up on the bed surrounded by stuffed animals, flowers, and boxes of candy. Her long, tumbly auburn hair was tied back with a pink ribbon to match her frilly nightgown. She sat there, nervously fingering the charm on her necklace.

"Who's there?" She turned her face toward the doorway that we had just walked through. "Is that you, Renie?"

I could not reply. The lump in my throat did not let me.

"Yes, it's us, Mrs. Greenberg and Renie," my mother answered reassuringly. "I just wanted to come inside and say hello, Nechama." She went to the bed, lightly kissed Nechama on the cheek, and warmly embraced her. "And now I'll leave the two of you alone. I am sure you have much to say to each other."

I looked at my mother as she went to the door and turned toward me. Her kind eyes met mine and regarded me for a long moment. Silently I pleaded with her not to leave me alone with Nechama. She smiled and shook her head gently, as if to tell me, Don't worry, you'll be all right. The door closed softly behind her.

Awkwardly, I stood in my place, immobile.

"Renie?" Nechama broke the silence.

"Yes?"

"Come, sit down over here, next to me," she patted a space on the bed. "And have a chocolate," she added cheerfully.

She reached over to where the boxes of candy lay and took one box. Ripping off the plastic covering, she placed the cover under the bottom of the box and held it out toward me. I just sat there, dumbstruck and open mouthed. I could produce neither a word nor even a sound.

"Hey, Renie, what's the matter with you? Did you lose your tongue or something? Yum, these are delicious," she said, helping herself to two chocolates at once and swallowing them in a single gulp. "Here — try some. The marshmallow and jelly ones are my favorites."

"N-no thanks," I said helplessly, glancing in the direction of the window. I could not look at Nechama. I was afraid I would see her eyes.

"Who's over there?" she asked, turning her head in the direction of the window, suddenly frightened.

"No one. I- I was just looking out the window."

" What did you see?"

"Um — a bird," I lied. "I saw a bird."

"What kind of a bird?"

"Uh — a bluejay."

"Are you sure?"

"Sure, I-I'm sure," I said slowly, my eyes filling with tears.

"Liar. You are just afraid to look at me because I am blind."

"No, no, that's not true."

She reached over towards me, following the direction of my voice. I was still facing the window, staring straight ahead at nothing in particular, the tears spilling over onto my cheeks. She turned my chin towards her and touched my face. I felt her fingers groping hesitantly over my nose, eyes, lips, and cheeks. I sat motionless and stiff, afraid to move or breathe, unable to utter a sound.

"Renie, you're crying."

"I know." It was the first honest statement I had made since entering that room.

"You don't have to be so sad," her face was earnest.

"I-I can't help it." I turned away, trying to stifle a sob.

"Don't cry," she said simply.

"I'm sorry I'm acting like this . . . I-I should be strong for you."

"We have to be strong for each other, Renie."

"Oh, Nechama," I turned and for the first time looked directly at her. "How could you be so good?" Impulsively, I reached for her, my despair suddenly giving way to hope.

" Well, we're best friends, aren't we?" She asked rhetorically, her voice muffled, as she buried her face in my shoulder. We hugged each other comfortingly, the huge barrier of tension melting like snow. For those few precious moments it did not matter that one of us could see and the other was blind.

I do not remember how long we sat there and talked, but it was almost like old times. As we spoke, I felt my old, irrational, prejudice and fear leaving me. Blind or not blind, she was still Nechama, my best friend, and I realized that I had nothing to fear from her.

Not one to hold myself back from enjoying something that waited to be relished, I helped myself to some chocolates. Of course we did not speak about the accident, but we did discuss everything that had happened since then. I told her about the *shmiras halashon* club, progress on the yearbook, and my newly formed friendship with Feigy. Then I made the mistake of informing her that it was *she* who was voted to be the school representative for the Mitzvahthon.

"Well, I'm not going to do it," Nechama said abruptly.

Stung, I stood up, "Why not?"

"What kind of question is that? You know, why not!" She said the "why not" in a high-pitched tone, obviously trying to mimic me.

"Is it because . . . because you're blind?" I asked rather bluntly, with my usual lack of tact, as I began to pace from one side of the room to the other. "You know those keys, you always knew those piano keys by heart as if they were attached to your fingers." I lifted the vase that was holding a bouquet of roses and, eyes closed, inhaled the delightful aroma. "You never needed to look at notes or at the piano. Music is part of you."

"Nothing is part of me anymore . . . just these eyes, these eyes that can't see anything," she said despondently.

"Nechama, don't let that stop you. I know you can do it. We need you." I sat down again and took her hands in mine.

"Why? Just so our school could win?" She pulled her hands away from me and continued, with an uncharacteristic tone of sarcasm in her voice, "So that everyone can look at me and have pity? No thanks, I can do without that honor."

I swallowed hard. "Nechama, why are you being this way? It would be good for you, as well as beneficial for the school. You see . . . " I stopped in mid-sentence.

"No, I don't see and probably never will."

There was an awkward silence. Finally, I broke it.

"Ne-Nechama, I w-want you to know . . ." I paused, took a deep breath and went on, "that I will always be here for you." The words I had been holding back burst forward like water when a dam breaks. "From now on you'll have nothing to worry about, Cham. I've become really studious and organized. You — you would be so proud of me. I'm doing it for you . . . Just like you've always been there for me, now I am here for you," I reiterated.

Looking at her troubled face, I saw that she was trying to force her lips into a smile. "And something else," I hesitated, and then determinedly told her what I had been thinking about since last night. "In the future, Cham, I will be your eyes."

"Thanks, Renie," she said politely but mechanically, "I know you will."

"And I know that we'll continue being best friends as always," I said sincerely, but felt my heart sinking lower and lower. I knew just then that although I fervently wished we could go back to the past, nothing would ever again be the same.

❧ ❧ ❧

At dinner that evening my mother served my favorite

meal, meatballs and spaghetti. I do not remember if I ate anything but I managed to drink at least two glasses of juice. Playing with my fork and knife, I sat quietly, immersed in my own thoughts. I noticed my parents exchange a few serious looks.

I could not stop thinking about Nechama.

Finally, it was time to *bench*, and then wordlessly I washed, dried, and put away the dishes. My mother swept up and cleaned off the table. As she was folding the tablecloth and I was putting away the last dish, my father entered the room. Clearing his throat, he announced that he would like to go for a walk and would anyone care to join him. I looked at my mother who shook her head and claimed that she had some mending to do. My father turned to me. Normally, I would have jumped eagerly at the thought of having my father to myself, but circumstances for me were not normal and just then I felt that I needed to be alone. Nevertheless, I agreed to go, not wanting to hurt his feelings.

Struggling into my parka, I met him at the back door as he was putting on his hat. Wordlessly we walked down the three steps. As we continued down the street I began to feel the night air sober me and lift me out of my despondent mood.

Feeling more optimistic, I tried to convince myself that despite Nechama's sightlessness, maybe we could still continue our friendship as it had been before the accident. And who knows, I thought hopefully, maybe she will regain her sight. Maybe she could conquer the darkness. After all, miracles do happen. Maybe . . . just maybe.

"Leba Rena," my father slowed his pace as he turned to me. "Your mother told me about your visit with Nechama today. We're very proud of you."

"There's nothing to be especially proud of, *Abba,*" I said modestly. "Things went more smoothly than I thought they would . . . but, well, Nechama has changed so much."

"I think that under the circumstances it is quite understandable, Renie," he commented, stroking his beard thoughtfully as he talked. "But it is important for you, as her good friend, not to abandon her and to have the patience and understanding that she so badly needs right now."

Ashamed, I looked down at the pavement.

"Anyway, Renie, there is something else that I would like to tell you."

"Yes?" I asked inquisitively.

"Your mother and I were not sure as to whether or not we should inform you about this." His kind eyes regarded me for a moment before he continued, "We've concluded that perhaps it is best for you to know . . . to be prepared . . . for Nechama's sake."

"What do you mean, *Abba?* What is it that you have to tell me?" I urged him to go on.

We had reached the corner. I followed my father across the street and we began to walk back in the direction of our house.

As we passed under a street lamp, I saw the solemn expression on my father's face. He cleared his throat and began gravely. "As you know, Nechama suffered a severe blow to her head during the hayride. This head injury caused Nechama to be unconscious for quite some time. The doctors did not always believe that she was going to make it." He took a deep breath. "*Boruch Hashem* she survived the coma."

"Yes, but look at her now. Doesn't it say somewhere that a blind person is like a dead person?" I questioned.

"True," my father answered patiently. "When Yaakov *Avinu* had the dream in Bais El and *Hashem* spoke to him, He referred to Himself as *Elokei Avraham* and *Elokei Yitzchak*. *Rashi* explains that *Hashem* attaches His name to *tzaddikim* only after they die, and in this case, although Yitzchak was still living he was considered dead — since he was blind."

"But why?"

"Because the *Gemara* tells us that the *Yetzer Hara* doesn't affect blind people . . . and therefore, they're excused from doing *mitzvos* . . ."

"That doesn't seem fair," I protested. "It's not their fault that they can't see. It's — it's as if the Torah considers this person's life useless."

"No, Renie," my father's voice rose slightly. "Just the

opposite. When the blind person does do the *mitzvos*, he's showing a special love of *Hashem*. He's doing it without *schar*, without any reward in mind. In fact," he continued vehemently, "there have been numerous great *tzaddikim* throughout the generations who were afflicted with blindness and yet *Klal Yisrael* could not have managed without them! Take, for example, Reb Yosef bar Chiya."

"Who?"

"Reb Yosef bar Chiya," my father repeated. "He was a great *talmid chacham* who was blind, and the *sefer Seder HaDoros* tells us that he attended the *shiurim* of great Rabbis and had many students who themselves became great leaders. So you see," he reiterated, "by no means does the blind person's life have to be useless. To the contrary, it could be quite productive."

I remained uncharacteristically silent.

"Anyway, Renie, I would like for you to understand exactly what happened to Nechama." I looked up at him curiously and met his gaze. He explained in his professional teaching voice what occurs when a person sees. "The light energy received by the retina is transformed into nerve impulses that travel along the optic nerve and nerve pathways into the brain." He studied my face thoughtfully before continuing. "When Nechama's head received the strong impact that it did, she suffered from ischemia, meaning that there was an inadequate blood supply to the optic nerve." He paused, giving me a chance to absorb this information. I nodded slowly, indicating that so far I understood what he was saying. He then steadily went on. "Renie, this trauma damaged the visual nerve pathways that connect the optic nerves to the brain. Unfortunately," his voice lowered somberly, "disorders of one of the nerve pathways behind the optic nerve crossing always affect both eyes. And . . . that's why Nechama can't see from either eye."

"*Abba,*" I asked guardedly, "why are you telling me all this?"

"Because," he hesitated choosing his words carefully. "Because nerve cells and tracts in the brain do not recover their function if they have been destroyed."

"D-does that mean," I stammered, "th-that it is impossible

for Nechama to ever regain her s-sight?"

"I'm saying, Renie, that it is almost impossible. Today, while you were speaking to Nechama in her room, out in the hallway her mother had a conversation with Mommy."

"Yes?" I asked earnestly.

We had reached the area directly across the street from our house. We stopped walking, and my father continued to speak.

"Nechama's parents have consulted many specialists in the visual/neurological field. Most doctors wouldn't even speak to Nechama's parents when they heard about the damage. They feel that it's unquestionably irreversible. But finally, on the advice of *rabbanim* and specialists, they consulted a young but quite experienced neurologist from Australia who is presently in the United States attending medical conferences here and in Canada. He will be in New York in two weeks, and has agreed to look at Nechama at that time."

Seeing the hopeful look on my face, my father regarded me for a moment, and shook his head slowly. Pensively, he walked across the street. I hurried along to keep up with him.

When he reached our front gate he stopped walking and, leaning against it, turned his head toward me. His voice was grave when he spoke to me. "Renie, you must remember that even if this specialist agrees to operate, there are no guarantees. Right now, Nechama knows nothing about this. Her parents have decided not to tell her anything until this doctor meets with her. Needless to say, you are not to discuss this with her or with anyone else until we are told otherwise. O.K.?"

"O.K., O.K." I sang out, feeling more light hearted than I had felt in the last twenty-four hours. "Oh, *Abba,*" I looked up at him, my eyes dancing. "I know everything will turn out just right. I just know it, I just know it," I reiterated with great emphasis, skipping up the steps leading to my house.

As I entered the hallway of my home I felt rejuvenated, as if I was entering a new and hope-filled chapter of my life.

Chapter Twelve

"Try on this green sweater," Feigy beseeched me. "It'll bring out the color of your eyes."

I took one look at the price tag and felt the color drain from my face.

It was the first Sunday in November, and before having our customary weekly visit with Mrs. Finkelman, we decided — or rather, Feigy strongly suggested and I, grateful to be asked, went along with her proposal — to go "winter" shopping at the mall. But things were not turning out as I had hoped they would. "What's the matter?" she asked. "It'll look gorgeous on you. Come on, try it on."

I could not tell Feigy the truth. So I lied. "I hate the color green," I told her.

"I don't know why," she said, astonished. "You would look great in it, and it's so stylish."

I looked at the sweater again. It had a cowl neck, small gold buttons and shoulder pads. I touched it and felt the softness of the fine wool. It really was very pretty, and I had saved up enough — well, almost enough — money from baby-sitting.

"O.K., I'll try it on," I said nervously, my heart beating wildly. I took the sweater to the dressing room and carefully slipped it on. I turned to face the mirror, stared at my reflection, and gasped.

The sweater fit me perfectly. The shoulder pads broadened my slight and narrow shoulders and I saw that Feigy was right about the color. My green eyes were shining brilliantly, my cheeks were a blushing pink, and the smile I could not suppress showed off my deep dimples. I could not believe it. Was that Leba Rena Greenberg, I wondered incredulously. I actually looked pretty. Very pretty!

"I like it," I said with a lilt in my voice. "I really like it!"

Feigy was looking over my shoulder at my reflection in the mirror, and when I met her gaze, I saw that I-told-you-so look in her eyes. "Now, all we have to do," she said approvingly, pushing my bangs back into a "bump" as we both stood in front of the mirror, "is let your bangs grow in. And you'll definitely need a perm to put some body into your hair," she added imperiously.

I studied my reflection. I liked what I saw, but I did not like what I was beginning to feel. I knew for sure that my parents would not feel very proud of me if I spent this exorbitant sum on a sweater at this stage of my life. Not that they would forbid me to — after all, it was my own money — but I could well visualize their disappointment if I did so. It was not just the financial issue, I knew, but they would be against the idea of an eighth-grader buying something that was more suitable for someone much older. Sure, they liked me to look nice and tried to get me to care about being neat, but I remembered hearing them once tell Sima that there is a time and a place for everything.

"Stop staring at yourself, Lady Di. Let's go to the cashier and pay," Feigy interrupted my thoughts.

"Well, I don't know," I said, blushing as I heard the disappointment begin to creep into my voice.

"You mean, you might not take it?" Her blue eyes were wide with surprise.

"I-I didn't say that," I hesitated, afraid of what Feigy would think of me, "but, I w-would like to ask my mother."

"Sure," she said automatically. "I'll wait outside while you change. You'd better hurry if you also want to go visit Mrs. Finkelman before dark," she called out from the other side of the curtain.

It was incredibly difficult to tear my eyes away from my reflection, knowing that as soon as I removed the sweater I would turn back into the same old Renie Greenberg. I saw the disappointed look in my eyes and felt doubly dejected, assuming that Feigy would think me dull and unsophisticated and would not want to be my friend anymore.

Mechanically, I took off the sweater and slipped on my old, familiar blouse. As I buttoned it, I began to feel the spell of the sweater leave me. I caught the new look of confidence in my eyes and resolved that if someone could not be my friend just because I did not dress like her, then I would manage well without her.

I repeated this to myself several times and then purposefully stepped out from the other side of the curtain. We did not converse much as we left the mall and caught the bus returning to Barclay. We could not find two seats together and so, for the first fifteen minutes of the ride, Feigy stood at the front and I sat in the back of the bus. Finally, at the third stop the seat next to me became vacant and Feigy slipped in beside me.

We did not speak for the first five minutes of our ride together. I sat quietly, melancholically staring out the window. Finally, Feigy broke the silence.

"Renie, I envy you," she said quietly.

"What?" I swung around, incredulous.

"Y-yes," she stammered, "y-you and your mother have such a lovely relationship."

"Huh?" I was still speechless.

"I mean," she said blushing, "your mother and you seem to be so involved with each other. For example, me . . . if I want something, I just go ahead and buy it. As long as it's nice and in good taste, my mother is glad not to have to bother shopping with me. And," her words tumbled out as I gave her a surprised but encouraging look, "friends . . . my mother never seems to have the time to talk to my friends and get to know them like your mother does . . . And she never has time for baking and stuff like that. You're really very lucky."

"And I always thought that you were the lucky one."

"What do you mean?"

"Well, like today in the store. I was too embarrassed to tell you, but I knew that the sweater was outrageously expensive and my parents wouldn't want me to spend so much on a sweater at this point in my life . . . And, in general, you always look so good and so neat and put together . . . You're head of dance and always manage to get the main parts in plays . . . "

"And you consider *that* lucky?"

I nodded, unable to speak. She stared back at me, momentarily speechless, and then began to laugh. "I guess it's true when they say that the grass always looks greener on the other side of the fence." She hesitated for a moment and added, "But, boy, what I wouldn't do to be closer to my mother, like you are to yours."

I turned away and did not respond, as I felt tears of gratitude fill my eyes, and I knew I should be eternally thankful for having been born on this "greener side of the fence."

❁ ❁ ❁

We alighted from the bus when we reached Main Street. I felt a strong breeze lift my hair and a sprinkling of raindrops tickle my nose. I wrapped my scarf around my neck. It was only the first week of November, and yet, it felt as if winter was already upon us.

I watched Feigy open her umbrella and suddenly felt incredibly happy. Everything was almost perfect. Feigy and I were becoming closer and closer. In less than a month it would be *Chanukah.* And this year it would be extra special because of Linda and Abe's wedding, and the *Shabbos sheva brachos* that was to take place in our home. And wonder of wonders, Nechama was coming home in ten days. The specialist from Australia had seen her a few days ago and agreed to do the operation. He had not yet scheduled the surgery, but felt that in the interim, it would be wise for Nechama to return home and resume as normal a routine as possible.

I felt wildly optimistic that Nechama would have a full recovery and I knew — I just knew! — that everything was going to be the same again. The only thing that put a damper on my spirits was that I could not bring myself to make up with Etty, and I felt a pang of guilt whenever I thought of her.

The rain was heavier now and I was glad for the shelter of Feigy's umbrella. I felt utterly content as we walked on closely together, careful to keep to each other's pace. I began to hum a tune and Feigy quickly joined in.

By the time we reached Mrs. Finkelman's apartment building, we found that even the umbrella could not keep us dry. Our shoes and socks were soaked and I welcomed the shelter of the building.

Surprisingly, there was no response when we rang the bell. Figuring that it was probably out of order, we knocked. There was still no answer. I pressed my ear against the door and suddenly froze. Someone was shouting, "Get him, get him, grab him by the arm!" The voice was Mrs. Finkelman's!

I motioned for Feigy to join me. After a few seconds of listening to what was going on behind the door, she looked up, a terrified expression on her face. It sounded as if Mrs. Finkelman was in the center of some kind of a fight, and it was essential that we go for help immediately !

I tiptoed quietly to the staircase and signaled for Feigy to follow. Cupping my hand around my mouth, I whispered my idea softly in her ear. She nodded conspiratorially.

We went down the stairs and knocked at the door of Apartment 1E. Without a greeting, Mr. Petrovsky looked us up and down, a blank expression on his face. Finally, he turned abruptly and motioned for us to enter.

Breathlessly, we explained the situation to him and I watched the expression on his face change from blatant indifference to one of genuine concern. Quickly, we gathered the "ammunition" we thought we might need and ran back to Mrs. Finkelman's apartment, hoping that it was not too late.

Mr. Petrovsky pounded on the door and received no response, either. With blazing eyes and in a hushed whisper, he informed us that he would break down the door. We had to rescue Mrs. Finkelman!

My heart pounding, I stood to one side of the door, a mop in one hand and a can of insecticide spray in the other. Feigy, with a look of steely determination, held a ceramic vase with both hands over her head, ready to knock down the intruder should he choose to flee through the door. Mr. Petrovsky took a few deep breaths and then heaved his strong body against the door.

It flew open easily. Fighting our fear, we all walked into the apartment. We could now clearly hear Mrs. Finkelman's voice coming from the living room.

"Get him," she screamed. "Come on and grab him!"

Trembling, we slowly edged closer. We were able to see her sitting on a chair, her back toward us, unmoving. They must have tied her up! I almost screamed.

Again, we heard her cry out, "Come on, you can get him!"

We looked around. Strangely, we did not see anyone and, except for the occasional cry from Mrs. Finkelman, we did not hear anything, either. I turned to Feigy, and Feigy turned to me, her forehead creased in perplexity. Unquestionably, something very mysterious was going on, and I no longer felt very brave.

Mr. Petrovsky went forward courageously. Nervously, we followed. Aware that someone else was in the room with her, Mrs. Finkelman abruptly swung around and, upon discovering us, her eyes filled with pleasure.

We could see that she was wearing earphones and all this time must have been listening intently to the radio. She seemed too excited to notice the shocked expressions on our faces.

"Oiy, Mr. Petrovsky, Renie, Feigy . . . I so happy to see you! I vas just listening to de best wrestling match ever . . . I tell you it vas so exciting."

I do not remember how long we stood there staring, but I do recall hearing Mr. Petrovsky mumble something to himself about old ladies, teenagers and wrestling matches as he walked out the door, an exasperated expression on his face.

It was about two hours later that Feigy and I waved good-bye to Mrs. Finkelman and rushed down the steps anxious to make it home before dark. But when we reached the lobby of the building I suggested to Feigy that perhaps, since we were there already, we could stop off at Mrs. Ross' apartment and say hello to her and her cute baby. Glancing at her watch, Feigy agreed that we had a few minutes to spare before catching our respective buses.

We headed towards the mailboxes to find out Mrs. Ross' apartment number. Each box was labeled, but the name Ross was not listed!

It would be some time before we discovered the terrifying reason that this was so.

Chapter Thirteen

I made it to the meeting with about thirty seconds to spare. Breathlessly, I slipped into the seat beside Peshy and quickly took out a pen and my yearbook notebook before *Rebbetzin* Leibowitz began to speak. I noticed the disapproving look she gave me, and embarrassed, I turned away. I glanced around the room. There were not many of us present, but then again, for a small-town school, the yearbook staff could not be that large.

Mrs. Ross, as the G.O. adviser and eighth-grade English teacher, sat up front beside our principal. Peshy, our "in-house" Israeli, was the Hebrew editor and sat in the second row. I was right next to her. Suri, Feigy, and a few other girls who were working on the class diary sat grouped together near the window. Zehava and I were to work jointly on art and I saw her sitting in the front seat, next to Etty, the yearbook photographer.

When I looked at Etty I felt a troubled feeling deep inside. I remembered how Etty and I had been such great friends since nursery school, but due to my obstinacy and sensitivity to her criticism about "my changing," I could not bring myself to forgive her and forget. I knew I was wrong, or at least not one-hundred-percent justified, yet found that I could not help myself and give in. Besides, I thought with indignation — but not without some guilt — now I had Feigy. Just then, unexpectedly, Etty turned around and her eyes met mine. I quickly turned away.

I opened my notebook and absently began to doodle as *Rebbetzin* Leibowitz spoke to us. It wasn't my fault that I was late, I thought defensively. Nechama needed me! Nechama. She had been home from the hospital for just about a week and already we were inseparable. I was constantly at her house, teaching her what she had missed in school, talking to her, comforting her, and helping her get around.

At first I loved spending every spare moment I had with Nechama. If I was not in her house, I was speaking to her by phone. Mrs. Leverman was grateful for the respite I gave her and gladly left the two of us alone. But, I had to admit, I was beginning to feel overwhelmed. I was still active in the *shmiras halashon* club, there were my obvious obligations to the yearbook, and in a few days Linda and Abe were getting married. I knew I was neglecting other friends and I did not seem to have the time to take care of my many responsibilities. Besides, Nechama had changed so much that sometimes I found it all so frustrating.

It was as if we had reversed roles. Now, I was the organized and studious one. In the hospital Nechama had always worn her nightgown, and so it was not until she returned home and dressed in her regular clothing that I noticed how much weight she had gained. She was constantly eating candy and chocolates, which was so unlike her, and I could see that she was beginning to break out terribly. If I tried to convince her to stop, she would say that since she could not see herself she did not care what she looked like and if I did not like what I saw I should not look. It was not so much her changed appearance that worried me. I found myself mostly disturbed by her apathetic attitude towards herself.

When we were together and the time came for me to leave, she would become sullen and try to detain me. Feeling remorseful, I would prolong my visit and comfort her. Sometimes I felt as if Nechama had me tied to a long and invisible leash. I knew that all this was no fault of hers, and I felt overcome by a new surge of guilt for complaining — even to myself.

I found it comforting to fantasize about the day that Nechama would emerge from surgery completely well, with her sight recovered. She would look for me and I would be there by her side, as usual. In front of her parents and the medical staff she would turn to me and, smiling, thank me for being a loyal and true friend and being there through the hard times. Nechama would be back to her old self, and our already strong friendship would continue forever, strengthened by the hurdles that it had had to overcome.

"Renie, is there anything that you would like to add?"

I looked up quickly, shaken out of my reverie. There was absolute silence in the room. I could see that everyone had turned in my direction, waiting for me to speak.

"Um-er, n-no thank you, *Rebbetzin* Leibowitz." I stammered, "I-I mean, I have nothing to a-add."

Frowning at me, she turned away and addressed the rest of the girls present. "Is there anyone who has anything else to contribute?"

Peshy raised her hand and announced that we were still short on Hebrew articles. A few suggestions were made and it was not until around twenty minutes later that the meeting was finally concluded.

I had no time to stay and chat with anyone and so, as soon as we were dismissed, I hastily slid out of my seat and took the short-cut home. Panting slightly, I ran up the porch steps, swung open the back door and rushed into the kitchen. My mother was calmly removing some potato knishes from the oven and she looked up, a surprised expression on her face.

"Renie, what are you doing home now? Is everything all right? Weren't you supposed to go to Sima today to watch Shuey?"

"Oh, Mommy, I totally forgot about it. I promised Nechama that I would go to her house as soon as I finished the shopping that you wanted me to do for the *sheva brachos.*"

"I had told you, Renie, that the shopping could wait until tonight," my mother said patiently. "The grocery store stays open late during the week before *Chanukah.*"

Just then the telephone rang. I ignored it, and continued talking with my mother.

"Yes, I know, but later I'll be busy with Nechama and I have no idea what time we'll be finished."

"But, Renie . . ."

The telephone continued to ring insistently. I reached out my hand to pick up the receiver, but my mother intercepted me.

"Take some lunch, Renie," she sighed, wiping her hands on her apron. "I'll get it."

Quickly, I took a fork out of the drawer and slid a knish onto a plate.

"It's for you, Renie. It's Feigy," my mother announced, handing the receiver to me.

"Hello, Feigy," I said, swallowing a large mouthful of knish. "What's up?"

"Have you forgotten that today is Sunday, Renie? Mrs. Finkelman's expecting us. You rushed in and out of the yearbook meeting so quickly today, I didn't get a chance to talk to you."

"Yikes, I did forget," I exclaimed worriedly. "Anyway, Feigy, it's impossible for me to make it today . . . I have a million things to do! Tell her I'm sorry."

When I hung up with Feigy, I turned to my mother anxiously. "Mommy, what am I going to do about Sima?"

"That is for you to decide, Renie," she said, not unkindly, as she rolled up her sleeves and went to the sink.

Guiltily, I dialed Sima's telephone number and informed her that I could not baby-sit for her that day.

I gulped down a glass of orange juice, said a *brachah acharonah,* and zipped up my jacket. My mother stopped me by the door and asked, "Renie, don't you have off from school this Friday?"

Chanukah was to begin that Friday night and we were given Friday through Tuesday off as *Chanukah* vacation.

"That's right," I said happily. "I can't believe I had almost forgotten about my vacation."

"I believe it," my mother sighed. "Oh well," she turned to me good-naturedly, "if you would like to have Feigy and some other girls over for *challah* lessons this Friday morning, it would be fine with me. I don't know when you'll have another free Friday."

I gave my mother a quick but warm hug. "Oh, that will be great, Mommy," I told her. "It's a wonderful idea. I'll call Feigy from Nechama's house and, oh," I opened my eyes wide with excitement, "maybe Nechama could join us, too."

I was out the door before my mother could respond.

❧ ❧ ❧

It was Friday morning. My mother had already kneaded the dough and allowed it to rise. The day's lesson was to be on how to braid the *challah.*

Everyone who was to be there was there — everyone, that is, except Nechama and I. Her mother had ordered a car service to take her to my house, but Nechama had insisted that she did not want to go in the car by herself and that I had to go along with her. Therefore, I had to wake up early that morning, take the two buses that would bring me to Rorey, and then pick up Nechama and join her for the ride back to Barclay.

The memory of that drive stays with me still.

Her mother had helped her dress and brushed her long, thick hair into a ponytail with a white bow clipped on top. She wore a new black-and-white checkered skirt with a coordinating sweater. As we rode through the quiet suburban streets, the early morning sun slanted in through the car window, bringing out the red and gold highlights of Nechama's auburn hair.

I do not know why I said it just then, but I felt something inside me stir as I looked at Nechama. Gently, I told her, "Cham, I know the operation will be a success."

"So do I, Renie," she said in a voice that did not sound as convincing as we both would have liked. "So do I."

The driver took us past the town of Barclay and then drove along the streets that led to my house. He stopped the car to let us out and collect his fare. I handed him the money that Mrs. Leverman had given me and went around to Nechama's side to help her out.

She was fumbling awkwardly in her shoulder bag, obviously trying to find something. The driver was impatiently tapping his fingers on the steering wheel and sighing noisily. I tried to hurry her on, but she informed me that until she found her sunglasses, she refused to leave her seat. Understandably, she did not want anyone to see her without them, yet I found myself becoming frustrated when she insisted on being the one that had to find them. Finally, after a full five minutes had elapsed, she allowed me to check her pocketbook. Irritated, I handed the glasses to her. It had taken me only a second to find them and I was feeling somewhat annoyed with her. She put them on and then told me that she was ready to go in. I took her hand and led her up the stairs to my house where the others were anxiously waiting.

Of course, I had invited Feigy. Feigy suggested that we also ask Suri, who gladly accepted. I had considered calling Etty and asking her to join us, figuring that it would be a good opportunity for us to make up, but pushed it off since it was something I really did not feel comfortable doing. I knew Miriam would enjoy being here, and often included her in group activities. However, I did not think that she and Feigy would mix too well and somehow never got around to calling her, either. At the end it was just the four of us: Nechama, Feigy, Suri, and I.

Lately, it seemed, I had been so busy and so involved in important projects that I simply could not find the time even for people who were important to me. I felt guilty for neglecting old friends, and I knew it was true that I was changing.

I was lifted out of my reverie when my mother removed the towel that had been covering the large bowl of rising dough, and told us that she would now be doing the *mitzvah* of *hafrashas challah*, separating *challah*. She then explained to her enraptured audience that in the time of the *Bais HaMikdash* the piece of dough was given to the *Kohanim* but since we do not have our *Bais HaMikdash* today, we nevertheless must set it aside — to be burnt. It is no longer ours and therefore we may not derive any personal benefit from it.

She made the *brachah*, *"Lehafrish challah min ha'isah,"* removed a small portion of dough, and put it on a piece of aluminum foil on which it would be burnt in the oven after the *challos* baked. As she did that she recited the prayer beginning with, *"Yehi ratzon sheyibaneh Bais HaMikdash,"* the one that we all say at the end of *Shemoneh Esrei,* and explained to us that just as we continue to do the *mitzvos* that were done in the *Bais HaMikdash,* so, too, may we be *zocheh* to participate in the rebuilding of the holy *Bais HaMikdash*, speedily in our days.

We responded with a fervent "Amen," and took our seats around the kitchen table. I made sure to sit next to Nechama in order to help her in case she should need me. My mother sprinkled the table lightly with flour to prevent the dough from sticking to it.

Then she gave each of us a large handful of dough to work with. It felt soft and supple. When she handed Nechama her portion, I was quickly by her side, checking the dough, wanting to assure myself that it was not too sticky for Nechama to handle. After all, I told myself, it was hard enough for Nechama not to be able to see what she was doing, and I felt that it was my responsibility to make sure everything went as smoothly for her as possible.

My mother announced that we would be making six-braided *challos* and instructed us to roll out our dough into six equal strips. Clearly, she explained how we were to lay out the strips evenly and pinch them together at the top. I watched as Nechama carefully worked with the dough, studiously trying to follow my mother's directions. As my mother continued with the lesson, the braiding became more complicated.

Suri burst out laughing when she reached the end of her braiding and her pinched-together top came apart. Feigy tried hard, but finally raised her arms in mock despair and informed us that she thought that she would stick to making round *challos* in the future. My *challah* was not too bad, as I had had much more practice than the others.

And then we all turned to Nechama.

She appeared to be looking straight ahead, but her hands were busily working with her portion of dough on the table before her. She was almost finished with her braiding. We watched as she manipulated the strips of dough into a perfect pattern, crossing her right hand over her left, alternating from one side to the next. She continued slowly but determinedly until the strips were too short to work with. Open mouthed, we all watched as she pinched the ends together and smilingly picked up her perfect six-braided loaf of *challah*.

I looked at her proudly, feeling more reassured than ever. I knew then with certainty that Nechama was going to surpass us all.

Chapter Fourteen

It was early Friday afternoon, *erev Shabbos Chanukah*, and Abe and Linda's *Shabbos sheva brachos* was soon to take place.

Our house was full of the usual hustle and bustle that accompanies a *simchah*. The doorbell rang constantly, as cases of soda and groceries were delivered from various local stores, and friends came and went, dropping off their home-made cakes and cookies. My brothers had spent the last hour moving furniture, and Yerucham and Naftoli were now busy setting up folding tables and chairs across the dining and living rooms. The beds had been made up with fresh linen, the newly polished furniture gleamed, and the vacuum cleaner was still humming in the background. Meats, *kugels* and chickens were sizzling in the ovens, while sauces, soups and vegetables simmered on the stove. In the kitchen, a group of women was artfully arranging cakes and fruits on serving platters, and another team dashed back and forth with glasses and silverware, preparing to set the tables as soon as my brothers finished arranging them.

The delicious aroma of the cooking foods and the sweet smell of freshly baked pastries and warm *challos* mingled with the clean lemon scent of the furniture polish and cleansers. The pleasant combination of smells permeated the house, and an air of celebration and anticipation was tangible.

Linda's parents, married brother, sister-in-law, and younger sisters arrived and were shown to their rooms by one of my brothers, while another helped them with their suitcases.

I was in the kitchen cutting up what seemed to be hundreds of vegetables for salad, when my mother reminded me for the third time that day not to forget to go downstairs to the basement and set the *Shabbos* clock. On most *Shabbosos* it is set to turn the lights off at eleven-thirty P.M., but because of the *sheva brachos* my mother wanted me to disconnect the clock altogether.

As I headed out of the kitchen she gave me two large pans of ice cream to put in the freezer. I lifted one sheet of the aluminum foil covering the pan and stuck my finger inside, bringing up some ice cream to taste.

"It's delicious," I said, smacked my lips appreciatively and rolled my eyes.

"Renie . . ." My mother pursed her lips warningly and threw me a reproachful look as she gave me a light, playful shove in the direction of the basement steps.

I laughed and hurried downstairs. Just then the phone rang. Knowing how busy everyone was, I put down the pans and rushed to pick up the receiver from the basement's telephone extension.

"Hi, Cham," I said, recognizing the voice of the caller. "What's up?"

"Renie, can you come over to my house right now? It's urgent. I need to talk to you."

"Can't we talk on the telephone? The house is in turmoil right now because of the *sheva brachos.*"

"Please, Renie, I won't keep you long."

I could not afford the luxury of giving myself much time to make a decision. I figured that the sooner I got there, the quicker I would be back. If Nechama needed me, I could not turn her down.

"O.K., I'll be there as soon as I can."

I did not want to take the time to explain the situation to anyone, especially as deep down, I was not really sure that my mother would allow me to go. So, instead of using the kitchen door as I normally did, I bundled myself into my parka and hurried out the side door without saying anything to her. I promised myself that I would not be long, and felt the rush of the cool autumn air as I ran down the path towards the driveway. I saw Shimon unloading some last-minute groceries from the car and casually called out to him that I was going to a friend's house and would be back soon.

I was lucky to catch the bus to town just as the doors were closing and the driver was about to pull away. I was not as fortunate when it came to catching the bus to Rorey. I had to wait for ten minutes until the Express showed up, and when it did, it did not seem to move very quickly.

When I finally did arrive at Nechama's house, her mother answered the door with a surprised expression on her face.

The usually polite and well-mannered Mrs. Leverman hesitated for a moment and then bluntly asked me, "Renie, what are you doing here at this hour?"

I told her that Nechama had just called me and asked me to come.

She lingered uncertainly in the doorway a minute or so, remembered her manners and graciously invited me inside. It was obvious to me, though, that she was very disturbed about something. She led me into the living room and joined me on the L-shaped couch.

I leaned back against the comfortable cushions and looked around at the tastefully decorated living room. Everything was immaculately clean and in its place, as if in a showroom. A bowl of fresh fruit was positioned, as always, on the shiny glass coffee table, and the room was adorned with vases of fragrant freshly cut flowers. The familiar, black-lacquered, baby grand piano occupied its corner near the French windows. It was surrounded by several beautiful ceramic pieces, pleasingly grouped on the highly polished marble floor which bordered the lush Oriental carpet.

Mrs. Leverman sat wordlessly and stared at me. I thought that she wanted to say something, but did not quite know how to begin. The normal me would have come right out and asked her what was wrong, but the new me, the more sophisticated Renie, decided to be tactful and mature and wait until spoken to.

One minute passed. I waited. I did not say anything and neither did she.

I waited a little while longer. She continued to remain silent and so did I.

We could hear the ticking sound of time passing as the second hand gyrated its way around the clock. Another minute passed. I could wait no longer.

"Is something wrong, Mrs. Leverman?" I asked. The question seemed almost ludicrous under these circumstances. Evidently something was very wrong.

She took a sip of water. I watched her cross her legs first one way and then the other, apparently in discomfort. Clearing her throat determinedly, she forced herself to begin. "Nechama and you have always been good friends."

I nodded, but remained silent.

"She has always thought the world of you," I blushed and she continued, "and that is why I am asking you for your understanding and, well, forgiveness."

"But Mrs. Leverman, there is nothing for me to forgive."

"Yes, Renie, there is," she said slowly. "I don't know exactly why Nechama called you. Maybe she was just reaching out, or something like that . . . but, well . . ." She paused.

"Yes?"

"The fact of the matter is, Renie," Mrs. Leverman sighed deeply, "my husband took Nechama early this morning to meet with a specialist in New York. When they came home — only a short while ago — Nechama said that she had to make a phone call. She went straight to her room and I heard her speaking on the telephone." She paused and then continued in a low, even voice, "The strange thing is . . . is that as soon as she finished talking she claimed to be very tired and went to sleep. She asked me . . . not to wake her up for anything or . . ." Mrs. Leverman hesitated before finishing her sentence, "or . . . anybody."

"I don't understand," I said, mystified. "Then why did she tell me to come here if she was really too tired to speak with me?"

"I don't know." She wrung her hands together helplessly. "I just don't know." She stood up and walked nervously over to the window. "Maybe . . ." she paused, hesitant to continue.

"Maybe, what?"

"Right now, Nechama is going through the most horrible time in her life." She turned around to face me. I could see that she was trying to compose herself, unwilling to let me see her falter, bravely resisting the urge to let her tears flow. "We all are," she said quietly. She walked back to the couch and this time sat next to me. "Who knows why she called you . . . why she did what she did? We cannot blame her for not being herself these days." She shook her head sadly. "Maybe she was trying to test you," her voice throbbed, "to see if you would drop everything and come running at her request. Or perhaps," Mrs. Leverman's tone became more hopeful, "Nechama *really* did want to speak with you but was too exhausted . . . "

"It's O.K.," I said, seeing Mrs. Leverman's distress and not feeling too much at ease myself. "It doesn't matter. I . . ."

Just then the large grandfather clock on the mantel began to chime.

"Oh, no!" I cried out in alarm as I glanced quickly at the clock. "There are only two hours left until *Shabbos!*" I headed towards the hallway.

"Renie, please wait!" Mrs. Leverman turned to the telephone on the end table. "I'll order a car for you."

"No, thanks," I said heroically. "It's only a short bus ride back to Barclay. I'll manage all right."

With a quick good-bye I dashed out of the house, pulling the heavy mahogany door closed behind me.

❆ ❆ ❆

Fortunately, the bus arrived within two minutes after I reached the stop. I quickly climbed on board, grabbed the first seat I saw, and felt the bus start up immediately. I sighed with relief at my good luck. Leaning back comfortably against the vinyl seat, I closed my eyes, grateful that we would soon be reaching Barclay.

This respite was not destined to last long. My relief quickly turned to dismay. The bus was moving at an extremely slow pace. I was sitting up front near the driver and watched impatiently as he turned on his radio and began to casually switch stations, singing along as he leisurely drove down the road. I wished I could make the vehicle go faster and found myself pressing my right foot down harder and harder against the floor in front of me as if it could accelerate the speed of the bus. After the first ten minutes, the bus slowed down even more. Through the front window, I could see incoming traffic from the turnpike trying to squeeze in ahead of us. Our driver was obviously in no rush as he politely waved at his fellow drivers, allowing them to go first. Gradually the bus decelerated further until it came to a complete halt. Our driver honked, suddenly impatient, and was joined by the various horn sounds of the other drivers on the road. Of course, no honking or beeping made any difference. Traffic was bumper to bumper and we could only inch along.

Helplessly, we sat on the stationary bus. Impatient groans and frustrated complaints were heard from many of the passengers, but most of the people sat quietly, complacently reading or staring silently out the window, knowing that there was nothing they could do. We hardly moved more than a few yards for at least fifteen minutes. I looked at my watch. There was a little over an hour left until *Shabbos.* I knew that my parents were probably frantic with worry — that is, if they realized that I was not in the house. I was beginning to get pretty apprehensive myself.

Finally we saw the reason for the heavy traffic. The police and tow truck arrived, driving alongside us on the service road. A car was sitting in the middle of the road, immobile. I did not know if there had been an accident or if the car had simply stalled. Frankly, I must admit, I did not care either way. My only concern at that time was whether I should leave the bus and walk. Even if I ran all the way back to Barclay, I remember contemplating, I would not be able to make it home before *Shabbos*. The possibility of finding a taxi was virtually nil, as the traffic was backed up as far as I could see. I did not know what to do. I chided myself for managing to get into this mess in the first place. My heart was beating quickly and I felt myself perspiring in my warm jacket. Finally, after another fifteen minutes or so, the traffic began to move. My fellow passengers heaved deep sighs of relief, murmuring loudly as we passed the car that had been the cause of the delay. I just begged the driver to hurry as much as possible.

When we reached the Barclay stop on Main Street, I ran out of the bus and down the block as quickly as my feet could carry me. I wondered whether to wait for the other bus, but decided in the negative, as there was no bus in sight. I looked at my watch and saw that it was less than an hour until candle-lighting time. I took off, running through short cuts, down hills, passed the library, up President Lane, around the park, through Miriam's backyard — until finally I arrived, sweating and breathless, at my house. I rushed inside. I was relieved to see that no one seemed to be looking for me. I hurried up the stairs. Fortunately, I did not meet my parents. Unfortunately, I met Sima.

"Where were you? There are only twenty minutes until *Shabbos*, and look at you! You're a mess!"

I told her that I had no time to answer her questions just then and that I would be glad to explain later. Whether that answer satisfied her or not I did not know. I was in and out of the shower and blow-drying my hair within minutes.

☙ ☙ ☙

An hour later, when the men returned from *shul* and I stood near the beautifully set tables, gazing at the shiny silverware and the dancing flames on the glimmering candlesticks, I felt flooded with contentment at being surrounded by the security of my warm home and embraced in the peace and comfort of the *Shabbos* Queen.

I was wearing a brand new navy-blue sailor outfit that Sima had sewn for me and I stood up proudly when the *chassan* began to recite the *Kiddush*. I saw Abe and Linda exchange smiles and could not help but admire how beautiful the *kallah* looked and how tall and handsome the *chassan* was.

We had to wait for everyone else to make *Kiddush,* wash their hands, and eat their *challah*, fruit salad and *gefilte* fish, and so, by the time the first speech began, it was already quite late. Then steaming chicken soup with *lokshen* and *kneidlech* was served with crispy Chinese noodles, and this was followed by more speeches. Soon came the tasty chicken, delicious meats, hot *kugels,* and more side dishes. By that time the room had become quite crowded, as additional guests joined us for dessert. These included a couple of people who had not attended the wedding, and now were coming to offer their good wishes.

And then it was time for dessert.

My mother told me to go downstairs to get the trays of ice cream from the freezer.

I headed towards the basement. Suddenly I stopped short on the narrow staircase, unable to move my foot to the next step. I stood frozen in place. The words ice cream, dessert, freezer kept reverberating in my mind. Freezer. I was supposed to put the ice cream in the freezer. That was when Nechama had called.

I replayed the scene in my mind. I had walked over to the counter which was right next to the freezer and placed the large tray there before turning to the telephone. I squeezed my eyes shut, remembering how I had raced up the steps and out of the house totally oblivious to the melting dessert I had left behind.

"Nu, Renie, what's taking so long?" I heard my mother calling from the kitchen.

I did not move. What could I tell her? How could I excuse

myself for the muddle I had managed to cause this time? And to top it off . . . in front of all these people!

"Renie!"

Helplessly, I sat down on the steps. What do I do now? Do I go upstairs and tell the truth, or should I just say that the freezer was broken? Why do I, Renie Greenberg, always manage to bungle up everything? I sighed desperately.

All of a sudden, the door leading to the basement steps opened and I saw my brother Shimon standing there.

"Renie, Mommy said I should come and help you bring up the trays of ice cream," he informed me as he hurried down the steps. "Hey, what's wrong?" He stopped short when he caught sight of me sitting forlornly on the stair- case, shoulders hunched over in despair. I felt his brotherly concern as he asked me in a worried voice, "Why are you crying?"

The tears began to roll down my cheeks now that I had someone with whom to share my problem.

"Shimon, remember when I told you I had to run quickly to a friend?" I sniffed.

"Yes, sure, I figured you were going around the corner to Etty."

"I was not on my way to Etty," I explained. "I was going to see Nechama."

"Nechama? Nechama Leverman? Doesn't she live in Rorey?" When I nodded, he went on incredulously. "You mean you went all the way to Rorey at that hour? I can't believe it!" he said shaking his head. "But why are you so upset now?"

"Shimon, I was on my way downstairs to put the ice cream in the freezer, when Nechama suddenly called me, begging me to come to her. I couldn't refuse. She needed me." I stood up and looked at him pleadingly, "So what was I supposed to do? I knew it was close to *Shabbos*. I didn't give myself a chance to think . . . I just ran!"

" I see," he said shaking his head back and forth. "Now, let's see what the ice cream looks like."

I followed him over to the counter, and there it was. Shimon lifted up the aluminum foil. The colored layers had all run together, the crust had fallen apart. The whole thing was one big jumbled mess.

"It probably still tastes good," he said, grinning as he dipped his finger inside the pan as I had done that afternoon, "but . . ."

"But we can't serve it."

"That's just what I was going to say."

"Shimon, what should I do?" My eyes were brimming.

"Tell Mommy what happened."

"I can't, not now. I am so ashamed!"

"O.K., I'll go speak to her . . ." He smiled, seeing me sigh with relief. "And don't worry, Green-eyes, it'll be all right," he said soothingly. "Mommy will figure out what to do."

"Thanks, Shimon," was all I could say as I followed him up the steps. I made sure to linger behind an extra few minutes to give him a chance to talk to my mother before I made my appearance.

By the time I returned to the kitchen, I saw my mother and some other women cutting slices of rolled cake and placing them on individual dessert plates. I watched as Sima poured some *parve* chocolate syrup over each serving.

Trying to show my remorse, I contritely served the portions, cleared the table, and made myself as useful as possible. As I began to empty the leftover salads into the containers that would keep them fresh overnight, I heard hushed whispers and then the awed voices of the assemblage greeting the *Rosh Yeshivah* as he entered the dining room. Respectfully, I joined the women by the doorway so I, too, could see and hear him speak.

He had a very soft voice and while he spoke the people had to be absolutely still in order to hear him. There was not a sound in the room other than the *Rosh Yeshivah* delivering his message. People were sitting on the edge of their seats, in deep concentration, trying to grasp each and every holy word that came out of their teacher's mouth.

Suddenly, the room became pitch black. I heard a few cries of surprise, and even panic, as people unfamiliar with the layout of the room tried to grope their way through the darkness. I stood still, unmoving, for I knew what had happened. I had forgotten to disconnect the *Shabbos* clock as my mother had requested.

This was all my fault.

I will not detail what happened after that, or during the rest of that *Shabbos*, as I've endeavored to erase all that from my mind.

However, I will never forget the memorable conversation I had with my father late the next night.

❧ ❧ ❧

My father asked me to join him in his study after the guests had left and much of the cleaning-up was completed. Here it comes, I remember thinking, as I walked into the room.

As frustrated and angry as I was with myself for having caused the *sheva brachos* to flop, I justified what had happened by blaming everything on the hayride. After all, I thought defensively as I took a seat, if it had not been for the accident, then Nechama would be fine and healthy. She would not have had to call me in the middle of preparations for the *sheva brachos,* and I would not have neglected my responsibilities. None of this was really my fault, I determined, and therefore it would not be fair to hold me accountable for what had occurred.

Chin up and shoulders back, I proceeded to defend my actions to my father, reporting all this to him before he even had a chance to speak. After I finished my speech I looked at my father expectantly, waiting for his reply, anticipating his full agreement with my analysis of the situation.

I continued to wait. My father remained silent, his eyebrows creased, a frown on his face. I could tell that he was deep in thought, and suddenly I did not feel quite as confident as I had felt a few moments before. I squirmed uncomfortably until my father finally broke the awkward silence.

"So that's how you see it?" was all he said.

"Well, y-yes, *Abba,*" I stammered. "If it had not been for the accident, then none of this " I gestured with a wave of my hand, "would have happened."

"Are you telling me," he asked dryly, looking me directly in the eye, "that you had no choices, no decisions to make?"

"I was forced . . ."

"You were forced to neglect something your mother told you to do?" My father's voice was harsh.

"I only did what I thought was right," I murmured, holding back my tears. "Nechama needed me."

"Is it right to neglect other friends and all the other people that are important to you?"

"What do you mean?"

" I used to know a girl that shared herself with many different people." Now his voice was softer. "A girl who had time for her family, the new girl in school, the old friends . . . "

I remained silent, looking down at the floor. I wondered if he was referring to Etty when he said "old friends," and knew that I had been treating her unfairly. It was true that I never seemed to have time for Sima or my mother and that I was neglecting many of the people I cared about.

Etty had been right. I really had changed during these last few months. I would never again be the carefree girl I once was. Somehow, I felt the old me disappearing, and a new me, a new me that I did not particularly like, beginning to emerge.

Yet, I still felt justified.

"*Abba,* what should I have done?" I cried out defensively, "Nechama said that she needed me. Remember that night when we took the walk and you said how important it is for me to be there for Nechama?" I reminded him.

"That is true, Renie. You have shown us what a strong friend you are and we are very proud of you for that. But," he continued steadily, "in your attempts not to lose Nechama, you must be careful not to lose others who are important to you, too."

"Right now, this is the most important thing," I insisted. "After all, if it wasn't for me, nothing would have happened to Nechama." I took a deep breath, "It-it should have been me."

"Renie, G-d forbid, don't you ever say a thing like that!" my father's eyes were blazing.

"But, it's true," I protested, and could not suppress the words from coming out. "It should have been me in Nechama's seat.

Originally, I was sitting there, and then we switched. You see," I sobbed, "it was all my fault!"

And suddenly, the heavy responsibility, the pent-up emotions, the guilty conscience that was suffocating me all seemed to emerge together to the surface of my consciousness as I let the tears flow.

My father remained silent until I finished. Finally, I wiped my eyes with the handkerchief that he handed me and looked up at him searchingly.

The kind eyes regarded me for a moment, and then he said soothingly, "Renie, you know that you never had any right to blame yourself. You could not know what was destined to be . . . If it was meant for Nechama to go through this tragedy, it would have happened, hayride or not. You are not G-d and you cannot take the responsibility for what occurred." He smiled at me warmly and continued, "But you *are* accountable for your own acts, the decisions that you make, the priorities that you choose."

"I know," I said remorsefully, looking at the floor. "I am sorry that I let you and Mommy down and I guess I have been neglecting some people," I confessed.

"Anyway," my father said, changing the subject, "right after *Shabbos* Mommy received a telephone call from your friend's mother, Mrs. Leverman. Now, I don't want you to be overly optimistic," he warned, "nor do I want you to be falsely hopeful. You must be prepared for the worst . . ."

I looked at him, a puzzled expression on my face.

"The specialist has scheduled the surgery. It is to take place the day after tomorrow."

PART IV

Chapter Fifteen

Ifelt like a stranger when I walked up the familiar steps
that day.

I had known this house as a second home ever since I
was five years old. The large, welcoming porch creaked
beneath my feet as I took a few more tentative steps forward. I
looked around nostalgically. There was the old, squeaking,
grey swing with the two comfortable rocking chairs facing each
other, the deep wooden trunk that was aged and peeling but
somehow never quite made it to the junkyard, the large, green,
stone flowerpots . . . All were warmly familiar to me and yet, I
felt like an unwelcome outsider.

I took a deep breath and then rang the bell to Etty's house.
The curtains on the door window parted and a pair of dark

brown eyes peered down at me. Immediately, the door was pulled open and Etty's older brother, Dovid, stood before me.

"Oh, hi, I'll get Etty," he said, disappearing into the back of the house, leaving me standing uncomfortably alone.

To say that I felt awkward being there, at that time, would have been an understatement. Etty had really done nothing wrong to me, yet I had treated her unfairly. And now, on the morning after that long talk with my father, I knew that despite my discomfort, I had to apologize to her.

I heard her footsteps even before I saw her. I suddenly felt incredibly shy and tongue tied.

Etty's brother must have told her who was at the door because she did not seem especially surprised to see me. She did not invite me in. Instead, she suggested in a cool, but polite tone that we take seats on the porch.

I felt relieved. I was not sure whether Etty's family knew about our quarrel or not, but I did not feel brave enough to come face to face with them and find out they did.

I sat down on the swing and winced as Etty took a seat opposite me on the rocking chair. Before our dispute, whenever we were out on the porch, it had been the usual routine for the two of us to sit side by side on the swing. Sometimes we would end up talking for hours as we gently glided back and forth. Now I felt incredibly alone.

I did not have Nechama — that is, not the old Nechama — anymore. I had neglected Miriam and Peshy. I was too busy for Sima and my mother, and I had alienated myself from Etty.

She must have seen my dismayed expression because she then asked me in a slightly warmer tone if there was anything I came for.

"Uh . . . Etty," I stammered, and felt myself blushing, unaccustomed to being in an apologetic position. "I-I came to tell you how s-sorry . . ."

"It's O.K., Renie, forget about it."

"Forget about it?"

" Yeah," she said, with a nonchalant wave of her hand.

"No, Etty, I owe you at least this much," I tried to explain. "I want you to know that you aren't the only one I haven't been myself with lately."

"It's really O.K. You don't have to excuse yourself. You've been so busy these days," she murmured, and then added with some asperity, "especially with your *new* friends."

"You mean Feigy and Suri?" I asked. When she did not answer, I went on. "It's not the way it seems, Etty, really. You know how Feigy and I used to be with each other. You couldn't put the two of us in the same room!" I laughed and looked over at Etty hoping she would join in. Instead, she just stared ahead steadily, the expression on her face displaying no emotion. "Listen, Etty," I turned towards her pleadingly. "As we began to get to know each other better, we found that just because we're different in certain ways, it doesn't mean that we can't be friends."

"That's nice," she answered mechanically.

"Etty, it's not just them. Ever since the accident, I've been so confused. Everything around me, around all of us, was changing so fast. I guess I just reacted to you the way I did because I was feeling so mixed up. Especially when you started to criticize me about changing."

I could tell that she was not fully convinced. So I went on. By the time I finished telling her about all the mess-ups I caused at the *sheva brachos,* there were tears of laughter rolling down her cheeks.

She went to the kitchen to get two large, juicy, Granny Smith apples, and when she returned to the porch, joined me on the swing. We spent the rest of that hour swinging gently back and forth together, talking amiably and munching on our apples. For that short time my worries receded and I felt carefree, almost as I'd felt so long ago when we were just a couple of giggling first-graders.

We did not talk about Feigy, Suri, or even Nechama. We tried not to think about the operation that was to take place the next day.

❀ ❀ ❀

Later that afternoon, when Feigy called to ask me if I wanted to meet her on Main Street to go and visit Mrs. Finkelman, I told her that I did, but that I would be asking Etty to join us, too. I ended up calling Miriam and Peshy, also, and was glad to see that Feigy had Suri come along.

We were a lively group that went to call on Mrs. Finkelman that day. As usual, our time spent with her was anything but uneventful, and it was only when the sun began to set and we realized it would soon be Monday, the day of Nechama's operation, that we all grew quiet and our high spirits evaporated. As we were about to leave and I zipped up my parka, I noticed that my fingers were shaking. The familiar feelings of apprehension began to creep back inside me, and I found myself gripped with a renewed sense of fear.

I hardly slept that night, but twisted and turned anxiously, slipping in and out of nightmares and dreams without respite. The memory of one nightmare remains vivid. Eyes, eyes, eyes of all different shapes and colors were doing a macabre dance around my bed. And then, suddenly, one pair of large, round, brown ones stopped dancing, and turning in my direction, began to roll towards me. I tried to hurry away, but they seemed to pick up speed as if they were chasing me, and at the same time they were yelling that it was all my fault and that I would never escape. They were about to crash into me and then I awoke to find myself in a pool of sweat, shivering despite the turned-up steam and the warm quilt that covered me.

When I finally fell back asleep I dreamt that Nechama was completely cured. She was on a stage, thanking everyone for attending the Mitzvahthon, and then, in front of the packed auditorium, thanked Leba Rena Greenberg, her best friend, for sticking with her through the hard times.

☙ ☙ ☙

Early the next morning, my mother informed me that Nechama's parents had her admitted into the hospital the evening before. For the first time in a long time I was in school fifteen minutes before the bell rang. After getting permission from the school authorities, I walked around to all the rooms and wrote Nechama's full Hebrew name on each blackboard, with the word *Tehillim* written on top.

The operation was to take place at ten-thirty that morning.

Nechama's aunt was in touch with *Rebbetzin* Leibowitz, and as soon as the office staff was informed of Nechama's being wheeled into the operating room, *Rebbetzin* Leibowitz turned on the intercom in order for the whole school to say *Tehillim* together.

After trying, with little success to teach us, our teachers finally gave up, realizing there was no way we would be able to concentrate on our lessons. We used that time to say *Tehillim,* catch up on work, study, or just talk quietly amongst ourselves. At three o'clock that afternoon, *Rebbetzin* Leibowitz came into our classroom, wearing a somber expression. A hush fell over the room. For less than a minute she stood at the teacher's desk and regarded us solemnly, a kind look in her eyes. Those seconds seemed to last forever.

Finally she spoke.

"Girls, I know how anxious you all are to hear about Nechama. She underwent a very dangerous and serious operation, as you all know. I do not have to explain to you the complexity of entering the domain of the brain."

I felt as if I could not breathe. We were all on the edge of our seats, waiting. . .

"As of now, we must all be thankful that she has survived the operation. The anesthesia has worn off and she has, *Baruch Hashem,* woken up." I let out a deep sigh of relief as I looked around and saw that most of the girls were doing the same. Some turned to their neighbors, murmuring softly to them. One could surely feel the lessening of tension in the air. For the first time since entering the room, *Rebbetzin* Leibowitz smiled as she looked at us. However, a moment or two later, when the class had quieted down, she went on solemnly. "As for her eyesight being restored, girls, it will be at least a week until we find out whether the operation was successful. In the interim, we have to hope and pray."

My hand shot up. "Yes, Renie?" *Rebbetzin* Leibowitz turned directly towards me.

"May we visit Nechama in the hospital?" I asked anxiously.

"Yes," she smiled. "As a matter of fact, when I spoke to Nechama's aunt, she felt it would be most beneficial for

Nechama to have visitors. I have the schedule of the hospital's visiting hours. I would appreciate it, Renie, if you could arrange for the girls to visit Nechama in shifts throughout her stay, beginning tomorrow. Remember, girls," she looked towards the center of the room, "it is a hospital and I expect you all to behave in a fine manner, as Bais Yaakov girls should. It is also important not to forget that Nechama might tire easily, and you must not overstay your visit."

By the time *Rebbetzin* Leibowitz left our classroom there was not much time left until the four o'clock bell would ring, and so I spent the rest of the day trying to compile a schedule showing which girls would visit Nechama, specifying days and hours.

Of course I made sure that I would be the first one to go to Nechama the next morning. According to *Rebbetzin* Leibowitz's instructions, four of us were permitted to go together. I included Etty, Feigy and Suri in my group.

Happy that we would all be seeing Nechama the next day, and glad that we were all going together, we met at the school gate to discuss the next day's arrangements. We talked for a long time about Nechama, wondering what we could bring her. We were determined to surprise her with something special.

We stood there for a while immersed in an animated discussion, absently noticing the schoolyard emptying out and the teachers waving nonchalantly in our direction. Even *Rebbetzin* Leibowitz had left. The sky was beginning to darken and finally, acknowledging the late hour, we decided that it was time to part. Suddenly one of us — I think it was Etty — put one finger over her lips, indicating that we should not make a sound, and with her other hand pointed in the direction of the school's driveway.

Walking quickly and alone was Mrs. Ross. She had emerged from the side entrance of the school. It was usually used for deliveries, and not even the staff members used it as an exit. It was for that reason that we remained immobile for a few puzzled moments, speechless and extremely curious.

Finally, not thinking of the consequences, I impulsively suggested that we follow her home.

I had no idea what awaited us. I was soon to find out.

Chapter Sixteen

We hurried along as inconspicuously as possible. When we reached Main Street we were surprised to see that instead of turning in the direction of Wilson Street, where we thought she lived, Mrs. Ross slipped into the dark alley next to the bakery. By the time we arrived at that spot she was nowhere to be seen. We stood in front of the store, not knowing what to do.

What could she possibly be doing there, we wondered in hushed whispers. I knew the owners of the bakery, Mr. and Mrs. Dowlander. But what connection could Mrs. Ross have with them? And why all this secrecy?

We were too busy discussing our suspicions and therefore

did not notice when the tall, broad-shouldered man emerged from the dark alleyway. It was only when I caught a glimpse of Feigy's white face and frightened eyes that I turned around and saw the large figure looming before us.

"Mrs. Ross would like to speak with you girls," he said in accented English. Unconsciously, we moved closer together. Seeing our wary expressions he added softly, "You do not need to be afraid."

His voice was kind and we were eager to learn what was going on. We were also young and not very cautious. And so, after a few indecisive moments, our curiosity outweighed our fears and we followed the tall man into the dark alleyway, not knowing exactly where he would lead us.

We walked towards the backyard and down a few steps that led to the bakery's basement. He reached into his pocket, took out a key, and slipped it into the rusty keyhole. The large door squeaked open and he walked inside, leaving the door open behind him. We stood there immobile, uncertain and afraid to enter.

"Don't worry, girls, please come in," we heard a familiar female voice say. "It's O.K., Renie." I was startled to hear my name spoken as I stood wavering in the doorway. I was standing closest to the entrance and she must have seen me. "Tell Etty, Feigy and Suri to all please come inside."

I motioned to the girls to come closer. They followed me in. We could see that we were standing in a small, one-room apartment. There were two beds, a small table, a refrigerator, a hot plate, and a crib. There was also a small bookcase filled with *sefarim* and some eighth-grade English books. The room looked poor and bare, yet it was immaculately clean and neat.

Sitting on one bed was our English teacher and yearbook adviser, Mrs. Ross. In her arms was a baby who looked to be about half a year old. I had not seen him in nearly two months and had forgotten his curly black hair and large dark eyes. He looked at me curiously when I approached him and then, deciding that I was O.K., grinned at me, his face breaking into an adorable smile.

The other girls looked more bewildered than ever. I glanced

back at them, my eyebrows and shoulders raised questioningly, indicating that I, too, did not know what was going on.

Mrs. Ross must have seen our puzzled expressions because she laughed just then and said, "Girls, I guess I owe you a bit of an explanation. First, though, I would like to introduce you to my husband." She turned towards the tall man who by then had taken off his large coat and was leaning again the wall. "Avraham, this is Renie Greenberg, the girl who baby-sat for Cheli that Thursday evening." He smiled at me and then turned politely as his wife introduced the others, "This is Feigy Landers . . . Suri Shepinsky . . . and Etty Samuels. And girls," she turned towards the tall man, "this is my husband, Mr. Fariborz Avraham Kohanteb."

"Kohanteb?" I blurted out before I could stop myself. "How can that be *his* name if *your* name is Ross?"

I felt Etty pinch me from behind, and I blushed at my outburst.

"It's all right, Renie, I can well understand your perplexity. As a matter of fact, my husband and I will explain everything to all of you. But first," she rose from the bed and put the baby in his crib as she spoke, "I think you should all telephone your parents and let them know where you are, so that they will not worry. It's a quarter past five already," she said, pointing towards the alarm clock on the table.

Surprised that it had gotten so late and anxious about having, perhaps, caused our parents needless distress, we quickly took turns telephoning them. While we spoke on the phone, Mrs. Ross (or Kohanteb, or whoever she was) prepared some hot tea for us and put a box of crackers on the table. Her husband brought over some folding chairs from the closet, opened them, and pushed them next to the table.

After completing our phone calls, we removed our coats and laid them on one of the beds as instructed. Shyly, we took our seats around the table.

I sipped my tea slowly, as it was too hot to drink at once, and felt it begin to warm my shivering insides. I could see the uneasy expressions on my friends' faces and assumed they reflected my own. I was excited, but apprehensive, at the prospect of finally hearing her story. We waited impatiently for our teacher to begin.

"Well, girls, where shall I start? Let's see," she paused thoughtfully, "I guess I'll begin with my trip to *Eretz Yisrael.*" She sat back and began to talk. As she spoke to us we felt ourselves transported back a few years to a different place in another country. She stopped only to give Cheli a cracker and to offer us some more tea. We were anxious for her to continue.

"I was born and raised in Wichita, Kansas — not a very Jewish area. And although I did not have a religious upbringing, my parents were always proud of their Jewishness and therefore encouraged me to attend a college in Jerusalem upon my graduation from high school. Anyway, to make a long story short, my one-year stay turned into four, and my degree in literature became secondary to my acquisition of a religious Jewish education. After more than four years of studying, I became engaged to Avraham." She smiled at her husband. "He had been studying in a *yeshivah* in *Yerushalayim* for ten years. Although he came from Iran, he was almost like a true-bred Sabra. My parents flew to Israel to join us for the wedding and my happiness knew no bounds. Unfortunately," her voice changed, "my husband's parents were unable to join us. They were not allowed to leave Iran."

As these words were spoken she turned her face away, but we were able to see that her eyes had filled with tears. She looked at her husband, who was staring into the distance. We saw her dab at her eyes with a napkin that was lying on the table, and then she continued.

"We settled into a small but cozy apartment. My husband was able to learn in the *yeshivah kollel* while I spent my mornings teaching English at the Bais Yaakov. Fortunately, I had a second job which paid me well and enabled us to live quite comfortably. I tutored children of diplomats in literature and language. These subjects are my specialty and I enjoyed the job immensely. Often the work entailed my going in and out of foreign embassies on a steady basis. I found this to be quite exciting, yet it was wonderful to return to my *frum* neighborhood and my lovely apartment at the end of the day. We were very happy and looking forward to the birth of the baby I was carrying.

"One hot sultry day, as I was returning from work, the mailman handed me a letter addressed to my husband. When I saw that the letter came from Iran, my heart began to beat wildly with excitement. It was not often that Avraham received mail from his parents, and I was both thrilled and filled with anticipation as I put the letter aside and waited for his return from *yeshivah*. I knew how happy he would be to hear from them.

"As soon as he walked through the door that evening I smilingly handed the envelope to him. I was shocked by his reaction as he read the letter. I watched as his face changed expression and saw his dark complexion literally turn white. I was afraid he would faint, and quickly shouted for him to tell me what the letter said. He handed the two papers to me. The letter was not from his parents as I had thought, but from an elderly Jewish neighbor who knew Avraham from the time he had been a baby. He wrote that Avraham's father had died suddenly of a heart attack, and that now his mother had fallen deathly ill. He was sorry to write such bad news but felt that as the only child, Avraham — or Fariborz, as he called him — should know.

"I sank into the nearest chair when I finished reading the letter, and tried to commiserate with him, but he did not answer. Instead, he walked over to the dining room table and put his head down. There was absolute silence in the room except for the loud sobs that shook his body. I felt so helpless as I listened to his heartrending cries. There was no way I could comfort him, and I knew his only consolation lay in the future.

"Finally, after what seemed like hours, but in actuality was only about ten minutes, he stood up. There were no more tears. His face seemed to turn to stone. And in a voice that seemed devoid of emotion, he announced, 'I'm going.'

"I tried to pretend that I did not know what he meant, and asked, 'Going where?'

" 'To Iran,' he answered. 'Where else?'

"I pleaded with him, knowing they would never let him out if he went back. I couldn't stop my tears, and knew I was becoming hysterical.

"He looked at me, his stony expression softening with sympathy. I knew Avraham, and I knew that if he made up his mind to do something he would do it, regardless of the consequences. And I knew he felt that out of love and respect for his parents, he had to be there with his dying mother. There would be no holding him back. I also knew that I was determined not to allow him to give up his future, our baby's future, and our future as a family together. He had been through so much, and deserved the happiness I hoped *Hashem* had in store for us.

"You see, when Avraham was entering his teenage years his parents realized that there would be no religious future for their son in Iran, and therefore insisted that he go to *Eretz Yisrael* to ensure for himself a better Jewish life. They were unable to attain documents to enable him to leave the country legally, as these were very costly and buying them would mean giving up their life's savings. They would have gladly done anything to make their son's departure safer, but they were elderly people who could no longer work and Avraham insisted they keep the little money they had managed to put away. It was decided that he would leave secretly. This meant an illegal escape would have to be planned, and no one would be allowed to know that he was leaving, not even his closest friends and relatives. It meant days of traveling with hardly anything to eat, past dangerous checkpoints, hidden under heavy blankets in the backs of bumpy vehicles. It meant riding on camels through hot deserts and freezing nights with just the clothing on his back, relying on a guide who was doing all this just for money and who, at the slightest whim, could have abandoned him to the merciless elements.

"Finally, after a fearful journey he arrived in Afghanistan. From there he went on to Vienna, where he met *yeshivah* people who helped him settle in a *yeshivah* in *Eretz Yisrael*. The following years were spent learning the Torah he loved, the Torah for which his parents had given up their son.

"And now, dominated by the strong emotions of *hakaras hatov* to his parents and out of *kibud av va'eim* and love for them, Avraham was ready to give up everything he had in order to return to Iran. I was afraid it would be suicidal.

"All at once it hit me. He *could* go back and forth — if I went along with him. After insisting that it was the only way, I finally persuaded him to let me come. He was anxious about me traveling in my condition, but as I pointed out to him, I would be in a more precarious position staying home alone and worrying about him.

"Using my contacts in the foreign embassies, I was able to obtain two French passports and visas. We would be allowed to stay in Iran for only two weeks, and although it was a short time, we were very appreciative of whatever time was allotted to us. With the trip well planned, it seemed to us that everything would go smoothly.

"How wrong we were!

"When we arrived at the Mehrabad Airport via France, we drove to Kazvin, on the outskirts of Tehran, where his parents lived. We were shocked upon entering my husband's mother's house to find it empty. After a few subtle inquiries we discovered that she had been in the hospital for over a month. We were fortunate to have come when we did. For the next twenty-four hours Avraham remained by his mother's side. Sometimes she was lucid and sometimes she was not. At least, at the end of her life, she had the satisfaction of seeing her son, grown up and married, and his wife who was expecting a baby soon. Avraham was able to say *Shema* with his mother before she died.

"The day she died I went into labor. A few weeks still remained before my baby was actually due to be born, but I guess the excitement and tension of the trip must have triggered it off. I was hospitalized and soon gave birth to a healthy baby boy. By the time he was eight days old and had his bris, we were ready to return to *Eretz Yisrael.*

"And then we found out that in order to leave with our baby, Cheli had to be registered at the government offices — since we did not have a passport for him. This undoubtedly would have led to suspicions and, perhaps, even dangerous interrogations, and we were fearful for Avraham's safety. It was out of the question for us to leave Iran the same way Avraham had left years before, as we had the health of our newborn baby to consider. The only way to escape would be to somehow obtain an illegal passport for him.

"Our allotted time had expired and we were forced to go into hiding. Now we, too, would need new passports in order to leave. Through secret contacts, it was arranged for us to stay hidden in a shabby, two-bedroom apartment in the worst part of the city, with three other families who were in similar situations. Every night the men were out attending secret meetings, attempting to find a way for us to leave. I would sit in the apartment, my stomach churning with anxiety until Avraham returned. The situation was unbearable. The people I was with were not clean or quiet, nor were they the type of people a religious person wanted to be with. Days and nights passed. I hardly slept and felt weak from having just given birth.

"This went on for a while until one night Avraham returned from a secret meeting in an obviously good mood. His excitement was contagious, and I begged him to tell me what had happened. We hurried into another room so that we could speak privately, and he told me that he had procured two false passports.

"One was under the name Ross. It was for a mother and her six-month-old son. I looked at the picture and knew that I looked nothing like this woman. She was blonde and light skinned and I was the opposite. The baby in the picture did not look at all like my baby. My Cheli was a newborn, just a few weeks old. The baby in the picture was sitting up and smiling directly into the camera. Only a miracle could get us through.

"And then my husband showed me his passport. It was in the name of James Richardson. I was amazed when I looked at the man's picture and saw that he almost resembled my husband to a T. They both had the same dark hair, dark eyes and olive skin. He even had a cleft in his chin like my husband. They could have been identical twins. The only difference in their appearance was their haircuts and glasses and, of course, that was easy to remedy.

"These passports cost us practically everything we had, but it would be well worth the expense if they enabled us to leave this hateful and dangerous country. The passports were American. Although my husband spoke English with an accent we were sure he would have no trouble once he reached the United States. We were more concerned that I should be able to pass as Mrs. Ross. However, we could bear the situation no longer and so it was decided that I would leave with the baby within two days. For reasons of safety my husband would follow on the next flight.

"I am sure that I do not have to tell you girls the fear I felt at that time. Wearing a blonde wig that my husband obtained with relatively little difficulty, and trying to look like Mrs. Ross of my passport, I was physically weak and emotionally drained by the time I boarded that plane. Carrying my baby to safety, to the future, was my only comfort and the only motivation to keep me going.

"I arrived here in the beginning of the summer. Relieved to finally be in the U.S.A., I hastily removed the blonde wig, replacing it with my own dark brown one. I felt glad to be rid of the false Mrs. Ross and the fear of the last few weeks, and sat in the airport lounge anxiously waiting for my husband's arrival late that night.

"When his plane landed and he did not walk through the arrivals' gate, I continued to wait. Finally, when it seemed to me that there were no more passengers left, I went to the information desk and asked about James Richardson. The lady at the desk looked at me with a surprised expression on her face. She then turned to her bulletin board and looked at me again. She asked me what my name was, and I gave her my real name, Rochel Kohanteb. She fumbled with some papers, ran her fingers down the passenger list, and told me that there was no James Richardson on this plane.

"I walked away from the desk in a daze. I was exhausted and shocked by what I had just heard and, clutching my baby tightly, sank into the nearest chair. Cheli began to cry and I felt like joining him. It took a strength I did not know I had to keep my tears from flowing.

"All of a sudden a religious woman approached me and, seeing me sitting despondently in an airport in the middle of the night with only a little baby for company, she asked me whether I was waiting for someone. Looking into her kind eyes, I told her that yes, I was waiting for my husband who was supposed to have arrived on Austrian Air an hour ago but hadn't shown up. She suggested that perhaps he would be arriving on the next flight which was due early the next morning. She explained to me that she was at the airport to see some guests safely off, and invited me to spend the night at her large house with its many vacant bedrooms. She mentioned that all her sons were away at *yeshivah* and that her married daughter was visiting her in-laws out of town. Her youngest daughter was in summer camp and that is why I did not meet you, Renie, at that time.

"When I came to her warm home, Mrs. Greenberg gave me the pampering I so desperately needed. As tired and worried as I felt, I had not realized just how hungry I was, and encouraged by my hostess, I managed to eat a healthful, hot meal. This lady made me feel as if I was doing her the favor by coming to her empty home. She had appeared to me as an angel, and I felt embraced by her kindness. It was for this reason that I felt I could hold myself back no longer. I cried, releasing my pent-up emotions as I told her the story of our escape from Iran. I explained to her the situation I was in. When I told her about the false passports and that my husband was traveling under the name of James Richardson, who looked exactly like him, I barely noticed her face change color. She put the baby to sleep for me and, making sure I was comfortable, encouraged me to get a good night's sleep.

"I was up early the next morning. Mrs. Greenberg was already in the kitchen when I came downstairs. After making sure that I had my breakfast, she asked me to sit down in the living room. She said that she and her husband wanted to talk to me. I was anxious to get to the airport, as I wanted to be there as soon as my husband arrived, but felt it would be impolite to rush off after she had been so helpful. I sat down uneasily.

"Gently, they explained to me that the passport my husband was carrying, the one with the picture of James Richardson who looked identical to my husband, was not only an illegal passport but the passport of a convicted criminal. They told me that there were posters displayed across the United States — in airports, post offices, libraries and many other public places — offering rewards for the capture of this man.

" Though it came as a shock to me, I did not have the luxury of time to accustom myself to my new predicament. We had to think of a plan before my husband's plane would arrive. We decided that since I had been seen with my baby in the airport the night before asking for James Richardson, it would be too dangerous for me to go and meet him. Instead, your father, Renie, would try to get him before the authorities did. That is, if he was on the plane at all.

"It was a close call, but a few hours later we were all sitting together in your living room. I was relieved to see my husband, but feared for our safety. His only crime, and mine too, had been entering this country with illegal passports. Even though he was innocent of the terrible crime James Richardson had committed, we knew it would be some time until this was proven. They looked exactly alike and we had no way to prove that Avraham was not James Richardson. He would not be the first person imprisoned due to mistaken identity, especially as he was using the passport of the very person he denied being.

"It was decided that I would go under the name on my passport, Mrs. Ross, and that I would continue to try to use her appearance as my cover. Otherwise, we feared, I might be identified as the woman in the airport who was seen asking for James Richardson. We needed a safe place to stay in the interim, but felt we could not turn to my parents. They aren't young people and I didn't want to endanger them or upset them in any way. Besides, they live in a small town. People would notice our presence and would wonder about the peculiar situation we were in. We decided to remain in Barclay and for security, keep two apartments, this one here, and the other in an apartment house on Wilson Street.

"The Greenbergs explained the situation to *Rebbetzin* Leibowitz and I was lucky that there was a vacancy in the school. She told me that the former teacher and yearbook adviser, Miss Einstein, had been called away. She managed to convince me that I would be perfect for the job and that she was in a bind as to finding the right teacher. She succeeded in making me feel welcomed and needed.

"During the day when I was at school, the baker's wife, Mrs. Dowlander, who knew of our predicament, would help us out baby-sitting.

"We were thankful to have a place to live, a means of earning a living, and wonderful people trying to help us out of a very difficult situation.

"That Sunday before *Succos* when I bumped into you, Renie, I did not know whether I was coming or going. We were told that the police would soon be arriving at the apartment on Wilson Street to investigate, as they had been informed that someone looking like James Richardson was living in that apartment building. I was in the midst of transferring our things when I saw you. You can imagine what I was going through at that time.

"Similar incidents kept cropping up unexpectedly these past months. Finally, with G-d's help and the assistance of some important and benevolent members of the community, we were able to get in touch with our congressman who, fortunately, decided to take on our case. We had to attend a secret meeting that Thursday night, Renie, when I asked you to baby-sit, and of course it wasn't appropriate for me to bring the baby along.

"Ever since that meeting, things have been much easier for us. We gave up the apartment on Wilson Street, and Mrs. Dowlander has continued being very kind to us. My husband still has to stay secluded here, but at least he has his *sefarim* to help occupy his time, and he tries to help Mr. Dowlander in the bakery as much as possible.

"The congressman feels that in a short time they will be able to prove mistaken identity, as they presently have evidence that the real James Richardson has left Iran and is in Canada. The diplomats that I know from Israel are also trying to help prove that my husband is not James Richardson and is innocent."

She paused, clasped her hands together and placed them on the table before her. Then she concluded, "And so, girls, now you know our story."

I looked around at my friends' faces. There was not a dry eye amongst us.

Chapter Seventeen

Late that night, after my father had picked us up from the Dowlanders' bakery, I had a very long and serious talk with my parents.

They told me some things I already knew: how brave the Kohantebs were and what *mesiras nefesh* they had. They also mentioned something I was not aware of: that even when Mr. Kohanteb's name would be cleared, their situation, here in Barclay, would still be intolerable.

The trip to Iran and the circumstances that followed had depleted all their savings. They were forced to give up their apartment in Israel to meet their expenses. Presently, they had nothing. And, at the end of the year, Miss Einstein would be returning to her job as English teacher and yearbook adviser.

They were poor but proud people who would not accept the *tzedakah* money that had been collected for them. They considered anything that was not earned as not rightfully theirs, and felt that there were people in more dire circumstances who had greater needs than they had.

Living under the bakery on a permanent basis was out of the question. It was important for the Kohantebs to settle into an apartment where their baby would be able to get some fresh air and where they could be a bit more comfortable. Mrs. Kohanteb was an immensely talented and educated woman and in our small town of Barclay there were few positions that were open for an "overqualified" person such as she. As for her husband, he was willing to take any job however menial, but he was a budding *talmid chacham* whose learning, his wife felt, should not be interrupted. My parents explained that it would be impossible for them to remain in Barclay much longer.

Throughout the morning hours and all the way to the hospital, I could not get the Kohantebs out of my mind. I reported to the other girls what my parents had told me and we all felt helpless at not being able to do anything to improve the situation. Besides our having grown close to her and knowing we would miss her terribly, we also knew how hard it would be for them to be forced to move again. They already had some close friends in Barclay and we realized how difficult it would be to have to adjust to a new and strange community after all they had been through.

We sat on the bus, quietly looking out the windows for the duration of the trip, each of us immersed in our own thoughts. It felt incredibly frustrating to be ignorant of a means to help the Kohantebs, and I wished fervently for a way to keep them in Barclay. I could see the restless expression on my face reflected on the glass of the bus window as we passed by the rolling hills that surround the highways near Barclay. Yet I could think of no solution. When the bus came to its final stop at the hospital, I could no longer think of Mrs. Kohanteb and her problems. The familiar tension of facing Nechama began to set in.

As the elevator lifted us towards the floor that Nechama's room was on, I felt my heart quicken with apprehension. Watching the expressions on my friends' faces, it was obvious that they were just as tense as I. I was glad not to be facing Nechama alone.

We followed the nurse through the corridor, our footsteps echoing softly on the shiny floor. Knocking gently on the door to Nechama's room, the nurse slowly pushed it open and led our nervous group inside.

"How are we feeling today?" she chirped, walking towards the window. "Isn't it wonderful?" She swung the curtains open, letting the sunshine flood the room. "Already we have so many visitors this morning!"

"Who's here?" Nechama asked weakly. We could barely hear her. On the huge hospital bed, buried under a layer of blankets, the top of her face and head wrapped in bandages, she looked so fragile and frail. I do not think we would have recognized her had it not been for the familiar, albeit reedy voice we heard.

"It's us, Cham," I answered softly, approaching the bed. I had forgotten my initial uneasiness and could only think of wanting to protect this vulnerable girl. "It's me, Renie. Suri, Etty and Feigy are also here." I sat down next to her. "*Rebbetzin* Leibowitz allowed us to be the first ones to visit you."

"How are you feeling?" Feigy's pale face was earnest as she joined me on the bed and reached for Nechama's hand.

"Is there anything we can get you?" Suri asked anxiously. "A drink of water, something?"

"Isn't that sweet," the nurse said in her rather annoying singsong tone as she removed a tray from Nechama's night table. "We have such nice friends."

"Oh, I almost forgot," Etty said, handing a small box to Nechama. "We have something for you."

"We have a present. How very nice!" The nurse took the box from Nechama's hands and began to unwrap it, "Oh, how lovely. Chocolates! We do love chocolate."

"Thanks for coming, everyone." Nechama's lips spread into

a smile, but her voice still lacked its usual strength. "It's great to have you all here together."

"Oh, how happy we are today," the nurse sang. She picked up the vase of flowers and announced, "I'll go change the water now. We mustn't let our flowers wilt," and sauntered out of the room.

"WE hope you enjoy yourself," Feigy good-naturedly mimicked the nurse's high-pitched voice when the door closed behind her. "And WE hope WE have a good day today."

"Sh-h," Nechama chuckled softly. "You'll get me into trouble here."

We laughed conspiratorially, more comfortable than we had thought we could be. Nechama was weak and ill but she was still Nechama and we were her close friends. I soon realized that we need not have worried about our visit with her. Surprisingly, she seemed happier than she had been since the accident. There was a feeling of serenity and contentment about her. Of course we did not talk about the operation. Optimism was in the air and we could only hope and pray for good results.

The conversation flowed smoothly as we told Nechama our English teacher's story. With all of us trying to talk at once, Nechama had to laughingly quiet us down in order to understand all we were telling her.

"And so you see, Nechama, they'll probably end up leaving Barclay as soon as this mess is cleared up," Etty concluded sadly.

"Or at the end of the year at the latest." Feigy stood up and walked towards the window.

Suri sighed loudly. "It seems so unfair after all they've been through."

"There must be something we could do to help," I exclaimed fervently. "It just doesn't seem right."

"I was thinking. . ." Nechama began slowly.

"Yes?" we all asked her at once.

"I-I was thinking," she repeated, "that if our school had a library. . ."

"Then Mrs. Kohanteb could be the librarian," I finished her

sentence enthusiastically, easily grasping what Nechama was driving at.

"Yes," Nechama smiled, pleased. "After all, she's certainly well qualified for the job."

"And you know how *Rebbetzin* Leibowitz has always been saying that it's the only thing missing from Bais Yaakov of Barclay," Suri added excitedly.

"So, if we had a library, then Mrs. Kohanteb would have a job!"

"She wouldn't have to leave Barclay."

"They would be able to move into a decent apartment!"

"And her husband could learn in the Yeshivah of Barclay and maybe even tutor or something."

"Cham," I exclaimed, squeezing her hand tightly, "you're an absolute genius!" Etty and Suri were nodding their heads approvingly.

"Um, I hate to be the kill-joy over here," Feigy began dryly. We turned towards the window where she was still standing. "But setting up a library in a school is not exactly expense-free. What with the high cost of the books, organizing it, the librarian's salary. . .Why do you think we haven't had one until now?" she asked, tucking a strand of blonde hair behind her ear.

We all knew the answer to that question. Most of Bais Yaakov of Barclay's students came from Barclay itself. There were not too many affluent students amongst us. It was hard enough collecting tuition from the parent body and managing to meet the school's growing payroll. How could we expect the school to support the library they had managed so long without?

"Well, I thought about that, too," Nechama's voice was barely a whisper. "If we would —" abruptly she stopped talking and turned her face away from us.

"What, Cham? Tell us," I urged.

She shook her head.

"C'mon!" we pleaded.

She remained silent, her head still turned towards the wall, conveying to us in a most obvious way that she did not wish to continue this discussion. There was not a sound in the room. Nechama could not see our expressions, but we knew she could hear us clearly. We looked at each other uncomfortably, afraid to say the wrong thing.

Two or three tense minutes passed and I could take the strained silence no longer. I began to speak about something else, and the mood in the room slowly lightened. Within a few minutes we were all talking animatedly again.

There was no mention of a school library or the Kohantebs' situation for the duration of our stay.

When visiting hours were over and we had to return to school, we spent the time on the bus discussing the strange change of mood that had suddenly come over Nechama. What had she been thinking about, we pondered aloud, and why did she change her mind about discussing it? Something had obviously disturbed her, but what?

❀ ❀ ❀

Later that day as I sat in class, I found myself unable to concentrate on the social studies lesson. Puzzled, I kept reviewing the conversation we had with Nechama that morning. We had spoken about the predicament of our English teacher and Nechama had come up with the idea of a school library as the solution. Feigy had pointed out its uselessness without adequate finances to fund the program.

And then Nechama had said that she had an idea. We had all eagerly waited for her to tell us what is was. That was when the conversation had come to its abrupt end. What had stopped her, I wondered. What fund-raising idea had she had in mind?

I began to think. Could it have been a cake sale? A *Melavah Malkah* to raise money? No, these events could not bring us in the needed funds to finance a library and besides, why would it have bothered her to suggest it? It must have been something else, but what?

All at once it hit me.

The Mitzvahthon! That's what Nechama must have been thinking about. If we could win the Mitzvahthon, then funds would be allocated to us by way of the grant awarded to the winning school. And that must be the reason she did not want to discuss it. Because even Nechama would have to admit that the only chance our school had at winning was by having her play the piano. I sighed with relief. The pieces of the puzzle fit together perfectly.

If the operation would be successful, and if Nechama would regain her sight, I knew for sure that she would agree to play. But, if it was not successful. . .she would never get on stage, she would never play before an audience. Without Nechama, it would take a miracle for us to win.

I heard Miss Weiss mention something about a wall in China. As inconspicuously as possible, I scribbled a message on a piece of paper, folded it and passed the note to Etty. I wrote on top, "To Etty: Read and pass on to Feigy and Suri; Love, Renie." Looking obliquely over my shoulder, I watched as she read it and nonchalantly, pretending to scratch her back, passed the note to Chaya Leah, who was sitting behind her. It went one person further when suddenly it slipped out of that girl's hand and landed on the floor. Miss Weiss stopped talking about the wall in China and walked over to where the note lay. Holding out her hand palm up, she demanded the note. After seeing who had written the note, and to whom it was being sent, Feigy, Suri, Etty and I were told to remain in our seats after class.

At first it seemed it would not be easy to explain the situation to Miss Weiss. This was her first year as a teacher, and although she had always been a brilliant student, I suspected that she felt threatened by our eighth-grade class. She was only a few years older than her students and I knew that she was afraid we would take advantage of her. But with all of us talking at once, pleading with her to read the note that I had written to the other girls, we were finally able to justify our actions and exonerate ourselves. I could tell by the expression on her face that she understood the problem and knew that we did not mean any harm. We looked at her eagerly, waiting to hear what a good idea the school library was.

"Suppose our school does win the Mitzvahthon." She regarded us for a moment and then, in an even voice, asked us, "How do you know whether a library is a priority for the school?

Have you spoken to *Rebbetzin* Leibowitz about it? Have you discussed this idea with the members of the board?"

Morosely, we looked at each other and shook our heads in unison. We were surprised to discover that there might be obstacles that could impede our well-intended plans.

"Girls, you don't have to look so sad." Her voice warmed towards us as she saw how quickly our eagerness was replaced with disappointment. "I'm not saying that your idea will be approved or disapproved. I am simply telling you that before you get excited about a school library you should find out if this is what the school's authorities want."

Miss Weiss was right. We had taken it for granted that the idea of a library would automatically be accepted. We had not realized that the administration might have other priorities in mind.

"Forget it," I said glumly. "Who would want to listen to us anyway?"

"Yeah," Feigy continued, her blue eyes staring sullenly into space, "and that's *if* we win the Mitzvahthon. A great big If."

Etty and Suri continued to sulk.

"Personally," Miss Weiss smiled at us soothingly, "I happen to think it's a wonderful idea. As a matter of fact, I'll tell you what. As soon as my classes for the day are finished, I'll go with you to speak to *Rebbetzin* Leibowitz."

A few hours later we were all sitting in our principal's office. With Miss Weiss' encouragement and our enthusiasm, *Rebbetzin* Leibowitz promised to do all she could to get the O.K. from the board.

The next morning, I breathlessly slipped into my seat in front of Etty as the nine-o'clock bell began to ring. As soon as I had pushed my books under my seat and hung my shoulder bag on the back of my chair, I felt someone tug at my hair. Fortunately, before I could cry out, I realized it was Etty trying to pass me a note. Pretending to be fixing my ponytail, I tightened my hand around the small folded piece of paper that was placed in it. Carefully, I placed it in my notebook and, pretending to check my notes, I read the note that Etty had given me.

"Last night," she wrote, "the board had a meeting. *Rebbetzin*

Leibowitz and Miss Weiss both attended. Our idea of a school library was approved. That is, providing we receive the funds as winners of the Mitzvahthon." I turned around and grinned at Etty.

Now, all that remained was for Nechama to be convinced.

⚙ ⚙ ⚙

I was unable to go to the hospital that day or the next. When I went downstairs to the kitchen Thursday morning for breakfast, my mother greeted me with the latest news: The real James Richardson had been apprehended and Mrs. Kohanteb's husband was free! I nearly danced all the way to school. When I arrived there, everyone was in an uproar. The complete story had surfaced and everybody, faculty and students alike, could speak of nothing else. Feigy, Etty, Suri and I could only smile at each other conspiratorially.

On Friday I was finally able to visit Nechama again. Unfortunately for me, Nechama had loads of visitors that day and I was unable to speak with her privately. The topic of conversation was the story of James Richardson. Everyone was discussing it; after all, it was not often that the town of Barclay made such sensational headlines. Nechama and I squeezed hands tightly. The story was about our teacher and we felt proud to have had a closer relationship to it. We discussed this topic too, but there was still no mention of the library or Mitzvahthon.

Sima needed my help on Sunday. She had to attend a wedding in New York and, as Shuey had a fever, she did not want him to go outdoors. I went over to her apartment to baby-sit and spent the day there.

I had finals to study for, but I also had a novel that I had been wanting to read for a long time. While Shuey slept, I read. When he needed a feeding or a diaper change, I took care of him as quickly as possible in order to get back to my book. He played peacefully in his playpen while I continued to read. I was totally engrossed in my book when the telephone suddenly rang.

It was Nechama. She had tried calling me at home and was told that I was at Sima's. At first we spoke about neutral subjects — tests, schoolwork, the yearbook, and even the weather. And then I asked her the question that I was afraid to ask, but somehow felt she wanted to talk about.

"Cham, are you very nervous about tomorrow? I mean, about when the bandages come off?"

"A little."

"You know, Cham, that whatever happens. . .you and I. . .we'll always be best friends."

"I know that, Renie."

"And I'll always be there for you. You know that too, don't you?"

"Yes. . ." She paused, and after a few moments said, "Renie?"

"What, Cham?"

"Promise me that whatever happens, whether I, whether I'll be able to see again or not — promise me —"

"Sure, Cham, anything. What?" I urged.

"Promise me that you won't let it change you. That you'll still go on being your cheerful self. Promise me that you won't let it get you down."

"Nechama, how could you be worried about me? How could you be thinking of me when you have so much on your own mind?" I felt my eyes filling as the words tumbled out.

"Just promise me, Renie, just promise you'll be all right."

"Of course, Cham, of course I'll be O.K. I'll just be worried about you."

"And. . .and don't be mad at me if I don't play at the Mitzvahthon. I — I just can't get up in front of everybody if. . ."

Suddenly, it did not seem so important whether Nechama would play at the Mitzvahthon or not. The only thing that mattered was for her to see again. All I cared about was Nechama's happiness. All I wished was for her to be able to lead the normal life so many of us take for granted.

"Don't be silly, Cham." I swallowed, trying to hold back my tears. "Of course I wouldn't be mad at you."

"Are you sure?"

"Sure," I gulped. The tears were spilling down my cheeks now. "Sure I'm sure." I felt overcome with emotion as I heard myself say those familiar words. Words we had often used in playful banter ... words that had been used during happier times.

How could Nechama be so concerned about me and so calm about herself? I remembered that night after the *pidyon haben* when we stayed up late, talking. Nechama had said that lots of things are here today and gone tomorrow, and that cheerfulness and happiness are something no one can ever take away from you. Oh, Nechama, I wondered to myself ... Will you be able to be cheerful and happy if the operation is not a success? If, Heaven forbid, you will never see again?

When at last we said good-night to each other, I could neither read nor study for my tests. I walked over to Yisroel's *sefarim shrank* and found a *Tehillim*. I turned the pages to the first *perek* and, with tears streaming down my face, began to recite the words that had brought solace to so many.

It was quite late when Yisroel and Sima returned from the wedding and I was driven back home. It was much later when I finally lay snuggled under my covers, fast asleep.

There was much left to be desired of my performance on the *Chumash* test I took the following morning, but while taking it I felt entirely indifferent. I could only think of Nechama.

I knew the bandages were to be removed that afternoon, and was not unaware of the significance of this event. I told myself that G-d would not want Nechama to suffer, and that surely He would restore her sight to her.

When I returned home from school that afternoon, my mother was on the telephone. I could tell, by her side of the conversation, that she was speaking to Nechama's aunt. I felt overcome by a sensation of déjà vu. It was like the last time. Only this time I knew ... I just knew. My heart hammering, I saw the expression on my mother's face as she turned towards me.

And I knew without a doubt that the operation had not been successful. Nechama was destined to a life of blindness.

Chapter Eighteen

A few weeks after the surgery Nechama returned to school. By that time, helped by our parents and teachers, we had come to terms with the fact that Nechama would never see again, and we were finally prepared to face her. I was glad, though, that she could not see the pitying glances that were directed her way when she was with us.

At first I tried to spend as much time as possible with Nechama. Despite my father telling me that it was meant to be, my guilt was not easily overcome and I felt overwhelmingly responsible for Nechama's blindness. It was as if I had to be with her whenever she wanted me.

The funny thing, though, was that she did not seem to need

me as much as I thought she would. Of course, we were still quite close, but it was not as it had been during those weeks before the surgery. Rarely did she call me, and when I would visit her house unexpectedly, she seemed pleased to have me, but, well . . . I did not feel that I was as essential to her then as I had been in the past.

Nechama's parents had hired a professional tutor who worked with blind people. She was teaching her Braille and helping her build a life of independence despite her sightless-ness. Nechama's brilliant mind had little trouble grasping the new teachings, and her indomitable spirit adjusted valiantly to the situation in which she now found herself.

She was playing piano again and enjoying it immensely. Sometimes I would sit on the couch in her living room observing her as, lost in her music, her fingers danced along the keyboard. It was at those times that I would temporarily put Nechama's blindness out of my mind, and forget about the dent it made in our friendship.

It was on one such snowy Sunday afternoon in mid-February that she broke the news to me.

From the French windows in Nechama's living room, I could see the sparkling snowflakes falling gently. A white blanket of glistening snow covered the streets, making everything look pure and untouched. Nestled in the soft cushions of the L-shaped couch, I was pensively eating a large red apple. It felt warm and cozy indoors, and Nechama's music provided the perfect background accompaniment for such an afternoon.

Admiringly, I watched her sitting, straight backed and disciplined, at the large baby grand piano. Her forehead was creased in concentration as she filled the room with music. She was playing a tune that I had never heard before, a comforting tune . . . so full of hope. Her long, graceful fingers leaped from one key to the next, and as I sat there, entranced by her music, I felt pleasantly cut off from the outside world.

I reached towards the bowl on the coffee table and chose a bright orange. After peeling it, I lay back against the soft cushions, reflecting on these past few months and the changes that had taken place.

I thought of the accident and how it had forced me to face circumstances that I had never even imagined, and emotions I had never experienced before on such a grand scale: despair and desperation, hope and resolve, protectiveness and, yes, a degree of rejection. Nechama no longer seemed to need me the way she did immediately following her accident. Although I was still prepared to come running at her beck and call, she now seemed slightly distant, discouraging extreme closeness. It appeared to me that as she worked to develop her independence within her new life style, our paths were slowly growing apart. And I wondered sadly whether things could ever be the same between us again.

Suddenly she stopped playing the piano. Aroused from my reverie, I opened my eyes to face the real world. Nechama was sitting rigidly on the piano bench, staring straight ahead, her hands clasped in her lap.

"Cham, is everything O.K.?" I placed the remainder of my orange in the napkin and stretched my arms and legs simultaneously. "Why did you stop playing? The music was gorgeous," I added enthusiastically.

"Thanks, Renie . . . Renie?"

"Yes?" I swung myself around and looked at her intently.

"I'm going to play at the Mitzvahthon," she said with determination and then added a little less confidently, "do you think it would be all right?"

I sat up abruptly, shocked by the suddenness of her change of mind. "Of course it's all right. Everyone wants you to play! But will you be O.K.? I mean — getting up on stage and —"

"I know. I thought about that. But look," she sounded as if she was trying to convince herself more than she was trying to convince me. "This is what I am now." There was not an ounce of self-pity in her voice as she referred to her sightlessness. "And the Kohantebs . . ."

"But, Cham. If you're uncomfortable getting up there, you don't have to force —"

"Renie, I want to do it."

"Are you sure, Cham? Are you really sure?" I stood up and walked over to the piano bench and sat down next to her. All along, this is what I had hoped for — for her good as well as the Kohantebs'. But now I felt uncomfortable at the prospect of her playing at the Mitzvahthon. What if Nechama, because of her goodness, was forcing herself to take on something she was not yet ready to handle? What if she froze on stage, unable to continue, and ended up making a fool of herself? Would that not set her back? And would everyone blame me, saying that I convinced Nechama to do it?

After a moment or two of silence, she turned around to face me. "Sure I'm sure," she smiled. Grasping my hand with steely determination, she added unwaveringly, "If it's O.K. with everyone else. . .I'm going to do it. Yes," she reiterated with great emphasis, "I'm going to do it."

And I knew that Nechama's mind was made up.

❦ ❦ ❦

I was reminded of that conversation a few weeks later. It was the Sunday night of the Mitzvahthon and I was sitting between Chana Devorah and Etty in the G.F.S. High School Auditorium.

Rabbi Markowitz, the principal of Bais Yaakov of Lancelor, delivered the opening remarks. His speech centered on the history of the Mitzvahthon, and we sat spellbound as the story of its inception unfolded.

It all began twenty years ago with the demise of the rich and famous Dr. Rothstein. He had led a secular life up until a few years before his death, at which time he decided to become a *baal teshuvah*. His soul yearned for the ways of the past, the *mitzvos* of his forefathers, and in his dying days he became a different person. His children, unfortunately, did not understand the spiritual change that had come over their father, and thought that he had become senile in his old age. Perhaps, Rabbi Markowitz explained to us, they did not want to believe that their modern and educated father could return to something they felt was so old fashioned. The children became estranged from their father during those last years of his life, and when he passed away, they were left with bitter feelings about religion. He, on the other hand, left this world content to have chosen the path of *teshuvah*.

Dr. Rothstein's death made headlines around the world. He had been quite famous as, in his younger days, he had been involved in very important medical research leading to the development of a crucial new drug. But there was a sensationalist aspect to the newspaper stories, as well. After Dr. Rothstein's will was read, it became known that he had cut his children out of his will and bequeathed the value of his entire estate towards the establishment of a Mitzvah Foundation. His sons' lawyers publicly contested the will on the grounds that their senile father had been influenced by religious extremists. After a long and bitter battle that made its way from one court to the next, finally the conflict was resolved with the determination that the will was legal and that Dr. Rothstein was in full possession of his senses when he wrote it.

One of the functions of the Mitzvah Foundation was to arrange an annual assembly where girls about to enter high school would gather together at a different Jewish Day School in the United States or Canada each year. Dr. Rothstein had always been a man of culture and felt that talents should never be wasted. As he became closer to his Jewish roots he realized that everything a person does is supposed to be *leshaim Shamayim*. Aware of the many gifted and talented young women in the religious world, he decided to motivate them to develop their G-d-given skills for altruistic reasons. Each participant in the contest would pick a *passuk* from *Tanach* and apply her special talent to bringing out her chosen theme. The grand prize at the Mitzvahthon would be a grant awarded to the winner's school, to benefit various student programs. Thus, the doctor's love of culture was combined with his philanthropic zeal to benefit the students on a personal level, as well as, on a larger scale, the school of the grand prize winner.

Two decades later his legacy still lived on. Not only did the winning school benefit from his philanthropy, and not only did the talented girls representing the school thrive both in their abilities and in spirituality, but all the girls flourished from what became known as the Mitzvahthon. It evolved into a convention of sorts. There was the *Shabbaton,* the singing, dancing and eating together, the specially planned *shiurim* and programs, the touring of local attractions. It was a time to make new friends and gain pen pals from all over the continent. The contest itself was the highlight of the weekend, but there was so much more that was loved about the Mitzvahthon.

After Rabbi Markowitz finished telling the story of Dr. Rothstein, we stood respectfully as *Rebbetzin* Davidowitz, of the nearby Yeshivah of Hudson Valley, led the assemblage in *Tehillim.* I was awe struck as girls representing schools from all over the United States and Canada stood together and, in one voice, said the ancient and holy words in complete harmony. I could hardly believe that I had finally reached eighth grade and was now a participant of this great event.

Soon it was announced that the performances would begin. *Rebbetzin* Leibowitz, as the principal of the host school, introduced the girl who would be performing and the school that she was representing. We were able to refer to the list on the fliers that we had with us as she spoke. Before taking our seats, we had all been given programs that included the names of all the girls, the schools and states they were from, and the *pesukim* chosen.

The lights dimmed and the assemblage grew quiet as the first girl began her performance. It was a beautiful ballet. She seemed to be representing the Jew being torn in opposite directions, the *Yetzer Hatov* on one side and the *Yetzer Hara* on the other. She twirled about the stage gracefully, the spotlight trying to keep up with her and yet, I found it difficult to keep my eyes focused on the stage. Restlessly, I kept looking down at the fourteenth item listed in the program. It said:

NECHAMA LEVERMAN, BAIS YAAKOV OF BARCLAY, NEW YORK, WILL BE SINGING AN ORIGINAL SONG AND ACCOMPANYING HER-SELF ON THE PIANO. *PASSUK: KI EISHEIV BACHOSHECH HASHEM OHR LI* [MICHAH 7:8].

I looked towards the stage and then back down again at the

shiny paper being twisted and turned nervously in my hands. I felt a squeeze on my arm and looked up to meet Etty's dark, penetrating gaze.

"Don't worry, she'll be great," Etty whispered to me.

"I can't help it," I murmured back. "What happens if she trips or something? What happens if she just goes blank?"

"She w —"

Just then someone in back of us told us to kindly be quiet in a not very kindly way.

I threw Etty a helpless glance and she shrugged her shoulders.

The next hour passed as if in a blur. There were performances in dance and song and dramatic presentations. There was even a comedy act from Chana Devorah's school, done by the Grossman twins. Each and every performance was an original one by an eighth-grader and was based on a *passuk* from the Torah. And although I had looked forward to this night for the last few years, I could only think of Nechama.

I knew that if Nechama performed on stage as successfully as she did in the privacy of her living room, she would surely make our school the winner of the Mitzvahthon. We would have a school library and the Kohantebs would have a means of support. But more importantly, Nechama would have her confidence back. People would no longer treat her so differently, so pityingly, and perhaps this would enable her to lead a more normal life in the future. I even dared hope that it would help us resume our friendship as it had been before the accident.

But if she could not do it? What if she became too nervous at performing in front of this large audience and would suddenly freeze, unable to continue? I pictured her being gently led off stage and knew how disastrous this would be for her. She would crawl into a shell from which she would probably never again emerge. All her work, talents and efforts would be wasted, lost, and would melt away like the snow on the ground.

I could only sit there and hope.

The performers continued to enrapture their audience. After each presentation there was applause and the school song of that contestant's school was sung before the next artist was called to the stage. When the cheering died down, *Rebbetzin* Leibowitz would continue with the introductions. It felt as though I was not really there, as if I observed it all in a daze.

And then, suddenly, it was Nechama's turn.

I gasped and sat up abruptly when I heard her name and our school's name announced. My heart pounded as I watched her slowly climb the steps to the stage. I tensely squeezed Etty's and Chana Devorah's hands simultaneously, as we saw *Rebbetzin* Leibowitz lead Nechama towards the piano. There was not a sound in the audience. Even those who did not know Nechama personally, understood that she was blind.

I sat rigid on the edge of my chair, listening in stunned silence as Nechama began to play the tune she had composed that snowy Sunday afternoon. As she played she began to sing about a girl named Sara. I leaned back in my chair and slowly released my grip on my friends' hands. Eyes closed, face relaxed, I listened to Nechama's music and lyrics and began to picture Sara.

At first the music was slow and haunting as Nechama described Sara, with the long, dark, braided hair, trapped within the thick and high walls of the convent. She was now in the merciless clutches of the nuns who had kidnapped her and it seemed impossible for Sara to escape. Refusing to eat or drink the little that the nuns provided her with, and unwilling to kneel in prayer with them, she felt beaten and weakened. As Nechama sang Sara's story in first person, I felt her hopelessness and despair. She cried for her father and mother and for the home she had left behind and wondered if things would ever be the same for her again.

And then, the music quickened as Nechama sang the refrain:

> I sit engulfed in darkness, believing in Your light;
> I will never give up my fight
> As I cling to *Yiddishkeit*
> Oh, *Hashem*, I know that wherever I may be,
> You will not forsake me,
> "*Ki eisheiv bachoshech, Hashem ohr li ...*"

The music slowed down as Nechama continued to describe Sara's ordeal. Confined to a life that seemed worthless and futile, she surely would have given up if it had not been for her hope and belief in G-d and the future He would give her. Finally, one day as she stood hidden in the shadow of some trees, she saw that the gate had been left open. Not thinking, not giving herself a chance to change her mind, she slipped through the opening and started to run. Breathlessly, she ran through meadows and hills, through valleys and fields, until she reached the edge of the dark forest where at last she collapsed in exhaustion. When she awoke, it was completely dark. Which way led to freedom, she wondered fearfully, knowing that the wrong turn could lead her in the direction of the monastery and back to a life of imprisonment.

She began walking through the black woods. It was the dead of night, and she could clearly hear the cry of the coyotes and the howling of the strong wind. It began to rain. She was cold, hungry and wet. She knew she was lost. She sank despondently to the ground, weeping and praying. And then Nechama quickened the pace of her music and again sang the refrain. "I sit engulfed in darkness, believing in Your light . . ."

I looked around at the girls sitting near me. Tears were rolling down their cheeks and when I touched my own face I was not surprised to find it, too, was wet. We knew that Nechama was not only singing a song about the fictitious Sara; she was singing her own song, too.

Accompanying herself expertly, Nechama sang of how, despite the hopelessness of Sara's situation, she did not lose faith. After having cried and prayed she felt strengthened and ready to face the dark night ahead. She walked, not knowing in which direction she was going. She just knew she had to keep moving . . . she had to keep trying.

The forest was dark and dense and she could barely see a few feet in front of her. All of a sudden she saw a light and began to follow it. As she slowly made her way through the thick woods, the pace of the music quickened and she sang: "As I walk engulfed in darkness, believing in Your light . . ."

The light seemed to be leading her away from the impenetrable forest to a clearing in the woods. As she came closer to the light she recognized the luminous flames of *Shabbos* candles burning brightly in the window of a small cottage. Weakly she knocked at the door and was quickly enveloped in the warmth and kindness of the Jewish family that lived there. When *Shabbos* was over they helped her return to her anxious but grateful family. She never forgot how *Hashem* had rescued her .. how just when things seemed utterly hopeless, she saw the light in the darkness.

Expertly, Nechama continued playing the piano, the harmonious chords echoing throughout the auditorium. When she sang the refrain for the last time, the audience spontaneously joined her. Together, in one voice we sang: "*Ki eisheiv bachoshech, Hashem ohr li.*"

When Nechama finished, the audience burst into round of applause and, with tears streaming down their faces, gave Nechama a standing ovation.

Chapter Nineteen

Looking back, I often wonder how I did not recognize the signs. I know, now, that I should have seen it coming.

That night of the Mitzvahthon, no one doubted who the winner was. Nechama had not only played professionally, but the tune had blended beautifully with the words .. and the *passuk* had been so appropriate. It was not just the poignancy of a blind girl singing about searching for a light in the darkness that had affected her audience so deeply. She had touched on something with which we all could identify. Throughout life we are all forced to face certain hardships, and we find ourselves searching for that beacon of light to guide us. There was a celebration that night in our school's gym. Streamers hung from wall to wall. Bowls filled with potato chips, popcorn, pretzels and cookies crowded the tables. There was punch and soda to drink, and sherbet was being dished out of a large barrel as a special treat. Laughter, conversation and singing reverberated throughout the large room. In the background, coming over our school intercom, lively music could be heard. Girls were exchanging addresses and promises to keep in touch. Exuberance emanated from the faces of all those present. The room itself seemed to exude joy.

As the host school, we had planned this good-bye party for our guests, the many eighth-graders who had come to Barclay from all over the continent. At that time we did not know that we would be the winning school, and now that the contest was over, we had an extra reason to celebrate. Everyone seemed happy for us. I guess each girl felt that if her own school did not win, at least the school that hosted them for the weekend did.

Nechama was the unofficial guest of honor. For the first time in its history, our school was privileged to receive the Mitzvahthon Award. I was beaming with pride. She looked radiant. I now felt sure things would be the same between us. She had shown us that despite her handicap she did not give up, and with her special talents she managed to inspire us all. I stood by her side, basking in the praise that was heaped on her by faculty and students alike. Many parents and strangers offered their congratulations. From the corner of my eye I even noticed Mrs. Kohanteb approach Nechama and tearfully thank her. It was just as I had dreamed, and I felt wildly optimistic about the future.

"Cham, you must be famished!" I exclaimed, turning to face her. "Would you like me to get you something to eat or drink?"

"Thanks, Renie," her face was shining. "Just some punch or soda, please."

I led her over to a row of chairs where a group of our classmates were sitting. After making sure she was comfortably settled, I made my way to the tables that lined the walls of the room, exchanging greetings with people I knew as I passed them in the crowd. I was jubilant and must have been grinning from ear to ear. Everything seemed to be working out : Nechama was surpassing all expectations and doing far more than anyone could have anticipated. The Kohantebs would finally have the peace of mind they deserved, and it had come about through our efforts. I felt surrounded by the warmth of special friends. Chana Devorah was with us, Etty I and were great pals again, and to top it off, Feigy and I had become so close. Except for C.D., we would all be going together to high school next year, and Nechama and I would continue to be the best friends ever. Life was wonderful!

"Hey, watch where you're going!" Chana Devorah laughed as I bumped into her, almost knocking the cup of soda she was carrying out of her hand.

The cherry drink sloshed over both of us, but we we were so giddy that we took no heed. Her eyes met mine and we both burst into a fit of giggles.

"Sorry, C.D.," I tried to apologize, but I was laughing so hard that the words barely came out. "I w-w-wasn't watch . . ."

Just then the music stopped and the room became quiet. The silence abruptly sobered us, and we edged our way towards the wall to find out what was happening. It seemed that *Rebbetzin* Leibowitz was ascending to the microphone. She was going to speak to us. The crowd was impenetrable and I knew I could not make my way back to Nechama. I motioned for Chana Devorah to follow me as I climbed up onto the wide window sill on the back wall to get a more comfortable seat and a better view. From high up I was able to see that Feigy had taken a seat next to Nechama. I was glad that she would not be sitting alone.

Rebbetzin Leibowitz began to speak. First she thanked all the guests for coming to Barclay for the Mitzvahthon and hoped they had as nice a time as we did. She mentioned how wonderful all the performers were and how proud Dr. Rothstein would be if he could see the *achdus* emanating from this room. "It is a pity that his sons are not here tonight to see the beautiful results of their father's legacy. Who knows," she sighed and shrugged her shoulders, "one can never tell what will be . . ." She looked at us admiringly, allowing her eyes to roam around the gym slowly, attentively, regarding the faces of her students, faculty, and guests with pride. Her gaze finally rested on Nechama. "And, Nechama Leverman. What a true champion in every sense of the word! Nechama, you have taught us how one can beat the odds and how to maintain dignity in all circumstances. You have directly and indirectly brought about changes in our school . . . in our lives. Nechama, it was because of you that the girls took on a *shmiras halashon* campaign, have become more diligent in the *Tehillim* and *tefillos* that they say every day, and have learned to appreciate and show gratefulness to *Hashem* for all that He so generously gives." I was swelling with pride and felt as if my heart would burst with pleasure as I heard our principal praise my best friend. "Nechama, I think that *we* are the true winners. Winners for having known a person such as you." She paused for a moment and then continued. "And, now, Nechama, I would like to take this opportunity to . . ." her voice suddenly broke, "to publicly say good-bye to you. Yes," she turned towards the rest of her audience, "in a way this is a farewell party for Nechama, because she will be moving with her family to Australia on *Rosh Chodesh Nissan.*"

I felt as if a pail of ice water had suddenly been thrown on me. I was shocked. Moving away? To Australia! My heart was hammering, my head pounding, as I jumped off the window sill and ran towards the nearest exit, pushing anyone standing in my path out of my way. I heard Chana Devorah's voice in the background calling me back, but I continued to run out the door and up the steps, ignoring her. Panting, I kept ascending until I reached the steps leading to the roof. Finally out of breath, I collapsed onto the step nearest the landing.

How could she do this to me? How could she? I cried out hopelessly to myself. Why didn't she tell me anything? Why did *Rebbetzin* Leibowitz know and I didn't? I held my head in my hands, shaken. Aren't we best friends? Haven't I been there for Nechama whenever she needed me? Why must she leave and ruin our plans of being together for high school? And to Australia — so far away? Why? Why? Why? I stamped my foot three consecutive times.

"Renie . . . are you up there?"

It was Nechama's voice. How did she know where I was? I did not move nor utter a sound.

"Renie, I know you're there. I want to talk to you." One of the girls — Feigy or maybe it was Chana Devorah — must have led her to the staircase. I heard her slowly climbing the steps, groping her way through her darkness. Silently, I remained where I was sitting until she reached the landing. My nose began to tickle and I felt I could not prevent myself from sneezing a second longer. I laid my head in my lap to muffle the sound so that she would not hear me.

Immediately, she sat down next to me, placing a clean tissue in my lap. I looked at her. She had taken off her sunglasses and was wiping the perspiration from her face. Her sightless eyes were blanks on her face. Her ears, I thought, her ears compensate for her eyes. She must have heard me despite my stillness and knew exactly where I sat.

"How did you know that I was up here?" I asked her with a trace of asperity in my voice.

"I might have been in a terrible accident, Renie," she said without any self-pity, "but," she paused and added softly, "I haven't forgotten our special place."

I smiled despite my hurt feelings. Nechama remembered! Ever since fourth grade, this had always been our own area where we could talk privately and hide from the rest of the girls. If I needed extra studying time, Nechama would come up with me and help me memorize my study sheets. Over here she would test me on my spelling words before each spelling test. This was the spot where I sat and cried to her when I felt that a teacher had punished me unfairly. It was true — this really was our special place.

"Right, but from now on I'm going to have to come up here alone," I said more sharply than I had meant to, and began to rise.

"Renie, let me explain." She put her hand on my arm to stop me from leaving. I sat back down slowly, and waited for her to continue. "You see, there is this school in Australia," she went on enthusiastically. "It's supposed to help . . ."

"But, why," I swallowed, "why didn't you tell me anything until now?"

"Because you're my best friend, Renie."

"So, if we're such great friends, then why did I have to find out this way?"

"Because," she said slowly, "because it's hardest to say good-bye to you."

"Well, I don't understand," I muttered relentlessly, not yet ready to give in. "Why Australia? Why do you have to go so far away? Aren't there enough schools here?"

"Yes, there are schools here. But Renie," Nechama continued excitedly, her voice passionate, "this school is special. My doctor and my tutor have told me so much about it. They don't just teach their students Braille or how to walk around with a white cane. They're encouraged to lead an independent life, to have a normal existence. It's hard work . . . but they believe in us over there."

"But I'm always here for you," I protested ardently. "I'll always help you. I . . ."

"Renie, don't you understand? That's not what I need," she said fervently. "I must learn to get along by myself." She paused momentarily and then continued speaking, hesitating at first, then speaking in a louder voice and with more momentum. "Right after the accident, when I still thought there was a chance that I would be able to see again, I leaned on you for everything . . . maybe too much. Remember that Friday before the *sheva berachos* when I called you so desperately? I felt so lost . . . I didn't know who I was anymore. But after the operation, when I had to face the fact that the surgery might not have worked, that I might never be able to see again . . . I knew, I knew that I would have to deal with the situation, to face it." Her voice dropped as she said softly, "Renie, I have to deal with this alone."

"But, but I'm supposed to be your best friend."

"You are, Renie. And sometimes being a best friend means letting go."

"And I always thought that we would go on to high school together . . . that we would be friends forever."

"We will always be friends. We'll write to each other . . ."

"But why? Why do you have to leave so soon? *Rosh Chodesh* is only a few weeks away." There was a tone of urgency in my voice.

"My parents really wanted to leave immediately, Renie. But we decided to postpone the trip because of the Mitzvahthon. And now", she added, "we don't want to push it off any longer."

"But Nechama," I knew I sounded desperate but did not care, "*I'll* always need you. How will I manage without *you?*"

"Look how well you did after the accident," she answered reassuringly. "You organized the *shmiras halashon* campaign, you made sure to take notes for me, you . . ."

"Oh, Cham, I'll miss you so much," I said hoarsely. "We all will."

"And I'll miss all of you, too." Her voice suddenly broke. "Especially you, Renie. But," she paused for a moment and then went on determinedly, "don't you see, Renie? I have this dream for myself .. of a good, full life. I need the proper training. And with *Hashem*'s help I hope that one day, maybe . . ."

"If you're doing it, Cham," the tears were rolling down my cheeks, "it's probably the right thing. I just wish —"

"I know it's the right move for me," she said steadily. "In all my life I've never felt more strongly about anything before."

She stood up and walked to the door of the roof. I followed quickly behind her and felt the rush of the cold night air as she opened the door.

"You've got to understand, Renie," she turned to me, her face intently earnest, "I think I finally see a light in the darkness."

Epilogue

All that had happened almost thirteen years ago. Just as she had planned, Nechama left on *Rosh Chodesh Nissan.* And just as she had promised, she did indeed write to me. At first, we maintained our correspondence religiously. But as time went on, I found myself not quite comfortable with our letter-writing. I knew that someone had to read my letters to Nechama, and that probably that same someone had to transcribe Nechama's words on paper for her. She had not yet learned to type, and I did not know anything about Braille, and therefore the intimacy and privacy on which every friendship thrives was no longer there. In addition to those complications, I felt ill at ease telling Nechama about the usual problems, exciting happenings and events of high school — experiences that she no longer was a part of and that we could no longer share.

And so, by the time we reached tenth grade, we had virtually stopped writing to each other.

I finished high school and went on to a seminary in Israel along with Feigy and Etty, and there I received my teacher's degree. Upon returning to the States, I taught third grade in Bais Yaakov of Barclay. *Rebbetzin* Leibowitz was still my principal and I found her to be a wonderful mentor, guiding and helping me become the educator I was striving to be. It felt a little strange, though, to be part of the staff of a school that was so tied up with my own childhood.

During recess I would watch the children playing in the schoolyard and sometimes find myself reminiscing about the carefree days when I would run with my friends along those same paths. The games did not change and the students in their uniforms looked the same, only these girls belonged to a new generation — and I would marvel at the swift passage of time.

Later on that year I became engaged to Dovid Samuels, Etty's older brother. It was a great *simchah* in the neighborhood, as we both had lived in Barclay all our lives and everyone had seen us grow up. After our wedding that June we took an apartment in the same complex that Sima had lived in when she was first married. I loved being surrounded by friends and family, and our happiness was complete.

Almost a year later our Eli was born, and I remember thinking that it must be impossible for anyone to be happier. Soon afterwards, Etty married a friend of Dovid's and they took an apartment nearby. Yisroel and Sima had bought a house not far from my parents and we would all gather together often. It gave us great pleasure to see our parents basking in the joy of being surrounded by their children and grandchildren.

When Eli was two years old, his brother Tzviki joined him. I was still teaching every morning, and when I returned home at lunchtime, I would scoop up my little boys and shower them with hugs and kisses. We would often join Etty and her little girl in the park, or just enjoy a pleasant stroll down Main Street. Sometimes we stopped off for a visit with the former Mrs. Finkelman, who, when I was in the ninth grade, had become Mrs. Petrovsky. She and her husband enjoyed indulging the children with all types of treats and playing the part as our "adopted" grandparents.

My daughter Ruchi was born on my twenty-fourth birthday, and I could not believe that I finally had a little girl. We enjoyed dressing her in anything pink, and her big brothers seemed to adore her. My parents made a beautiful *Kiddush* for her in their home and many of our friends and relatives shared in our *simchah.*

That autumn, Eli began to attend kindergarten for a few hours a week and I took a temporary leave from my teaching job. My husband became a *rebbi* in the local *cheder* where he proved to be quite successful and very much in demand.

Life was wonderful at that time.

And then, when Ruchi was about a year old, my uncomplaining and energetic mother began to complain about back pain. After much persuasion on the part of family and friends, she finally agreed to see a specialist. The doctor had her hospitalized immediately and ran a series of tests. Gravely he told us how ill she was and that she did not have much time left to live.

Of course, we refused to accept this prognosis, and when she died that *Chol Hamoed Pesach,* the whole community was shocked. We were devastated.

It seems that of all the children, I took her death the hardest. Perhaps it was because I was the youngest or maybe it had something to do with that fear that had burdened me ever since I was a child. I had always wondered how one continues at a time like this and now felt I could not go on. I was inconsolable.

It was a small comfort to me when my second daughter was born a few weeks later. We called her Dina, after my mother, and as the months passed and she grew, I found it a little less difficult to get on with my life. Besides, my days were so busy I did not have the time to allow myself to think too much.

However, when the sun set and night drew near, I would be enveloped in sadness.

During the evenings, when Dovid was at the *yeshivah* learning with his *chavrusa,* and the children were tucked in for the night, I would sit by myself on the living room couch remembering my mother, missing her, and knowing that I would never see her again.

When Dina was almost a year old, I was quite glad to be thrown into the frenzy of *Pesach* preparations. The additional cleaning, cooking and baking, along with the usual caring for the children succeeded in taking my mind off the upcoming *yahrzeit* day. And so, when it finally did arrive, Dovid wisely took the children out to visit his parents so that I could be alone. He knew how strong my need was to think about my loss . . . and to finally face it.

Alone, I climbed onto a chair and reached for the heavy box that was on the top shelf of the closet. Carefully, I lowered it to the floor and then, cross-legged, sat down next to it and began to examine its contents. I remembered that day almost a year ago when the *shloshim* had just ended, and my grieving father brought the box over to my apartment. Solemnly he informed me that he thought my mother would have wanted me to have the items that were inside.

I did not open the box in front of him, and after he left, I told Dovid that I was not ready. He did not push me. He understood that I needed time and offered to put the box away in the closet. All these months had passed and I had not yet looked into the box to see what was inside. Today, on her *yahrzeit,* I finally felt ready.

There were some photographs of the two of us and I laughed aloud, remembering the incident connected with one of them. I could not help smiling as I examined the birthday card with the misspelled birthday wishes, carefully written in a childish scrawl with my new set of crayons. My eyes filled when I saw her recipe cards covered with her neat handwriting, some slightly smudged with ingredients that had spilled onto them.

When I saw the card titled *Pesach Sponge Cake,* I closed my eyes and remembered how I would sit near the counter licking the bowl after she had scraped out the last of the batter. And I tried to bring back that feeling of satisfaction that only a child could feel, secure in the safety of her mother's warm kitchen.

And then I suddenly had an idea. How about surprising the family with Bubby's cake? I went to the cupboard and made sure that we had all of the necessary ingredients, then began to assemble what was needed. I separated the eggs and proceeded to carefully follow the recipe. Before long my small apartment was filled with the remembered aroma of my childhood. I felt as if my mother was with me.

It was at that time that the telephone rang and Nechama called, informing me that she was in town and would like to drop by to visit me. I gave her my address and then nervously began to clear away anything that might obstruct her path, all the while wondering, almost resentfully, why she had to come.

I had had such a happy childhood, marred only by the tragedy of that year. My mind was suddenly flooded with the memories of all that had happened when we were in the eighth grade. It was something that I tried not to think about and yet . . . I found I could not suppress a feeling of excitement at seeing Nechama. She had been such an integral part of my childhood and we had shared many happy times together.

I allowed my imagination to go wild. Perhaps her sight had been restored. Maybe she did get married, have a family and continue to lead a normal life. And now, all she wanted was to get together and resume our friendship.

But what will we say to each other after all these years? And what if she is still blind, I wondered desperately. Perhaps all this time she has blamed me for what happened, I thought guiltily. Now she would come here and find me happy, with a husband and family. Building a stable Jewish home was something that had been so important to her . . . something she could never have.

I was suddenly jolted out of my reverie by the sound of the doorbell. Automatically, I stood up and hastily tucked some stray strands of hair under my kerchief. I glanced quickly at my reflection as I passed the mirror and then almost laughed out loud at the irony of it.

Nervously, I swallowed, then opened the door. Standing before me was a tall and slim woman. She was dressed in a camel-colored suit and a creamy white blouse. Her auburn wig was brushed softly off her face. She was wearing a stylish pair of sunglasses and I was not sure if they were worn to cover sightless eyes or to make a fashion statement. I took a deep breath. Standing before me, so proud and poised, Nechama looked beautiful.

"Mommy, is this your friend?"

I looked down. Grasping Nechama's hand and looking up at me with big brown eyes was an adorable little girl who looked to me to be about three years old. I had been staring so hard at Nechama that I had not noticed the child at her side or the tall man behind her, holding the baby boy. I just stood there gaping, too shocked to speak. "Don't tell me, Renie, after all these years you've grown short of words," Nechama lightly broke the silence. "Aren't you going to invite us in?"

"Oh — excuse me, I'm sorry. Please come in." The words came out awkwardly as I opened the door wider and motioned for the small group to enter.

"It smells delicious in here," Nechama said, sniffing the air as her little daughter led her by the hand into the living room. "It reminds me of your mother's home."

"Thank you," I said uncomfortably. "I'm experimenting with an old recipe of my mother's. Please make yourselves comfortable." I turned to the man. "You can put the baby here," I pointed towards Dina's swing. "You must be . . ."

"Reuben," Nechama intercepted, "I'm sorry. I've forgotten to introduce you. Renie, this is Reuben Fried, my husband," Nechama said proudly. "And this is Renie Greenberg, uh, I mean, Samuels." She turned towards me. "Yes, I was so happy to hear that you married Etty's brother. Now, you are sisters-in-law as well as good friends."

Nechama's husband turned to me and smiled warmly. "Nechama has told me so much about you and what good friends you were. I'm glad to finally meet you." I heard the slight trace of an unfamiliar accent in his English and wondered where he was from.

"Thank you," was all I could say. "I'll be back in a moment."
I escaped to the solitude of my kitchen and excitedly began to
cut the cake and arrange the warm slices on a platter.
Nechama actually has a husband and children, I thought in
disbelief. I filled a large glass bowl with some fruit and,
balancing the fruit and cake platters on a tray in one hand and
holding a container of ice water in the other, awkwardly
managed to carry it all into the living room.

As I entered, I could not believe what I saw. Nechama was
reading a book to her daughter, who was sitting on her
mother's lap looking at the pictures. I could see Nechama's
long, graceful fingers lightly skimming over the dots along the
bottom of the page, and knew that she was reading Braille. Yet
I realized, as I leaned over to place the snacks on the coffee
table, that the large colorful pictures in the book were for a
seeing child to enjoy.

Reuben must have noticed my surprised expression because
he immediately turned to me and in a low voice, so as not to
disturb the reading session, proudly said, "This is one of
Nechama's creations."

I looked at him inquiringly and he explained further.
"Nechama did not want parents or any unseeing adults, for
that matter, to be deprived of the experience of reading aloud
with their children, grandchildren, or other youngsters. So she
began to write books on Jewish themes, hired an experienced
children's-book artist, had the books printed in Braille, and
before we knew what was happening . . ."

"Oh, Reuben," Nechama stopped reading and modestly
said, "it was no big deal."

"Really, now?" He smiled and then turned back to me.
"Before we knew what hit us, we were being bombarded with
telephone calls from other publishers asking us to have their
books converted to Braille. It has been very successful."

"Well, thank G-d, it has helped those who needed it most,"
Nechama admitted softly.

"That's one of the reasons we're in the States right now," her
husband continued enthusiastically. "Nechama has been invited to lecture on the subject in schools for the blind here and

in Canada. We decided to take in *Pesach,* too. This way we could spend some time with friends and family."

"How long will you be here — I mean in Barclay?"

"Well, that depends," Nechama smiled, displaying a deep dimple, "on how welcome we are made to feel."

"Honestly," Reuben laughed, "it's hard to say. I'm sure you have heard about the school that Nechama started a few years ago in Australia . . . the Tikvah School for the Jewish Blind."

"No." My eyes widened in surprise.

"Well, Nechama had worked in the school in Australia that she had attended as a teenager. She began a program there that was so successful it eventually became an independent fully staffed school. She was asked to start similar programs in some of the schools here, in America. That is why we do not know how long we will be staying. It depends on how long it will take to train the right teachers, order materials, and to incorporate the program into the schools."

"Reuben, I'm sure we're boring Renie with all these details."

"No, please go on," I said, anxious to hear more.

"Yes, in fact, it was in that school that I first met Nechama," he continued, his eyes shining.

"Reuben. . ." Nechama said warningly, feigning annoyance.

He looked towards his wife admiringly and then went on. "My little sister, unfortunately, was born blind. My parents wanted to raise her as normally as possible and, luckily for us, there was a school in Ballarat, which is just a few hours away from East St. Kilda where my family lives. This school was known for its success in teaching its students independence. The school, however, was run by secularists and, of course, my parents only wanted a religious Jewish education for their child. Not knowing of any alternatives, they decided to at least go and investigate the school. When they got there, they were surprised to discover that there was a special program within the school that was run by an enthusiastic and idealistic young religious girl. The children, and even the few adults who were part of this program, were given only kosher food — as well as 'kosher' lessons. From *davening* out of Braille *siddurim,* to studying *Tanach* with *Rashi,* to learning about the *Yamim*

Tovim — their education could not have been surpassed in the best 'regular' schools. This young teacher consulted *rabbanim* who, buoyed by her enthusiasm, would often agree to come to the school to speak with her students." He stopped for a moment to catch his breath and then continued, "So they not only received the best Jewish and secular education, but they were also the grateful recipients of *hashkafah* lessons and strong Torah values. They were constantly encouraged to believe that despite their handicap, their lives were definitely worth living."

He paused to take a sip of water and then went on. "I was learning in *yeshivah* in *Eretz Yisrael* at the time. When I was home *bein hazmanim,* my parents and little sister would talk nonstop about the teacher in Ballarat. Finally, some four-and-a-half years ago, when I was home for the *Succos zman,* my parents asked me to take Shiffy — that's my little sister — back to school for them. It was a long drive, but well worth it. It was then that I met the famous teacher that Shiffy and countless others relied on and raved about . . . *Morah* Nechama Leverman. And it wasn't long afterwards that I succeeded in convincing her to become Mrs. Nechama Fried."

I felt my eyes filling with tears. Awed by the specialness of this woman sitting opposite me, I found myself totally and utterly speechless. I was literally "saved by the bell" because just then the bell really did ring.

I had barely unlocked the door when it was pushed open further and three lively children bounced into the house, followed by their rather exhausted father who trudged in after them, carrying a sleeping baby. I had no time to warn them about the unexpected company because within seconds they were all in the living room looking curiously at the guests seated on the couch.

"Hi, I'm Eli," my older son said, in his most grown-up voice. "Who are you?"

"My name is Reuben Fried," he answered with a chuckle. Then, turning to my four-year-old, he asked, "What's yours?"

"I'm Tzviki. Do you want to see me make a tumblesauce?" Without waiting for a response, he proceeded to do one.

Everyone laughed. Turning towards my husband, I introduced the two men to each other. Dovid was still holding our sleeping child in one arm. With his free hand, however he managed to reach out and shake hands warmly with Reuben.

Dina was beginning to awake and was squirming uncomfortably in my husband's arms. I took her from him and sat down on the couch next to Nechama.

"Me too! Me too!" Those seemed to be the only words that Ruchi knew. Smiling, I introduced her and she grinned proudly.

"And who are you?" my little Eli asked, looking directly at Nechama.

"This is Mrs. Fried," I explained, before he could ask any other questions. "We were very good friends when we were little children."

"Just call me Aunt Nechama," she said.

"Why are you wearing those funny glasses in the house?" The question was out of Tzviki's mouth before I could stop him. I threw a helpless look at my husband, who stared back at me, equally uncomfortable.

Tzviki just stood there expectantly, waiting for a reply.

"It's because," Nechama explained to him, "I'm blind."

"What's blind?" both Tzviki and Eli asked together.

"It means," Nechama went on smoothly, "that I can't see out of my eyes. And I wear these glasses to cover my eyes since they can't see the way yours can."

"But my Mommy can see in other ways, right, Mommy?" The little voice of Nechama's daughter piped up from the corner of the room where she had been sitting quietly, looking at the colorful pictures in Nechama's book.

"Right, sweety," Nechama said as her daughter returned to the couch, climbed up on her mother's lap, and wrapped her pudgy arms around her neck. "I'm able to picture things in my mind and in that way I can see anything I want to see. Sometimes I must use my hands to see, like when I want to read a book or bake a cake. When I am cooking, my nose and tongue tell me if the food tastes right. So, children, you understand," she kissed her daughter's forehead,

"Zeesy is right. I have my way of seeing things, even if my eyes don't work."

"Wow!" Eli was definitely impressed.

Tzviki turned to Nechama's daughter and, with eyes full of admiration, said, "You're so lucky that your Mommy has so many ways of seeing. Do you want to see me make a tumblesauce?" She nodded shyly and proceeded to follow him into the study where there was more room for him to show off his acrobatic abilities.

"Wait for me!" Eli was not going to be left out, even if they were younger and even if she was *just* a girl. She had earned the status of the daughter of a celebrity and was therefore definitely worth playing with.

"Me too! Me too!" Ruchi cried out, running after them. A few minutes later we could hear them all giggling as she also joined in the fun.

Nechama's husband accompanied mine into the dining room where the bookcase stood. I knew that with their friendly personalities and the *sefarim* on hand, they would have no problem conversing. With the four older children out of the room and the men in the dining room, it seemed unusually quiet.

Nechama and I were able to have some pleasant adult conversation, and before long I started to feel that familiar comfortable feeling in Nechama's company. It was not hard to imagine that the two of us had once been best friends.

Nechama's son started to squirm out of Dina's swing, while at the same time, Dina tried to wriggle out of my lap. I gave them each a cookie and within a short time the two little ones were babbling as they played with the blocks on the floor nearby.

I sat back down on the couch and looked across at Nechama. I felt my heart soar with admiration as I stared at her. How was this woman able to take a tragedy and turn it into something that not only gave her a normal, fulfilling life, but moreover, gave others the hope and desire to go on? Why were so many of us unable to make the most out of our lives, lives that were free from disabilities, unhampered by disaster?

I suddenly felt ashamed. Here I was as healthy as ever, surrounded all my life by a loving family and familiar friends. I was never monetarily rich, but I always had everything I needed. And now, a year after it occurred, I was still finding it difficult to cope with my mother's death. I knew that I had a right to mourn, but I also knew that my mother would have wanted me to get on with my life. She would have wanted me to learn from Nechama.

I now understood what my father had meant by giving me that box filled with memories and recipes. It was fine to miss those loved ones who have left us, but one must also try to remember the happy times. They would not want us to grieve forever.

"A penny for your thoughts." Nechama playfully shook me. "Where are you, in China?"

I laughed at the familiarity of that question. "I was just thinking of how lucky I am that you came today."

"Really?"

"Yes, really," I replied. "You see," I hesitated and then went on, "today is my mother's *yahrtzeit* . . . "

"Oh, I am so sorry, Renie, why didn't you tell me?" her face took on an expression of deep sadness. "I remember how close you were to her and how much she meant to you. I'll never forget that conversation we had that night of the *pidyon haben* and how afraid you were of the day that this would happen."

"Well, it happened," I said matter-of-factly, yet could not help but feel amazed that she, too, remembered that talk we had had so many years ago. "And when it did, I thought I would never get over it." I sighed deeply. "I've been having so much trouble dealing with my mother's death. . .coming to terms with it," I confided. "This past year I've found it difficult to get involved in outside activities or to even participate in family gatherings. I've just barely managed to keep my house together."

"That's not like the Renie I knew."

"You're right." I continued lightly, "I think that the Renie you knew needed the Nechama she knew to bring her back to herself."

"Come on," Nechama said, laughing.

"It's true," I said in a more serious tone. "I'll always remember the night of the Mitzvahthon when I found out that you were leaving, and you told me about seeing a light in the darkness."

"I remember that night, too."

"Well, you found it. And," I paused for a moment and then continued, "I guess I just realized that we all have our different types of 'darkness' to deal with. Your coming here today showed me that there is always a way to conquer the darkness. But, in your case," I hesitated again, and then went on unwaveringly, "you've managed to truly light up not only your own darkness but everyone else's, too."

"Wow! You sure know how to compliment someone, Renie," Nechama said, "but —"

"But nothing!" I was determined to tell her what was on my mind. "Ever since that first day you joined our class you knew how to take a difficult situation and make the best of it."

"And that was only because you were there to help me through it."

"Always shifting the credit to the other person." I smiled. "That's the Nechama I knew then, and that's the same Nechama I know now."

"Well I certainly hope that in the future, the Renie I know now will be a better letter-writer than the Renie I knew then."

"I definitely will," I promised fervently. "This time nothing will separate us. Not problems or differences, not distance . . . nothing!"

"Are you sure about that?" she asked teasingly.

"Sure I'm sure, Cham," I grinned happily.

And the world seemed pretty perfect just then.

Sources
and
Glossary

Sources

Chapter 3:

Information about *Succos* is taken from *The Complete Story of Tishrei,* by Nissan Mindel.

Information about the ceremony of *pidyon haben* is taken from *The Jew and His Home,* by Eliyahu Kitov. The liturgical selection between the *Kohen* and Yisroel Bradsky are quotations taken directly from pages 197 and 198 of *The Jew and His Home.*

Chapter 5:

The concept of a *shmiras halashon* club is derived from the well-known *Machsom L'fi* program sponsored by the Chofetz Chaim Heritage Foundation, 1301 Avenue I, Brooklyn, NY 11230.

Chapter 9:

Facts about disclosing private information are taken from *Guard Your Tongue,* by Zelig Pliskin.

Chapter 11:

The *Rashi* which discusses the status of a blind person, specifically Yitzchak *Avinu*, is in *Bereishis* 28:13.

The Gemara which teaches that the *Yetzer Hara* does not affect blind people, and that they are therefore excused from doing *mitzvos*, is *Bava Kamma* 87.

Information regarding Reb Yosef bar Chiya is taken from *Sefer Seder HaDoros,* where he is identified as Rav Yosef Sagi Nahor.

Glossary

Abba: father

Achdus: unity

Ananei Hakavod: clouds of Glory

Baal Simchah: person celebrating a joyous event

Baal Teshuvah, Baalas Teshuvah, Baalei Teshuvah (m., f., pl.): repentant sinner, returnee to Jewish observance

Bachurim: unmarried male youths

Baruch Hashem: "Thank G-d"

Bechor: firstborn male

Bein Hazmanim: between semesters (vacation in a *yeshivah*)

Beis Hamikdash: The Holy Temple in Jerusalem

Benched, Benching: blessed, blessing; recited, reciting the Grace after Meals

Bilkalech: small *challah* rolls

Brachah, Brachos: blessing(s)

Bris: ritual of circumcision

Bubby: Grandmother

Chait Ha'egel: sin of the Golden Calf

Chassan: a groom

Chavrusa, Chavrusas: study partner(s)

Chazanishe: cantorial

Chazarah: review

Chevrah: group of friends

Chol Hamoed: intermediate days (between first and last days of *Pesach* or *Succos*)

Chrain: horseradish

Dan lechaf zechus: to judge favorably

Davened, Davening: prayed, praying

Devar Torah, Divrei Torah: discussion(s) of Torah subject

Esrog: citron, used during the *Succos* festival

Ger: convert to Judaism

Hakaros Hatov: gratitude for a favor

Hashem: G-d

Havdalah: the ceremony marking the end of the Sabbath

Kallah: a bride

Kedushah: holiness

Kiddush: prayer over wine

Kohein, Kohanim: priest(s) from the tribe of Levi

Kumzitz: informal gathering; usually one of the group plays the guitar while the others sing along

Laining: Torah reading

Lashon Hara: gossip

Libeinu: our hearts

Leshaim Shamayim: for the sake of Heaven

Levi, Levi'im: Levi(tes)

Lulav: palm branch, used during the *Succos* festival

Maves vecha'im beyad halashon: death and life are in the hands of the tongue

Mazal Tov: "congratulations!"

Mesiras Nefesh: self-sacrifice

Mi ha'ish hechafetz cha'im . . . netzor leshoncha mei'ra: who is the man that desires life . . . guard your tongue from evil

Mitzvah, Mitzvos: one of the 613 Torah commandments, or good deeds

Nosh, Nosher: snack

Passuk, Pesukim: verse(s)

Pidyon Haben: the redemption of a first born male child

Pirkei Avos: Ethics of Our Fathers

Rav: Rabbi

Refuah Sheleimah: complete recovery

Rosh Chodesh: first of the month

Rosh Yeshivah: the dean of a *yeshivah*

Schach: covering of *succah*, usually bamboo sticks

Sefarim Shrank: bookcase

Sefer, Sefarim: book(s)

Shevah Brachos: Seven Blessings, recited at weddings and during the following week

Shabbos, Shabbosos: Sabbath(s)

Shalosh Regalim: the three pilgrimage festivals: *Pesach, Shavuos, Succos*

Shekalim: shekels

Shepping Naches: enjoying satisfaction, usually from one's child

Shiur, Shiurim: Torah lecture(s)

Shmiras Halashon: guarding one's speech

Shul: synagogue

Simchah: happiness: a joyous occasion

Simchas Torah: Rejoicing of the law, the last day of *Succos*

Succah: a temporary dwelling erected for *Succos*

Succos: the Festival of Tabernacles

Talmid Chacham: scholar

Talmidim: students

Tefillah, Tefillos: prayer

Tehillim: Book of Psalms

Tzaddikim: pious men

Upsheren: ceremony when cutting three-year-old boy's hair

Yahrzeit: anniversary of one's death

Yahrzeit Licht: candle to commemorate the *Yahrzeit*

Yetzer Hara: evil inclinations

Yiddishkeit: Jewishness

Yisrael: Israelite

Yom Kippur: the Day of Atonement

Yom Tov, Yamim Tovim: Festival day(s)

Zeeskeit: sweet one

Zemiros: songs of praise

Zman Simchasainu: time of our happiness

Zocheh: worthy

This volume is part of
THE ARTSCROLL SERIES®
an ongoing project of
translations, commentaries and expositions
on Scripture, Mishnah, Talmud, Halachah,
liturgy, history, the classic Rabbinic writings,
biographies, and thought.

For a brochure of current publications
visit your local Hebrew bookseller
or contact the publisher:

Mesorah Publications, ltd

4401 Second Avenue
Brooklyn, New York 11232
(718) 921-9000